Lady AND THE Camp

STEPHANIE J. SCOTT

Contents

Author's Note

Lady and the Camp can be read as a standalone, but is intended as the first full novel in a planned three book series about a group of former college roommates finding themselves at a crossroads in their careers and love lives.

A prequel short story **It Happened One Getaway** is available to readers who join my email list. Find it here: https://www.stephaniejscott.com/free-read

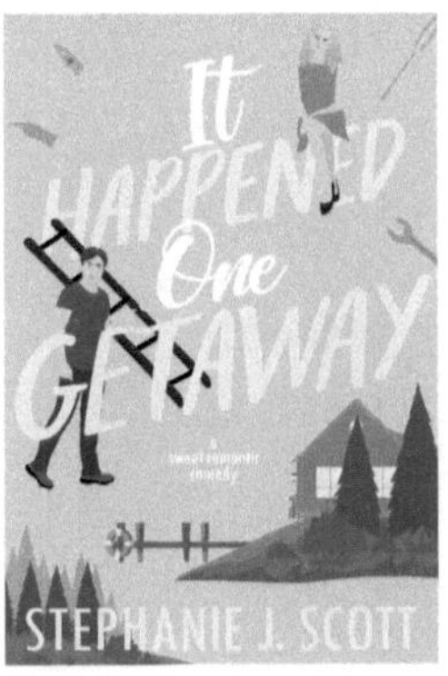

This book is dedicated to all of you with a soft spot for silly but heartfelt stories.
Because sometimes you're in the mood for an escape with a mildly bonkers plot.

Chapter 1

Hudson

HUDSON, WE HAVE A Problem

Give it up for the most basic click-bait headline of all time. Talk about phoning it in. If a gal's entire reputation had to go down in flames, could the media at least attempt some creativity?

Because I was that gal, that Hudson whose collective years of building a social media presence was about to be scorched to cinders.

"Hudson, did you hear me?" the aggressively agitated voice on the other end of the line prompted. "This is not great news."

Of course losing a golden opportunity brand ambassadorship with an up-and-coming organic beauty company wasn't great news. Of course having my supposed sure thing, my guaranteed airlift to the next level—next level! they'd said—completely fall apart, exponentially magnified on a world stage, was the total and complete opposite of *great news*.

"Listen, we both know I had no idea the feds would raid his offices and beach house," I shot back to my talent manager. "He's Kristoff freaking Krom, the self-proclaimed *most chill billionaire innovator* in the world. Why would I have seen through his lies if the rest of the world couldn't?"

"Stop being cute," my manager said, which was super insulting on several levels. Firstly, because I excelled at the business of cute. I'd made cute my literal brand. Secondly, none of *this* was cute, and he knew it. "Because he's your boyfriend."

"Ex. Very, very ex-boyfriend."

He snorted. "Huh. Tell that to the judge."

Okay, so my now ex-boyfriend faced serious charges for embezzlement and had implicated me as an accomplice. That was bad. Very, very bad. I knew I wasn't guilty, but Kristoff had a lot of clout on social media with his bro brigade—his legions of fans who adored every flashy move he made and fawned over his cutting edge views on investments.

Of which I had been, apparently. An investment. He'd told me as much. He'd chosen me, the online influencer known as the Beauty Butterfly, as the new spokesperson for Sheek Cosmetics, a company he'd recently bought. A departure from his usual digital currency and tech company investments.

My manager continued. "I don't think our relationship is working."

I choked and spit my cold-pressed kombucha outward, sending scattershot spray against my light ring and filming phone behind it. "*You're* breaking up with me? Can you even do that?"

"This is a business partnership. And you, Hudson, no longer have a business."

"I have Beauty Butterfly. Those are *my* followers. *My* brand."

"You haven't posted in three days."

Didn't I know it. "I can't talk about the case publicly. Besides, it's been a rough few days—"

"No content means no brand. The Krom case is what the public cares about. They don't care about your face masks."

Well, wasn't that a kick to the veneers. Not that I had them, but I had considered it once the check cleared from this deal.

Only there wouldn't be a deal. Certainly no check. Not even a wad of cash in small unmarked bills. Nothing. That's what I was looking at. A whole lot of no money and a whole lot of negative attention.

"Isn't there a saying—all press is good press, even if it's bad?" That definitely worked in some celebrities' favor. Bad press *created* careers.

My manager grumbled. "His bros are coming for me. The comments online—they're horrible. These people are scary. Anyone connected to Krom that they don't like, they aim to make them suffer. I'm out, Hudson. I'm out."

The cold stab of reality hit deep. Despite the online following I'd built, my name now connected to Kristoff Krom in a negative way.

You had a shot, brushing shoulders with a billionaire, but now that's over. And so are you.

Grabbing a tissue, I wiped my mouth, thankful I wasn't on video. My stomach tilted. And not from the kombucha. My career was headed into full free-fall before it barely left the ground. No manager to manage me couldn't be a good sign.

After ending the call with my manager that thusly ended our partnership, Agent Mulder flashed on my phone's screen. Not the actual Agent Mulder since he was obviously fictional. Adding the fake name to my phone provided a buffer between reality and fiction I found rather handy at the moment.

I squeezed my eyes shut and prepared for impact. I accepted the call. "Hello?"

"Hudson Hawley?"

"Am I required to confirm my identity?"

A barely audible sigh stretched across the line. "Yes."

"Okay. It's me." I swallowed past the hurt building in my throat. This sucked. All of it. "And you're not supposed to talk to me without my lawyer present."

"Hudson, it's me," the steel-edged voice of my attorney, Kelly Q. Pierce, cut in. I was dying to know what the Q stood for, but unsurprisingly, we'd had more pressing matters to cover. "I was on mute. I had a school program to attend. The nerve of these elementary schools to plan their programs during working hours."

"Ah, I remember those days," Agent Mulder said. "Had three little ones myself, each two years apart. Only saving grace was my middle child had stage fright. Refused to perform."

"Excuse me," I interrupted. "You both *called me*. What is going on?"

Not-Actually-Mulder cleared his throat. "It's a spot of bright news. You've cooperated and answered all of our questions. We've confirmed you are not linked to Kristoff Krom's embezzlement charges. We had to do our due diligence since he made those claims."

Claims Kristoff made in a video he posted to the masses. The one time I truly went viral and it involved being blamed for the financial downfall of someone I dated less than six months.

"We reserve the right to contact you for further questioning," the agent continued. "But for now, you're clear."

My breath caught. "So I can post online again?"

"Not so fast," said my attorney. "We're releasing a statement that you've been cleared of involvement in the embezzlement. You can post the statement, but given the pending investigation, no other comments should come from you about the case. Understood?"

I pressed my lips together, nodding to agree. But obviously neither of them could see me. Video was so ingrained in my routine, I had to remind myself to speak. "Okay." Okay, *but*. "I need to at least be able to defend myself. Kristoff's...*fans* are attacking my posts with nasty comments." One thing my manager had right—those fans were scary. "Regardless of the statement, they're going to keep blaming me. Threatening me."

"We're monitoring chatter online, but until we get a plausible threat, it's all hot air." Mulder's throat made a noise like knives in a garbage disposal. "We're going to need you to take it easy with the internet stuff for now. Lay low. A break can be a good thing. Think about it like a, what do you health nuts call it?"

"A detox?" Kelly Q. offered.

"Yeah, that's it. Detox. You young folk are online too much. Take a break. Go outside. Get a dog. Log off and tune in—*to life.*" He chuckled at his own quip.

The turning in my stomach intensified. Waves of hot and cold took turns pulsing through my body. Panic. This was pure, helpless panic.

I'd built my Beauty Butterfly brand the past five years and that brand was me. I had no idea how to pluck that identity out and simply stick it somewhere else. Let alone this idea of logging off. Like, out of *everything*? Even email? For how long?

"Your online presence is an area of concern," Kelly Q stated, since I obviously could not form a response. "To maintain the integrity of the case, we need your outward persona to align with the statement that you've been cleared of financial scandal. Videos and social posts can be taken out of context. The media is eager to scrutinize your every move, especially if they see you spending money or promoting big brands. They will pick you apart, even if just for enticing headlines."

"In other words," Mulder said. "No living it up and hobnobbing with celebs. It makes us—er, our case—look bad."

Oh, so as long as the *feds* didn't look bad.

I peeked out my bedroom window. A man stood on the sidewalk two stories below with a hefty camera strapped around his neck, checking his phone. He'd been there all day. Waiting.

My small apartment, my homey little sanctuary, felt like a ticking time bomb. Kristoff's bro base knew I lived in Los Angeles. If they were harassing my manager, what might they do to me? Would they snap photos of me out in public and claim I was a heartless partier as poor Kristoff suffered?

Despite my name being cleared in the investigation, I didn't feel safe. Relieved, sure, but not safe. "You suggested I lay low. Where should I go?"

"Where's your family?" Agent Mulder asked.

"Michigan, but that's not going to work."

"Ah, the mitten state." he mused. "You ever been to the thumb? Could be a good place to hide out. The thumb."

I could imagine it now. Curfews, required family dinners with detailed lectures about my choice of career. In my parents' mind, I didn't have a career. And now after all this, maybe I didn't.

Agent Mulder went on with what I assumed were essential details, only the buzzing in my ears drowned out his words. It was the oddest thing, hearing words I knew were English, but having no understanding of their meaning.

"My job is to represent your best interests," Kelly Q said. "I agree it's a good idea to find somewhere, even if temporary, to disappear."

Disappear. The absolute opposite of every goal I had. My entire existence was driven by the desire to leave a mark on the world.

I'd only recently left Nashville, where I'd lived for several years *hobnobbing,* as Mulder put it, with online influencers and alt-country stars (I'd dated *the* Shane Jordan before he went Hollywood, *thankyouverymuch*). Then to L.A. for more opportunity. Where I met Kristoff.

My mind raced. So much hit so hard so fast.

"Do you have any questions, Hudson?" Kelly Q's voice came a little softer, which meant steel lightly warmed in a forge.

I swallowed. "I thought he believed in me. That he really liked me."

I could practically smell the pity waves through the phone. The agent and attorney's silence spoke—screamed?—loud enough to sink me another layer lower.

I'd been so naïve. Kristoff hadn't cared about my vision that every person deserved to look and feel great even if they couldn't afford high-end brands. He cared about his own image. No, he was obsessed. His desperation to win over the coveted young, professional, female demographic led him to date one of their wholesome, cheerful stars, and buy up a company they liked that he could then profit from.

And for what purpose? The guy had everything.

Ego, it turned out. Pure ego.

"You take care, Hudson," Kelly Q said, back to sharpened metal. "You're young. You'll spring back."

The call ended, inviting silence free from the witness of adults in professional careers.

I'd truly believed Kristoff saw me as more than a pretty, popular face he could say he discovered. Nope. He saw me as an easy target to attach blame. A girlfriend who blabbed about his financial crimes to the authorities. Which I never did. Because I hadn't known he was *doing crimes*. Why would I be with a crime guy? Why would I sign on to be a brand ambassador with a company controlled by a shady guy?

But that didn't matter. The story worked to gain Kristoff favor with his base. My reputation now tarnished for snitching on an innovator who many believed to be above the law, I'd been tossed away, like a disposable face cloth (which were totally bad for the environment).

Disaster. Total disaster.

I curled smaller on my bed and buried my face in a pillow, smooshing my skin against the silk cover. *Give me wrinkles. I dare you.*

The headlines should have been: *Wealthy Man-Boy Tanks Company Mere Weeks After Takeover.*

My phone buzzed beside me. And again. And again.

For some unknown reason I flipped the device over. Ignoring the infinite notifications piling up from my social media accounts, I hit my new friend, the phone keypad. I had a call to make. And it was going to be a doozy.

"Jillian?"

A pause. "Hudson? Is that you?"

I sat up, rubbing my bleary eyes. The silk pillowcase, now stained with mascara and shimmer n' shine highlighter, served as a visual reminder of my disintegrating brand. "It's me. I'm sorry. I've been a terrible friend. I owe you apologies for unanswered calls and texts, and for ditching the trip you planned. I am so—"

"The nerve of that man," my friend interrupted. "The nerve of that obviously orchestrated video. His constant deflection. Did you see the interview in *Fame*? Does that man even employ a PR rep?"

Words failed. Jillian should have been burned I'd flaked out on our weekend getaway a few weeks ago. I'd ditched not only Jillian but our other friends, even when I'd promised I wouldn't.

"Marcy's texting me," Jillian said. "Can we add her in? Can we do video? Noah wants in too."

Could I handle video with friends? Were they even still my friends?

Well, I *had* called them. Er, Jillian, and by default the others, since news traveled light-speed with the besties. Former besties. I had no idea what to call them. I knew I was on the outs.

"I'm switching to video," Jillian decided before I could protest. Jillian, the smartest of all of us, had a PhD in brain science. She was so smart she literally *studied brains*. "Hanging up and I'll be back in a flash."

A moment later, my phone cheerfully announced an incoming video call. Smeared make-up and all, I answered.

Jillian's fair-skinned face appeared, her blond hair artfully tousled. A switch from her usual ponytail. Two more squares popped up, filling my screen with four faces, including mine.

"Hudson," Marcy declared. "You look—"

"*Shh*. The woman just went through a public breakup," said Noah, a.k.a. "Noah the girl," because she'd been questioned so often why she was named Noah when it was "a boy's name." As if gender neutral names hadn't rocked the world for decades. I'd experienced a bit of heat myself as a *girl Hudson*.

The four of us had been thick as wolverines (University of Michigan's school mascot) during undergrad. Friends I'd thought I could never survive without, until I'd done exactly that.

The past five years, we'd grown more distant. Scratch that—I'd become more distant.

"I know I look a mess," I started. This was my chance to be real with people who knew me. No filter, no extra lighting, just me with damp eyes, dried fermented juice crusted on my chin, and dark roots betraying my cotton candy pink hair. "Truth: I *am* a mess. Big time. I...need help."

I assumed I'd hit bottom, but who could be sure this wasn't merely the first layer of earth? Toss in a shovel. Surely a deeper level existed.

The three of them spoke at once, all overtop each other. Marcy raised a hand. "May I speak? I'd like to speak."

"Go ahead," Jillian said as Noah gestured with her hand to continue.

Marcy leaned closer to the screen, showing off her impeccably maintained skin. When we lived together, she used only soap, water, and SPF, and wow, look at that gorgeous warm complexion. "I think we need to hear from Hudson what she wants from us." Marcy's voice softened. "We miss you. The stuff online is madness. I can't tell what's real. How are you holding up?"

"I have a lawyer," I answered. "She's intense. A statement is going out." I pressed a hand against my throbbing head. "But that's not what you're interested in. I'm trying to figure out my place in all this. I feel so completely stupid."

"I'm sorry," Noah spoke up. "But what were your *friends* doing for you while this whole 'blame Hudson for a billionaire's scams' went down? Those mega blonds from TV? Hmm?"

My new BFFs, or so I'd thought. Those sisters on the home renovation show everybody loved, with the impossibly gorgeous hair, who never seemed to break a sweat when they tore into drywall. (Their secret: they picked up a sledgehammer for the shot, and handed off the tool to hired help.)

The text response I'd received from Brenna, the older of the sisters, came to mind, as chilling as when I'd first read it:

So sorry to hear of your troubles, Hudson. We feel like distancing from your toxicity aura is needed during this difficult time. Later!

I couldn't admit to the friends who'd known me when I still wore braces with rubber bands (yes, as an eighteen-year-old—I was a late bloomer) that my supposed famous besties bailed via text. "They've been busy," I began. Aw, screw it. "They're protecting their brand. Right now, aligning with me is a bad idea for most influencers."

Noah loudly scoffed. Marcy removed her glasses, fanned her face, and put them back on. Jillian stared open-mouthed.

They spoke at once all over again.

"Okay, hold up." Marcy clapped for our attention. "I know what we need to do. I'm calling us in. It's the 9-1-1 back in action. You hear me? Two words: emergency sleepover."

Chapter 2

Hudson

AFTER A THANKFULLY UNEVENTFUL flight from L.A. to Detroit, a ride share brought me to suburbia to the address given to me. A modern apartment complex with little alcove doorways and white painted trim.

I'd barely set foot on pavement when familiar faces and arms and voices came at me.

"Get her inside!"

"I could have picked you up, you know."

"Don't ever go this long without checking in!"

"Will you stop shaming her? She's been shamed enough."

"Sorry, it's just—"

"Inside. Let's hustle!"

We made it to the second floor apartment in a whirlwind of chaos. Through a door and closed in tight. My luggage was taken from me and wheeled off down a hall. My body herded into a living room and positioned on a deep seated couch. Her living space offered a homey sensation, unlike most of the apartments in which I'd spent my recent years. A collage of framed photos featuring her large family filled the stretch of wall between two windows. More framed photos lined up along a low bookcase, including one front and center of the four of us at college graduation. On a coffee table, a lopsided stack of magazines sat beside a clear plastic case of nail polishes. Manicure set beside it.

A mug of tea appeared in my hands.

"Herbal okay?" Noah asked.

I nodded, dazed.

Marcy emerged in front of me. "Slippers? I keep an extra pair for guests."

The slippers were of the white and fluffy variety, stopping just short of bunny ears. "Yes," I whimpered. I'd arrived in another dimension, a cozy one with people who knew a long-past version of me.

"Drink the tea!" Jillian moved past me in a flurry of activity, gathering blankets and pillows.

"Girl, it's June," Marcy told her. "What are you doing?"

She stopped, overloaded with throw pillows and a whole duvet cover pulled from a bed. "There's a chill in here. We need comfort. Blankets are comfort."

Finally, the flurry settled. My friends arranged themselves on the furniture while Jillian took the floor among her hoarded blankets.

"We're all here," Marcy stated. "We're glad you're here. Everything is going to be okay."

Jillian's head cocked. "Are you wearing a wig?"

I looked at each of their concerned faces and promptly burst into tears.

Noah swatted Jillian. "Now you made her cry. Of course that's a wig. You think that's her real hair? It's like straw sprayed with aerosol paint. Or that bark stuff in garden beds."

"Mulch," Marcy added. "I think you mean mulch."

I yanked off the wig. My real hair, faded pink, was now flattened and damp from an afternoon wig sauna. Worse than garden mulch. "It's a disguise," I admitted. Assembling a wig, hat, sunglasses, and schlubby clothing combo had been my only intentional accessorizing for days.

Questions poured in about paparazzi and the menacing media. Too much to follow and respond to.

Jillian clapped once, loud. "Come on, ladies. *Focus.*"

The women descended on me. Hugs and more hugs.

"I knew that rich boy was a creep," Marcy muttered.

"It's the power," Jillian said. "It's the power that does it to them. Makes them feel invincible."

I wiped at my eyes. "I'm not crying over him. Or my hair. It's you all. I've missed you so much. I don't have a clue what you've all been doing." The tears came again. "I'm the worst friend." I pulled a pillow onto my lap and wrapped my arms around it. "I'm really sorry for losing touch. Until all this happened, it was like I existed in this bubble and only so much fit inside." I'd sure made enough room in that bubble for VIP access parties, trips to posh day spas, and hours and hours connecting with strangers online.

Guilt hit in a new wave. This just plain hurt.

"We can get to what we've been up to after you tell us the real deal with this drama," Marcy said.

I took a breath. "I messed up. I shouldn't have trusted him. I shouldn't have believed..." *I was special.* That my brand, my life, would leave a lasting mark anywhere, unless that mark was a stain. An oily, chemical-laden foundation stain. My nightmare stain.

"Everybody messes up," she responded. "Not everybody messes up with a worldwide audience. The important thing is, you're here. And we're here for you."

When my eyes closed, the viral video played, streaming free in my brain from now through eternity. A video call I'd assumed was private.

Despite blocking his number, I couldn't block the memory.

I told my friends exactly what I remembered feeling as it unfolded, wincing at my own replay.

"You sold me out," Kristoff had fumed, waving his hands frantically. The Krom Industries logo faced prominently behind where he sat at his massive clear plexiglass desk.

"I don't know what you mean," I'd stammered, sounding painfully naïve.

"You tipped off the feds. You just couldn't stand sharing the spotlight. You had to sabotage me. All for attention. All for more likes from your followers. Now look. I stand to lose everything. Because of you."

Fear struck me cold. He was blaming *me? "That's not—what are you talking about? I signed on as a brand ambassador with your new business. Why would I sabotage that?"*

But it was like I hadn't spoken at all. He'd gone on and on, almost as if reading from a speech, with bursts of anger and at one point, near tears. I'd sat there in a panic freeze, like watching an oncoming semi-truck barreling toward me and aiming to total my life and career.

And then the ranting stopped. Kristoff grew calm, cool, almost serene. His posture shifted as he sat back. "I know you're not capable of this level of machination. But it sure will get clicks."

Guess which part went viral. And which part was conveniently cut.

Now my breakup could be replayed for anyone and everyone to assess, judge, and critique. As the federal investigators uncovered, Kristoff had been stealing from investors to feed several hollow projects for years.

Marcy shook her head. "That dirty rotten—"

"The audacity!" Jillian interrupted.

"Where's this man right now?" Noah smacked a fist into her open palm. "Can we find him? Give me ten minutes, alone, with my brass knuckles."

Marcy shot her horrified look. "Who owns legit brass knuckles?"

Noah shrugged. "Look, I ran with a rough crowd as a kid. You know this."

Their chattering finally eased, so I went on. "The spokesperson deal meant I'd be the new face of the natural beauty company Sheek—that's s-h-e-e-k like *chic*, but branded to be its own thing."

Noah scrunched her nose. "Aren't they one of those—"

"It's a many-tiered operating triangle of independent consul-tants," I responded on instinct. "Yeah, it's *a make a killing at the top level and profit off the consultants who sell the products* type of company."

"Only this one doubled as a laundromat," Jillian added.

Noah looked at me. "Sheek sells clothes?"

Jillian threw up her hands. "Hello, *laundering*. As in laundering things that *aren't* clothes. Like oh, dirty cash or shady real estate transactions. That's why billionaire bro wanted it. To funnel cash through."

I let them piece the details together. Then, like everyone else in the world, surmise that I was a total idiot for signing on to a deal that looked so impossibly shiny on the outside but rotted to the core beneath one flimsy surface layer. And it was a real shame because their waterproof vegan eyeliner glided on the eye in the most magical way.

But my friends didn't call me an idiot. These were my real friends. Not like the renovation sisters who'd ghosted at a whiff of bad news.

"What do you need?" Jillian asked. "How can we help?"

I willed the tears back. Being here surrounded by their support felt like a literal rescue, even if I had no vision of my next steps. I told them about the photographer lurking outside my apartment. "The agent and my attorney suggested I take a break. I called you all. And now I'm here."

"Easy," Marcy said. "Stay with me. The second bedroom is my office, but I've got a futon in there and I can move my desk into the dining room."

Tears welled again. "I can't ask that of you." Except I'd already made it known I needed help and I'd flown all the way here.

"You're not asking, I'm offering," she said. "You know me well enough that I don't offer my home to just anybody. Now bread, on the other hand. That I give away all the time. I'll be right back."

She returned with a freshly baked loaf cooled from the oven. A vintage shallow dish with butter followed.

Marcy leveled a look at me. "Don't tell me you're on some no bread diet. Unless, it's due to allergies, of course."

My mouth watered. "No allergies."

We all dove into the bread. Sweet, delicious carbs could solve almost anything.

I needed to think through my next steps. Because while I told myself I'd boarded that plane for a sleepover invitation, deep down, I knew wouldn't return to California for a while. I'd have to figure out what to do with my stuff and my apartment, but I needed a plan first. I couldn't hang out at Marcy's apartment without doing anything.

"I need more than a place to stay," I admitted. "I'm going to need a source of income. I have some money saved, but..." This was brutal. "I wasn't...well, see, I had followers and the free samples, but they were more like supplemental..."

"You still worked a job," Marcy finished.

"More like jobs, plural." My secret, like a clogged pore. "I wasn't raking in the influencer money. That's why this brand deal was a such a big get for me." I picked at chipped polish on my fingernail. "I did temp work in offices. Freelance jobs. Stuff like managing social media accounts for other influencers, skincare consults, an assistant to a make-up artist. I did make-up for a few weddings."

"I'm sure we could figure that out," Marcy said. "I've got a friend who does event planning. I bet she'd love your touch with social media. Maybe she could use your talents."

Talents. The word felt like an insult, especially around these three who worked in successful careers. Jillian, a PhD Neuroscientist with a fancy new job in Detroit, Marcy, an accountant, and Noah working in insurance at a high-rise in downtown Chicago. The type of jobs parents could name at a dinner party and not get questioning looks from their friends.

Time for more humbling self-reflection. "I can't blame the evil ex for everything. I got swept up in a life that matched the image I wanted. Especially when he paid for everything." I'd literally been wined and dined and had lapped up every morsel. I cringed. "Now I have attorney fees. To keep me, you know..."

"Out of the clink?" Noah filled in.

Marcy burst into laughter. "The clink! No one says that."

"I was trying to lighten the mood," she said.

I took out my phone. "They suggested I take a break from social media. I've never had to do that before. Please don't make fun of me, but I'm not sure how."

"I do no phone Sundays twice a month," Marcy said. "I put the phone in a drawer for the day, or at least out of sight. If it's a real emergency, my family knows where to find me."

She didn't get it. I *lived* online. "It's already been rough not responding to the trolls."

"Ugh, never respond to the trolls," Marcy said.

Jillian nodded toward my phone. "I could respond to posts on your behalf. Let you know what needs to be followed up on and do that for you."

The idea of someone else controlling my brand, even a friend like Jillian, made the horror of my situation sink in further. I really, really didn't want to let go. No, I *couldn't*.

I shook my head, determined now that I'd at least made one decision. "I'll monitor my accounts. But other than the prepared statement, I won't post anything. It's too hard knowing I can't say what I want."

My phone lit with a text. An unknown number. *Ugh, block.* Either a telemarketer or worse. Anyone I needed to answer a text from I'd saved as a contact.

Another text came in.

Kelly Q. Pierce: *Call me when you get this.*

"My attorney." I held the phone out. "I need to take this."

I stepped into the kitchen and called. "Yes?"

"Hey. Where are you?" Kelly Q asked, all business.

"Michigan. With friends."

"Good. Out of abundance of caution, please stay there and don't post your location online. Turn off your GPS and all that."

My heart thundered. "What? What's going on?"

"We're examining a few online threats related to the case, but please don't worry. None are directly focused on you, and we are taking every precaution. I'll let Agent Shoney"—Mulder— "know you left the state."

So many questions. So many. I asked them, rapid fire, and came away with not much more information than when I'd started. Lay low. Let the agents do their investigation.

The call ended, leaving me numb.

"Hudson?" Jillian found me staring at nothing.

Quickly, she returned me to the living room where I recapped for the group. "I'm thinking a job with a caterer for public events might not be the best idea. And if I'm supposed to be offline, I basically can't do any of the things I know how to do." This was the pits. "I don't know what to do with myself."

The room quieted.

And I had no idea how I'd keep my mitts off my phone. I'd reached for the stupid thing six times since I'd set it aside. *Six times*.

"Maybe you should get a burner phone," said Noah.

Marcy nodded. "Yeah, like a flip phone. I've got a cousin who still uses one. Can you imagine?" She cackle-laughed until suddenly she stopped. "Hold up." She reached for her own phone and winced my direction. "That phone reach is such a subconscious instinct. I swear I have a reason."

She tapped at the screen. Even watching her interact with the device sent a wave of dread over me. How would I ever manage to detox from my online life? My online life *was my life.*

Marcy suppressed near glee as she tapped and swiped her screen.

"What?" Noah prompted. "Spill."

She turned the phone's screen to face me. An outdated website with a photo of a lake and trees and some cabins stared back. "Hudson, what do you think about summer sleepaway camp?"

Chapter 3

Lucas

CRISP MOUNTAIN AIR HIT my skin. The sun hadn't yet broken fully from the horizon, leaving the day to be explored. The lake shone in tones of blue, deepening farther out. Brisk waves lapped against the side of the sailboat. I felt alive. Free. Adventure waited. All I had to do was take it by the—

"Lucas? Lucas, did you hear me?"

A shrill voice cut through my perfect morning boat ride. All that was missing was the boat, the sea, and the feeling that actual adventure waited anywhere close to where I existed.

"Luu-caaasss!"

I grit my teeth and left the storage room, my solace. When I didn't respond fast enough, the woman called after me as if I were one of her grandkids.

I found the seasoned administrator perched at her desk as if she hadn't just hollered loud enough to wake the dead. Today, her graying curls attempted a jail break from whatever hair do-dad she had clipped in. "Twila, it's honestly too early for this. The coffeemaker's still on the fritz."

She looked at me simply, though simple did not accurately describe Twila. An agent of chaos, more like. "I offered to bring you coffee from town. *On me*. You turn me down every time, so I stopped offering."

That was before my Dr. Coffee machine gave it up to the big bean in the sky. "I'll go into town later and buy a new one."

"I can order you one now. Something more...current."

"I like what I have. They just don't make parts for it."

Twila snorted as she slid her reading glasses from the top her head onto her face. These glasses were even more obnoxious than the last pair. Multi-colored plastic with jewels along the side surrounding the word *Guci*. I could have sworn the brand had two Cs in the name. "No one makes parts for antiquated small appliances that were cheap to begin with. How about this? Come here and look."

I walked over to her desk. "Those are hats for dogs."

"Ope. Wrong screen." She clicked to a new screen and the desktop computer displayed rows of fancy chrome machines fitting for a coffeehouse in a city.

"No."

The screen blinked and another set of machines appeared. More realistic, but with price tags I didn't care for.

"No." I shook my head. "You know I hate online shopping."

"It's like our generations got mixed up," Twila mused. "Oh wait. My generation of old fogies all shop online."

"I can just as easily go to a store and support a local business." How did we even get on this topic? "What were you calling me in here for?"

"Oh!" She clasped her hands together. "That Marcy woman—your cousin, did you say? She is a *delight*. I called her back since you hadn't gotten around to it. About the hire. For the office."

I grunted. "I told you I'd handle it. And we need the hire out at camp, not in here."

Twila had been begging for more help after she'd, without permission, run some kind of ad attached to a school program resulting in more families enrolling their kids for camp sessions.

Enrolling as a last resort, obviously. We were gaining all the families who realized the big name camps filled months ago.

And cost more. And had top-of-the-line facilities.

Camp Junebug? Not even close.

But we were open. And we'd hung onto our camp accreditation. We were deemed safe; we just weren't exactly popular.

"Sounds like she has marketing experience," Twila went on. "A real smart cookie. Graduated from U of M."

My head throbbed from the lack of caffeine. I'd need to head into town sooner rather than later. The thrift shop by the diner had a rack of household appliances. That would do the trick.

"Are you even listening?" Twila asked.

I rubbed my forehead. "Sorry. Coffee."

Twila loudly huffed and rolled back her chair, which knocked against the knotty pine wall behind her desk. She moved to the kitchenette in the adjoining room. She banged open a cupboard and pulled out something crinkly. "Instant coffee. For emergencies. I'll heat up water."

I could have sworn the words *you baby* followed, but the microwave door slamming shut clipped the insult.

The hiring thing *was* important, which I'd ignored. Not intentionally. I didn't want to be doing any of this office management stuff. It wasn't Twila's fault I'd gotten stuck with administrative tasks when every breath of my being screamed to be outdoors. Out in the woods. Or on the lake. Eventually, I'd lead hikers on mountain trails in Colorado.

I needed to be patient.

I cleared my throat. "Bring the hire in for an interview. Make sure they get the background check or it's a waste of time." I coughed. "Please."

"Already on it." She handed me a chipped Camp Junebug mug with a liquid smelling vaguely related to coffee.

I sipped and winced. "Thank you."

"She should be here at any minute."

"Sorry?"

"The new hire. She's on her way."

Talking to Twila frequently felt like time traveling, as if entire conversations occurred in some past reality.

The door burst open. Maggie, the head counselor, nudged in a camper wearing tie-dye from head to toe. Even the canvas shoes had the funky print. "We've got another one asking to call home."

Twila edged out the stool beside her desk. "Sit here, darlin'. I'll ring up your folks. How's that sound?"

The little girl's lip trembled as she nodded.

They said you'd build leadership experience. They said you'd be outdoors every day. Some days, the big mountain sky seemed further and further off.

Maggie, now momentarily free of her charge, walked over to me. She had an imposing presence at nearly six feet tall and a sense of directness demanding respect. "You found a hire yet? I don't know much longer I can take it. The girls are undoing all of my restorative energy work."

As I tried to make sense of that, she continued. "Not the campers. The *teenagers.* Sixteen and seventeen-year-olds should not be trusted as authority figures. They don't listen. It's like herding cats who are also stuck-up and obsessed with themselves. So, I guess, cats." She blinked. "I miss adults. Rational, trained adults."

"You've got adults out there."

She narrowed her eyes. "College students. They're all children as far as I'm concerned."

Point taken. Legally speaking, age eighteen or older meant adult status, which mattered for our camper-to-staff ratio. Which could not dip below regulations or we'd all be out of a job. "Twila's got someone coming in."

We only had the budget to hire one more person. We needed another adult out there with the campers and teen counselors, despite Twila asking for support in the office. It pained me not to hire another body for the office since I was desperate to get work off my desk. More like ditch the desk altogether.

Office work involved calls from parents. I liked trees. Trees didn't talk back.

The list of camp maintenance tasks came to mind. I'd need to get going to finish everything—

"Are you even listening?" Maggie looked at me, her pale freckled arms folded.

Wow, was I bad at this. "I'm repairing the roof over the rain shelter." It's why I'd gone into the storage room in the first place, to fetch my tools, only I'd gotten sidetracked daydreaming of being anywhere else.

"Well, we need that done, for sure. It's hard for the girls to do crafts there on rain days when water is dripping in." Maggie's features softened. "Look, I know this new director gig has been hard for you. We're all trying to hang in there. You know, for the girls."

My gaze went to the little girl on the phone. She wiped her eye with the back of her hand. Poor kid.

Maggie lowered her voice. "Hey, you did an incredible thing, Lucas. Taking this job so we could keep the camp going means so much to the families who love this camp."

I shook my head. "Don't make me out to be some hero. Somebody needed to keep Camp Junebug going. That's it."

"Most people jumped ship to the other camp."

"Guess I'm not most people." Most people didn't prefer trees to actual human conversation.

Maggie returned to the camper, who seemed less trembly and sad.

"Ready to get back to camp?" Maggie asked the girl.

She nodded, staring at the floor.

Maggie knelt in front of her. "Want to do a special, exclusive, super secret craft?"

The girl's eyes widened. "What kind of craft?"

"Let's go to the craft room and I'll let you pick."

The kid perked up and smiled. She and Maggie left together, leaving the office quiet again.

"You're a cold one, Mr. Grinch," Twila said from across the room.

"Me? What did I do?"

"Not even a cracked smile with that sweet little girl in here?" She shook her head. "Just over there scowling."

"I was thinking about that awful coffee."

Twila huffed. "I bet if you had a woman in your life, you'd be less a grump."

I let out a clipped laugh. "I'm surrounded by women." Through all the chaos of the past year, I'd ended up running a children's camp. *For girls.* "Besides, you shouldn't tell me that. I'd never suggest you start dating. It's inappropriate."

"Of course it's inappropriate. I've been married nearly forty years."

My head pulsed as if speaking to me. *Get out. While you can.*

"You know I mean well." She grinned while she said it. "Go off now. I'll hold down the fort."

I really needed to try harder. Maggie and Twila were dependable and had stuck around after the big split siphoned most of the staff to Camp Trail Blazers across the lake. If I could manage to stick it out for the summer, prove my leadership skills as camp director and score a recommendation from the camp owner, I'd have what I needed. Experience for the real job I wanted. Off to mountainous terrain leading wilderness expeditions for adventure-seekers who didn't need to call home to mommy.

"What about the interview?" I asked Twila.

She saluted me. "I'll take care of it, boss."

Enough for me. Already, the stale office air climbed down my throat, strangling the sense of adventure out of me. Roof repair beat conference calls and camp budgets any day.

I grabbed my tools and stopped by the locked shed behind the office. I headed to the rain shelter with my tools and ladder, and got to work.

Despite the safety cones on the ground, I kept watch for darting children. Working at the camp took patience and incredible amounts of attention. If it wasn't children running out in front of you, it was the threat of tipped canoes, random trips and falls, and general crying. There was *just so much crying*.

My patch work now complete, the sun beat down, sending sweat dripping across my back and neck. But the air was clear and I had a nice view of the lake from the roof. Moments like this helped me feel like myself again.

Maybe I'd stay up here the rest of the day. Move over to the end of the roof beneath shade and take a nap.

The ground clear below, I chucked the garbage bag of old roof tiles over the edge. I gathered my tools and swung my leg to the ladder, carefully lowering with the toolbox in my free hand.

Halfway down, a child's ear-piercing squeal split the air.

Everything happened in slow motion.

First, my body left its skin.

I jerked my head toward the scream, scanning for hurt or endangered children, and pain shot through my neck.

My foot slipped.

The toolbox left my hand and clambered to the ground.

Gravity pulled me down.

My knee hit a ladder rung. Hard.

Another scream followed, this one closer, louder, overtaking shrieks of laughter in the distance.

Somewhere in there I braced for impact, trying to remember my limited eighth grade martial arts lessons on how to take a fall.

I tried to relax into the fall despite the shooting pain in my neck and knee.

And then I hit...something squishy.

Flat on my back, I looked up. A woman. With pink hair.

She gaped at me. "Are you *okay*?"

Chapter 4

Hudson

A MAN FELL OFF a ladder. Right in front of me. And I'd been powerless to stop it.

"Are you okay?" I asked a second, no, third time. The guy was blinking at least.

His face scrunched. "Plastic..." He managed to sit upright and pat the bag he landed on. "Is there a blanket in here?"

"A comforter," I answered. "See, my friend Jillian has this thing about blankets. She insisted I bring one, and well, I'm carrying all this stuff and it's really hot out, so I set it down. I forgot about the humidity here after being in L.A., which is more of a dry heat—"

The guy scrambled to standing. "I'm sorry, who are you?"

"Oh, hi. I'm Hudson." I stuck out my hand, and when he reached to shake it, he grunted and instead grabbed for his neck, the muscles seeming to seize in pain. I detoured my unshaken hand to finger comb hair from my face. "I was told to find you to be let into my cottage."

The man stared as if I'd asked him which way to the day spa.

From the looks of this place, I highly doubted a day spa hid beyond a grassy knoll. At this point, I prayed for indoor plumbing. Something I never imagined required divine intervention.

"Cottage?" he asked.

I shifted my purse to my other shoulder. I should have worn my wide brimmed disguise hat to shield me from this unrelenting sun. "Or cabin. Whatever. Twila in the office said I'd find you out here."

"Twila."

Just the one word, he repeated. "Uh huh."

"Said you'd find *me*?" he finished.

Okay, this conversation would take forever at this pace. "I'm the new office assistant. I'm looking for my lodgings."

This guy was a case study in facial expressions. The sheer number of changes in ten seconds had to set some kind of record. And he was so *sweaty*. But weirdly, not in a bad way. Almost like the sweat suited him. I definitely wasn't minding how his shirt clung to his lean, toned arms.

Dark hair, cut short on the sides, longer on top, beard. Me into beards? No. His wasn't long at least but it wasn't shaped either. It looked almost accidental. Like he'd told the hair follicles: *Have at it!* to explore new areas of his face.

I shook sense into myself. This was my *job*. Marcy delivered. I had a place off the grid to lay low, rent free, and I might even make a few bucks in the process.

Besides, the guy just fell halfway off a roof. "Do you think you have a head injury? Those are no joke. Can I walk you to the camp nurse? I'm assuming you have on-site medical."

He rubbed his neck again, wincing. "I don't have a head injury. Did you say you're the new office assistant*?*"

"Yes."

"Not here for an interview."

"Correct."

"You passed the background check?"

I nodded. "All clear."

He seemed to be taking in my whole look. "What are you wearing?"

I was confident he wasn't asking for brand names. I'd never been to summer camp myself, so when Marcy told me where I'd be riding out this bad PR wave, my mind thought resort and thus resort wear collections. A breezy tropical print kaftan over a minidress seemed practical enough. My heels were only a measly two inches tall. Totally reasonable for an office setting. I considered this look as upscale casual resort which should be applicable for camp.

I kept this to myself. "I wanted to set a professional impression."

"Your hair is pink."

I pressed my lips together to seal shut the first response that came to mind. "How quick of you to notice." Dangit. Second response wasn't much better. "Twila didn't see my hair or clothes as a problem."

"I bet she didn't," he muttered. He appeared to want to say something further but held up his hand instead. He walked past me. Scratch that—limped.

I spun. "Hey, where are you going? Am I supposed to wait here?"

He paused. "I have no idea."

So, wait here then.

No, this was fine. Everything was fine. I just needed to adjust. And wait.

The roof he'd been on attached to some sort of large covered area with picnic tables inside. Open walls on three sides and a dusty looking fireplace along the far wall. I left my suitcases and the comforter in its giant plastic bag on the grass and sat at a table facing out at trees and scrubby grass and dirt.

The urge to reach for my phone came so automatic, I couldn't stop myself. I made contact with the device in my purse, but let it slip from my fingers. It wasn't even my real phone with all the temptations of the internet. Nope. This sad piece of plastic came prepaid from a gas station. A behind the counter purchase, which added an even more surreal sense to this unexpected life twist.

I peeked at the rectangular device in my purse. To use for calls only.

Calls only. I shuddered.

Thankfully, my smart phone, *my precious*, existed a mere few feet away, tucked deep in a suitcase. I'd keep tabs on my Beauty Butterfly accounts and think through how to relaunch my career. I'd rebuild my reputation as a friendly expert in the world of natural beauty and skincare. I'd find myself a new brand to work with, one not run by a shady guy with an honest-to-goodness Slurpee machine in his penthouse.

So many red flags ignored.

I had to give Marcy credit. Working in the camp office would make my social media monitoring even easier. I could use Twila's desktop computer and not even bother with my phone.

Voices sounded from the path emerging from the trees. A group of girls walked toward me in a single file line. The leader, probably in high school, and the rest grade school-aged, maybe ten-year-olds if I estimated right.

"Hello, future friend," the teen girl leading the pack called over. She had frizzy black hair and a killer brown complexion. I imagined she used a good toner and vitamin C serum. She smiled in the effortless way only those who hadn't been part of a viral scandal could.

I waved a tentative hand. "Um, hello."

"All stop," the girl announced, holding her hand in front of her like a stop sign. The younger girls stopped, though a few stumbled into the girls they followed. Little giggles and chatter followed. "Have you lost your way?" the girl asked.

Had I ever. "I'm waiting on Luke to show me to my cottage."

She raised a dark brow. "Are you the new counselor with Maggie?"

The name didn't ring a bell. "I'm working in the office."

She pouted a little at that. "Bummer. You have an amazing aesthetic." She moved her hands up and down in the air. "Like, all of it. But those shoes will die here. You need some of these." She tilted her foot to show off her boots.

Hiking boots paired with thick socks. And cargo shorts. It was a real...look.

"We'll see," I said lightly. "After all, I'll be working in the front office most of the time."

"Who is that?" one of the younger girls asked.

"Are you our new counselor?" another chimed in.

"Bianca is mean!" a voice called from the back.

Chastising shrieks and gasps cascaded through the line.

The teen girl swung around to her minions. "I heard that. And I'm not mean. I'm *precise*."

I could respect precise.

Bianca returned her attention toward me, then past me. "Oh, here comes your *Luke* now." She gave me a sly grin before alerting the girls to "Forward march!"

The guy now wore a clean heather gray T-shirt. The unpretentious kind that probably came shrink-wrapped in a package of four. He had on a faded cap with the Detroit pro baseball team logo—a casual look I was definitely into. Not gonna lie, he was hot. In that natural, not-trying-hard way that no guy in L.A. seemed to pull off. Nashville had those guys, but every one of them wanted you to listen to their demo.

He jingled a set of keys as he breezed past. "Follow me."

Well, well. Hiding out at Camp Whatever might not be so bad after all. For eye candy purposes only. Because I obviously wasn't in the market for anything more during this exile than a little ocular dazzle.

Men right now—I couldn't trust them. Any of them. Honestly, *The Golden Girls* had the right idea living in that breezy pastel house together. Maybe when all this drama blew over, me and the girls could arrange our own late twenty-somethings ladies living scenario. We'd need a cute name—

"You coming?" Luke, many feet ahead of me, made his annoyance clear in his tone.

"Sorry." I gathered my stuff and rolled the suitcase along the path. It rumbled a few feet until the wheel angled into a muddy patch. "*Gross.*"

I shifted the suitcase out of the muck, only for it to get stuck again. Ugh, mud in the wheel parts. The giant bag with the comforter pressed against my skin like a sauna. Why was everything so sticky?

The guy returned to where I stood. Scowling, he lifted the suitcase by the handle and walked again.

"Thank you." I truly was grateful. That thing was heavy.

He veered into a wooded area where the path split off in a new direction. I'd dressed for an office, not off-roading, so these heels really might lose their life. I could take them off, but who knew what kind of nastiness I'd step on? With a bare foot? Thank you, no.

Finally, we emerged at a clearing revealing a single shack. Weathered wood that may have been painted blue in a past century stared back in jagged horror. Gaps between the slats provided barrier-free entry for whatever creepy-crawlies wanted in.

And it leaned. The whole thing leaned.

Luke unlocked the door. "Home sweet home."

I stood, struck dumb. "This is uninhabitable. I can't stay here."

"It's the only free cabin."

I ventured forward. Maybe just the outside looked like a murder hut. I peeked inside. Nope. Straight from a thrasher flick. Was that a *stained mattress?*

Static sounded accompanied by a woman's voice. "Lucas? Where are you?"

The guy plucked a two-way radio from his belt. "I'm at the cabin."

"*I'm* at the cabin. She's bunking with me. Over."

I could swear the guy held back a grin. "Simple mistake. Over." He shut the door without looking at me and walked ahead, still carrying my suitcase. "Let's go."

I breathed in relief. At least I wasn't a tired plot from a horror movie. My actual life felt horrific enough.

I followed Luke—Lucas—to where the trail had split, joining the main dirt path again toward several brightly colored cabins. They looked a bit worn, but at least the yellows and greens were identifiable, happy colors.

A tall woman with wild straw-yellow curls wearing a polo shirt with the camp's name and logo walked out from a smaller cabin with a covered porch. "Hiya. You must be the new hire. I'm Maggie."

I smiled my friendliest smile. "Nice to meet you. Hudson."

I'd briefly considered a fake name to embrace the full lay-low life, but lying on a job application that required a background check to work with children seemed a step in the wrong direction. I'd earn a lecture with Agent Mulder for a stunt like that.

Maggie jacked Lucas in the side. He winced. "Ow! What's that for?"

"Lucas Russo, you played a dirty trick on Hudson taking her out to that run-down shack."

So it *had* been a trick.

He shrugged one shoulder. "It's the only cabin open. How did I know you two were sharing?"

I hadn't known I'd be sharing a cabin either, but I also knew basically nothing about the job. Twila and I mainly talked shoes, facial fillers (she had some hot takes), and the latest season of *Celebrity Houseboat: Escapades*, which I hated to admit I watched, but I totally watched.

Okay, focus. Maggie had called him by his full name, Lucas Russo. Marcy's last name was Russo. Because they were cousins. So, why did Lucas act so confused about me? "You're Marcy's cousin," I stated. "You should have known I was coming."

His cheeks colored. "I had things to do and let Twila handle everything."

He muttered something about mistakes and maybe coffee makers, but that didn't make any sense.

Huh. So maybe he didn't know my real reason for being here or any of the sordid details.

Which was great, actually. The fewer people who knew about my situation, the better. Marcy said she'd covered what she needed on the phone, so that must have been with Twila. I wasn't sure what that had entailed. I'd been devouring another chunk of Marcy's homemade bread and internally spiraling about an internet-less future when she'd made the call.

Twila never questioned why I wanted to live on the grounds. She'd only asked if I'd want her to bring in coffee from town in the mornings. Me and Twila would get along just great.

"Well then, let's get you settled." Maggie opened the door and gestured for me to follow.

The small front room featured a floral couch I swore was a duplicate to one currently in my grandmother's basement, along with odds and ends lamps, tables, and an old desk with one of those wooden roller covers domed over it. Window unit air conditioner. Beyond it was the bedroom, and I spied a bathroom—indoor plumbing! Along the left, a counter with a microwave and hot plate. A minifridge on the floor with a healthy plant on top.

Sparse, but cozy. Very cozy for two.

Marcy had gone to bat for me so I wouldn't make this weird. "Thanks. This looks great."

A grunt sounded by the door. Lucas, smoldering in a very rugged outdoorsman way, gave me a disparaging look only rivaled by judgey teen girls on the internet. "Sure thing. Make yourself *comfortable*."

He sauntered off like some kind of scorned cowboy, letting the screen door slap shut.

"Well that was…interesting," I stated. Fascinating, truly. Who knew hot, grumpy men worked at children's camps? I sure didn't.

Maggie rolled her eyes. "He is *so* difficult sometimes. But he's been through a thing or two this year. We all have. Okay, come on. Let me show you around."

That tour took twelve seconds since I'd scoped out the place from the doorway. The bedroom wasn't large enough for two beds, therefore, bunk beds.

"I never took this apart," said Maggie. "After my last partner in crime was—" She cut herself off.

"Oh no, what? Are they…okay?" Was the murder hut involved? Were those horror movies based on real camps?

"Yeah, she's fine. She works at the other camp." Maggie stared out the small window for a beat. "If you don't mind me keeping the bottom bunk, that's where I've been since we opened again this season. Otherwise, I hit my head on the ceiling."

Top bunk, sure. I could do this. Never mind a month ago I'd been partying on a superyacht with the daughter of a shipping magnate and the now-adult child star from that early 2000s sitcom everybody quoted in memes now. Because they were friends with my billionaire boyfriend.

Ex. Very, very ex.

"I don't use the closet for much, so you can have that," she went on. "I have my stuff in the dresser."

I scanned her outfit. Wrinkled shorts. Faded polo shirt. Thick socks and hiking boots. Well, the woman did work at a camp.

"I hope you brought more shoes." She looked at my dirt-caked heels. "The girls will think you're cool, but your feet won't last an afternoon in those."

"Right. Of course."

I felt ridiculous. Heels, dress, and my resort wear bangles and chunky necklace? I really hadn't thought this through. I'd envisioned my lodgings in some sort of suite in a large log cabin, more hotel than actual cabin.

I rummaged through my suitcase. I'd packed hastily. My jewelry and accessories I'd swept into zippered cloth bags. Probably a hot mess in there. Not that it mattered. I wouldn't be wearing any of that here.

Finally, I found my phone. I tapped the link to open the browser for a quick peek at email and my socials.

"Oh, and no cell phones."

Maggie's voice registered, but not what she said. "Huh?"

"No cell phones. At camp."

I continued looking at her. She returned a mildly uncomfortable gaze. "Okay, technically the adult staff are allowed to have them. The teen counselors have very limited access and none of the campers can use them. It's part of our camp mission."

I stared. It was rude and I knew it, but I'd lost all chill.

"Sounds like maybe that wasn't covered in the interview." She threw me a weak smile. "After hours here in our cabin, it's no big deal. Not like we get much of a connection out here anyway. Just don't have your phone out around the campers." She tapped a two-way radio clipped to her belt. "We'll get you one of these."

My focus shifted to the blocky ancient tech *physically affixed to her body*.

I wouldn't survive this.

"There's an extra camp shirt and some shorts on the top closet shelf. I'll give you space while you change." Maggie eased out of the room. "You'll want to head to the office to talk with the boss."

Whew, this was a lot to take in. The camp, the job, the surrender of any fashion sense. "Oh, Twila said to take my time."

Maggie laughed. "Yeah, wouldn't that be nice." She closed the door.

An ominous sensation crawled across my skin. This coming from a woman who'd purchased a disguise wig and a burner phone in the last three days.

Chapter 5

Lucas

"WHAT DID YOU DO?" I kept my voice measured and professional despite the absolute trainwreck I'd just witnessed.

Twila held up a finger at me while she continued a phone call. "That's right. Dressing on the side, but two containers. Your dressing is *the best.*"

I felt my teeth tighten. Which made my neck muscle spasm. "Gah." I rubbed my neck, which reminded me my knee throbbed. It'd been a dang miracle I'd landed on that blanket or I'd be in even worse shape.

But why had there even been a blanket on the ground? My cones clearly signaled to steer clear.

All of this made my head ache. Not to mention my looming conference call. I had reports and a budget to prep ahead of the call. The plan had been roof: fix; office: budget. Not escort a fashion model through camp for a job she shouldn't have been hired for.

Finally, Twila hung up. She directed a pleasant look at me. "Yes, boss?"

I snorted. "Oh, I'm the boss now?" I paced the floor in front of her desk. "Twila, you hired that girl without consulting me."

"She's a full-grown woman, sir."

"I'm not—don't call me sir." I stopped and took a breath. "You hired her behind my back."

"She passed the background check."

"She looks like some fashion diva from a magazine. Does she even have experience working with children? Or any outdoors training?"

"Working with me in the office, I'm not sure why those skills would be necessary."

I stared at Twila. She stared at me. I stared some more until she flinched. There—I knew it. She knew I needed that hire out with Maggie and not as her own personal sidekick.

"Twila," I said slowly. "Did you actually—"

The front office door opened, and a whirlwind of sounds tumbled in. The pink-haired diva returned, in slightly less obnoxious clothing. A camp shirt and a normal looking skirt with shoes that at least weren't high heels. No weird jewelry. She carried a huge purse and held an ancient alarm clock with the cord dragging against the floor.

She huffed out a breath. "Hi again. Got back here as quickly as I could."

"Hudson!" Twila stood and gestured to her chair. "Take a seat. I'll get you something to drink. Tea—iced or hot?"

"Oh, um, iced. Thank you." She looked at me. "Do you do electronics repairs? This clock doesn't work and I don't have a watch. I usually use my phone but it seems there's a severe lack of cell tower coverage out here." She bit her lip and something stirred beneath my anger that I pressed back. Far back. "Anyway, I'll need to know what time it is at the cottage. You know, to report to work on time."

She handed me the clock, smiled, and walked to Twila's desk and sat.

The broken clock was the least of my concern. Where did I even start?

"So, where would you like me to start?" she asked.

I blinked, irritated. "Have you worked with kids?"

She perked up. "I was a babysitter certified in first aid."

"Was?"

"Yup. In high school."

"When's the last time you babysat?"

She looked thoughtful. "High school."

"And how long ago was that?"

Her expression turned mildly heated. "You're not supposed to ask that. Never to women. And probably never in an employment scenario."

Twila arrived with a clinking glass of iced tea. "I've tried to tell him just the same, Hudson, but he doesn't have a filter."

"*I* don't have a filter?" I gestured and the alarm clock cord collided with the desk leg. I set the thing on a nearby table. "Okay, how about wilderness training? Camp experience?"

The woman—Hudson—at least had the decency to look humbled. "I'm afraid I don't. Though, I did once sleep in a VW bus at Coachella, and bartered with other festival-goers. I mainly traded plant-based sheet masks for fair trade coffee and organic protein bars. I always carry skincare samples on me. In fact—"

"That's enough." I turned my ire at Twila. "This is what I'm talking about. We need someone qualified to supervise the campers and work with Maggie running the programs. She ain't it."

The room deadened to silence. I braved a look at Hudson whose earlier confidence shrank to nothing. Twila shot me a scornful expression layered with disappointment.

I sighed. "We only have the budget for one hire. I know you need help in the office, Twila, but Maggie needs support. It's not safe *by law* if we get a single additional camper. If a counselor is out sick or quits, we're screwed." I took a breath. "We intended for this to be a regrouping summer. Keep things small and work out the kinks."

"Respectfully, I'm great at working out kinks," Hudson announced, then blushed, looking surprised by her own comment.

I couldn't help it, I laughed.

"That came out weird," she said. "I mean, I can adapt. I adapt all the time to shifting algorithms and trends."

"Algorithms?"

"She's a social media star," Twila announced with pride. "I looked you up," she told Hudson.

Her face drained of color. Whose skin worked like that? Blush and pale and blush and pale. Couldn't be healthy.

She tugged at her hair. "You did?"

Twila nodded and looked at me. "She's got a whole YouTube channel with a million followers! Skincare and wellness. I subscribed today."

Hudson stared into the distance. "I'm hoping that part of my life can stay separate from here. If that's okay."

Twila placed a hand over Hudson's. "Of course, dear. Marcy said to keep your employment details discreet. A secret celebrity. I'm honored she trusted me with your fame secret." She inched closer. "You know, I was thinking, Hudson. You can store any of your fancy things here in the camp office. We have a cabinet that locks."

"Oh...sure. What will I wear here?"

"We can order you a couple camp shirts in your size. Maybe some shorts."

I looked between them. None of this mattered. "I'm sorry, this isn't going to work. I've got my own boss to answer to, and we've got a call in—" I checked my watch. "Ten minutes. About the budget. I can't say we've already hired somebody when the budget to hire anyone hasn't been approved."

Twila gasped with excitement. "Maybe you can ask for more money. For *another* hire."

She thought she was so clever. "Look, we're barely hanging on." I hated worrying over camp budgets. I'd much rather lead survival expeditions and tackle advanced trails in the mountains. At least as a guide at the old camp, I'd taught the next generation how to build fires and identify poisonous plants. Now? Now my stints in the woods involved yarn crafts and walks that required constant stopping to treat "ouchies."

Scratch that. I'd take an afternoon of ouchies over budget calls.

Hudson stood. "I need this job. I'm sorry I'm not what you expected, but I really am adaptable. I have a lot of...varied skills."

I doubted fashion sense and YouTube translated to camp life.

"She graduated from University of Michigan," Twila added.

I grumbled. "You told me that already. Unless your degree is in outdoors activities or children's crafts, I don't know how it helps."

"I'll do whatever job you need." Hudson straightened, seeming to call up that confidence, despite her silly hair color. "Marcy said you'd pull through," she said more quietly.

Marcy. I kept forgetting she knew Marcy. She was practically my sister, and her brothers like my own. They'd lived on the block behind ours, a quick cut through two neighbors' backyards and through their gated fence. Her mother and my dad were siblings, and stayed close. I'd experienced my first taste of the outdoors camping with my aunt and uncle along with Marcy and her two brothers. My own parents weren't fond of roughing it, so they happily sent me off with enough food to feed a well-equipped regiment.

Our adventures had been simple. Unpretentious. We pitched tents and slept in sleeping bags my uncle found at an Army surplus store. None of those water-repellent synthetic insulated types that set you back hundreds of bucks. We toured state parks and mom-and-pop owned campgrounds. I still loved that little camp-ground ten miles out of town where we'd escape for a campfire and hiking fix. Probably why I ended up with a soft spot for an aging camp like this when I'd dreamed so much bigger.

"How do you know Marcy?" I couldn't recall any mention of a Hudson, though I hadn't exactly been up-to-date with my cousin's life. Mostly my fault. Nope—all my fault. I wasn't great at keeping in touch.

"College. We were roommates."

"Hmm."

"She's looking out for me," Hudson said. "She's good people."

Yeah, wasn't that the truth. Marcy took after her mother, who'd taken on the role of tirelessly planning events to keep our extended Italian family gathering regularly. Marcy did her own version of that with us—her cousins, brothers, and her brother's best friend, who we'd absorbed into our little clan in high school. Marcy cheered me on at the extreme mudder obstacle races I'd done during my obsession with course competitions. She made the effort first to message me if a chunk of time had passed. She and her brothers ragged on me for not being on social media. I had a phone and they could text—seemed good enough.

They ragged on me for a lot of things, like my dating life, or absence of one. Like I had time for any of that when I could barely handle directing a run-down camp named after a bug. Try putting that on a dating profile.

Static sounded on my two-way.

"Lucas? How soon can I get Hudson here?" Maggie's voice squawked from the radio. "These kids are wearing me down. It's not even noon."

"Won't I be staying here?" Hudson asked Twila.

Twila nodded and I snapped. Part of good leadership meant seeing what had to be done and using the resources available. "No. She will not!"

Good leadership most likely didn't include shouting at subordinates.

I held the radio to my face. "She'll be on her way. Over." I pointed the antenna at Twila. "She passed the background check." I pointed at Hudson. "You. Go find Maggie."

Hudson grinned. "So, I have a job?"

I grabbed the broken alarm clock and headed to my office. "Yup. It's your lucky day."

Chapter 6

Hudson

I LEFT THE CAMP office with my head held high. A small but key victory. So what if that hot grouch saw me as unqualified? I'd show him. I had *charm*. I could talk my way through just about anything. And sure, I was out of my element here at this rustic excuse for a resort, but I had Midwest roots. I only needed a little time to dig into those roots.

The important part was I'd secured my hideout spot. Off grid and off Wi-Fi. I'd lived in Michigan my entire life up until four years ago and had never heard of the tiny town nearest to camp. Now I had to bide my time and lay low doing whatever it was people did at summer camp.

Back at camp proper, Maggie's shift from desperation to grateful mentor brightened my mood. She was seriously so appreciative of my presence, it sent little dopamine hits through my body. Like real-life comment notifications, no online interaction required.

A wistful pang hit thinking of my videos. Every new video was an attempt at getting those dopamine hits. Affirmation that me and my brand mattered. Any time a video clocked lower views I blamed myself for becoming unlikeable or worse—irrelevant.

It struck me how I'd seldom felt the good and appreciated sensation the past few months. I experienced a taste with my college friends pulling me back into their inner circle, but before that? I should have sensed the warning signs. The slow creep of people distancing themselves. The creep had been hard to identify while I'd been blinded by the charm of a fame-worshipping billionaire.

I spent the next hour flexing my non-existent craft muscles with the girls. We were stationed at the picnic tables under what they called the rain shelter, where Lucas had tipped from the ladder. He couldn't even thank me for cushioning his blow with the blanket. Jillian would be happy to note her comforter had saved a frustratingly hot man in need.

I should text her—Gah! No phone!

A new group of campers arrived at my picnic table station. The girls rotated through different craft stations, and after completing each, they received a sticker for their guidebook, which each camper made out of construction paper. Cute. Why hadn't I ever gone to camp? I would have loved making my own guidebook.

The girls, perhaps ten or so, like my oldest niece, settled around the table. They weren't as shy as the last group.

"Why is your hair pink?"

"Is Hudson a fancy name?"

"Are you from New York?"

"Do you get manicures?"

"Are you on YouTube?"

The last question froze my smile in place. I dipped into the yarn bucket and pulled out a true reject—frayed, knotted orange. "Do you mean like, my own channel?" I asked.

"You look like this girl who does skincare videos that my older sister watches," one of the teenage counselors said from the next table over. She was full-figured and pale-skinned with mousy brown hair pulled into a low ponytail. Cute red-framed glasses.

Amy was her name. "Only she didn't have pink hair. At least not that I remember."

"Oh, how funny." I pretended to consider the comment as my mind frantically worked up a logical response. Of course these kids would be all over the internet outside of camp. At least here, they couldn't immediately search for me and out my location. Thankfully, I'd only done the pink hair in recent months, so most of my videos showed me with a different look. Longer, lighter hair with varying color streaks depending on my mood.

Amy's eyes narrowed as she looked to where Maggie sat at another table. She leaned forward, keeping her voice low. "Maggie's allowed a cell phone but we aren't? As counselors? It's totally unfair. We have to ask Maggie for hers or use the office phone."

I shrugged, as if I didn't fully agree with her. "It's not so bad. It's like a vacation from your real life." Ugh, dorky.

Sure enough, Amy visibly cringed. Not exactly subtle. "That's what my parents said. It's why they wanted me to be a counselor here. Camp Junebug *gets back to the basics*." She made a gagging sound and the little girls around us laughed but declared it gross.

"The boys' camp lets them have phones," one camper stated as she wound yarn around her popsicle sticks.

Amy scoffed. "The boys get all kinds of stuff."

I rifled through the yarn box and pulled out a knot of sparkly pink. "What's the boys' camp?"

"You don't know?" Bianca, the teen counselor I'd run into earlier, sauntered over and sat across from me. "The Trail Blazers? Across the lake?"

I shrugged. "Never heard of them."

"You *are* off the grid," Amy remarked.

Definitely. "That's the plan. So, tell me about these Trail Blazers."

"We used to be one big camp," Bianca stated, clearly the expert on camp history. "Us here, and them across the lake. The old folks who owned it started it here, but built on after a waterfall."

"That's a *windfall*." Maggie appeared behind us. "A sudden influx of cash they received from an inheritance."

Bianca flitted a hand in the air. "Sure, okay. Anyway, they built the new lodge and new cabins and a new dock and all that. But one of them got sick with Old Timer's—"

"Alzheimer's," Maggie corrected.

"That's what I meant," Bianca went on. "And they gave the camp to their evil son."

Maggie *tsked*. "Bianca. That's unkind."

"'S true." She didn't appear the least bit remorseful. "The son is one of those earthy guys but like, has all the expensive gear. He acts like the guys you see in those romance movies at Christmas time where the bad guy from the city goes to the small town and says, 'we're gonna tear this all down.'"

"A scrooge," one of the younger campers added.

"Well, that's accurate," Maggie said.

Riveting. "Then what happened?" I pressed.

"Evil guy—er, the owner's son—he said he wanted to tear down the old camp and make everything modern. Build a big sports building and bring in all these rich kids with trainers and junk, and make everything really expensive. See, my parents used to come here as kids, and now I'm here as a teen counselor, which was always my dream since I was little, but we wouldn't have been able to afford the new camp, so a bunch of us were totally against it. And the staff and the parents and everybody all argued and got lawyers involved—"

"Careful," Maggie warned. "There are legal aspects we aren't at liberty to discuss."

"Right, right," Bianca plowed ahead. "So anyway, they struck a deal—the old folks, the son, and the staff—had to split up. So the old camp, that's us, Camp Junebug, would stay going like we used to, and the new camp the son bought out so he could run it himself the way he wanted. He doesn't even *talk* to his parents anymore. My parents would kill me if I ever stopped talking to them." She sighed with emphasized drama. "And evil son made a contract with all the scouting groups for boys in the state so they'd all use his camp. The only girls over there come later in the summer to train with sports teams."

That left the option for girls as Camp Junebug, the *before* in this makeover scenario. How wonderfully equal.

"The rich girls go to other camps," Amy said. "Not that there's anything wrong with not having money."

"Not everyone gets to go to summer camp," Maggie added. "Camp Junebug offers a simpler alternative to slick and modern. The way camps ought to be."

Amy grumbled while Bianca beamed at Maggie. So many fascinating dynamics here.

I tapped at the table with a pink nail. "With all this camp splitting, that divided the staff. Your top bunk," I said to Maggie.

She nodded. "Yeah."

"She was your friend." I wished I could take back the comment after seeing hurt flash across her face. "Sorry. That must be hard."

And Lucas. Grouchy Lucas who I'd assumed handled the maintenance around camp, when it turned out he ran the place. Seemingly unwillingly. There sure must be a story there. Probably real clickable content in the camp world.

"I could have left too," Maggie said. "But then I'd miss all this." She squished herself between two campers, making oinking sounds, which sent the younger girls into a giggle frenzy. Must be an inside joke.

Cute, though. A real chill vibe existed here, despite the bare bones look to the place. I was super curious on these Trail Blazers. I reached for my non-existent phone and swore.

Gasps cascaded around the table.

"Language," Maggie declared.

Seemed obvious. "English?"

She gave me a stern look. "*Your* language. Around the girls. No salty words."

It wasn't as if I'd dropped an F-bomb. But yeah, I should have been more aware being around impressionable young minds. "Sorry. If you have a swear jar, I'll add to it."

"What's a swear jar?" a girl with crooked front teeth asked.

Maggie appeared less appreciative than she had earlier. "It's where Miss Hudson will put her money if she says bad words again."

Oh, bleep.

Okay, I needed to watch my mouth. And quit reaching for a phantom phone. As for my curiosity about the other camp, I'd just have to go over there myself.

For the remainder of the day, I joined each new camp activity, all with an accompanying commentary by the teen counselors and Maggie.

The girls got swim time at the lake that afternoon. A rocky section of sand bordered the water. Nothing to rival Venice Beach, but I scoped a few more-sand-than-rocks patches that could make for a decent spot to park a patio chair. Would a bikini be too much here?

Buoys bobbed in the water, marking a swim zone. As the campers took to the lake, I heard all about the water rules—and there were a lot of them.

Across the lake, a large windowed structure with a mega deck gaped at us. "Is that—"

"Trail Blazers' lodge," Maggie finished for me.

"Wow." I clipped my adoration short. Being a Junebugger made the other camp the enemy. Seemed odd to be loyal so quickly, but something about Bianca's recap of the camp split felt both cruel and familiar. People with money and power excluding others with that money and power.

As swim time ended, Maggie and Amy took the girls to their cabins to dry off and change.

Bianca hooked an arm into mine. "We have some free time. Let's go to the Mess."

I couldn't wait to hear what *that* was. Given I had nothing but time, I followed her willingly.

The Mess Hall, aka the Mess, instantly gave me flashbacks to elementary school. Like a cafeteria stock photo pulled directly from my memory.

The kitchen staff appeared obscenely chipper. Bianca introduced me to the head cook who wore a faded shirt from a famous metal band.

"Hey." He nodded my direction. "I'm Pocket Pete."

"Pocket?"

"Used to be two Petes here. Now I'm the only Pete. The name stuck. Because I'm short." He shrugged. "Any dietary restrictions?"

Oh, good call. "I do a light Keto with Mediterranean influences. Fermented juices if you have them, but if not, I have a probiotic supplement in a pinch."

Bianca steered me away from the kitchen. "You sound like a snob. The cooks are cool, so just eat what they have or give them a normal suggestion."

Normal. What a word. Nothing was normal here. We were pretending to live in the woods while using a cafeteria with food cooked by paid staff. Camps were a real trip.

"Sorry," I found myself saying as I scratched my legs. They were so darned itchy. "I wasn't trying to be difficult."

"No problem. Anyway, here comes *Luke*." She snickered as none other than Lucas Russo himself entered the Mess.

"I know his name is Lucas..." I trailed off as my gaze followed him in.

He cleaned up well. Over the gray shirt from earlier—or a different shirt? Maybe he liked gray—he wore an unbuttoned plaid shirt rolled at the sleeves. No hat. Dark, well-fitting but not tight jeans. Work boots.

He stopped at the counter, looking into the open window to the kitchen. He called over to Pocket Pete and the two had a friendly conversation. Nary a grunt or growl from the big boss. His general demeanor appeared more relaxed. Comfortable.

A poke hit my ribs. "You're drooling."

I flashed a look at Bianca. "Am not."

She bit her lip. "You *like* him."

"He's my boss."

"Mmm, naughty."

I swatted her. "You're sixteen."

"*Seventeen.* Nearly eighteen."

"I'm your superior," I said with zero authority and we both knew it. "Besides, I am not here to find a boyfriend."

"Why, do you already have one?"

"No, I—" I stopped myself. No wonder Maggie needed support. She was out here with the wolves. Here, the wolves wore camp shirts and scrunchies. "This conversation is not appropriate."

"You sound like Maggie already," Bianca whined. "No fun."

The remaining campers and counselors arrived for what was apparently dinner. The big clock on the wall read five o'clock. I couldn't remember the last time I'd eaten food at this hour and labeled it dinner.

"Line up over here," Bianca instructed.

We grabbed trays and waited single file behind a group of campers. I noted colorful bins set against the wall ahead of us. "Looks like recycling is a priority." Cool. I could get behind that.

Bianca nodded. "Totally. You'll need to remind the campers which color bin does what. There's one for cans, one for plastic, and two for food waste. Only certain foods go in compost—the gray bin. That bin gets mulched. That's where worms go town at the garbage and make it into fortified dirt for gardening."

She went on about dinner rules, clean-up duties, and how the campers required reminders about all of it.

My head spun. *Think of it like content management.* All those shifting pieces that had to be set in order, scheduled, detailed, edited, curated. Only for content creation and management, I had tools. Digital tools. Here, I had bug spray. And needed more of it based on the itch screaming from my legs.

Dinner options involved a plethora of carbs and a surprising array of vegetables. Nothing too greasy looking. I took my tray and warily scanned the long tables with bench seats. This was like being a transfer student at a new school. Where did I sit? Who were my friends?

As instructed by Bianca, I sat at a camper-filled table to provide supervision. Hello, Hudson the cafeteria lady, like the lunch moms at my old elementary. What a far cry from the L.A. club scene.

I tried to focus on the girls and their chatter, but my attention drifted when their questions and stories jumbled into nonsense. I didn't mix much with this age group. These kids didn't watch the same shows on streaming or subscribe to what I did on YouTube. I had nothing to offer as far as conversation, so I listened. Or tried, at least.

Across two tables, Lucas looked up at the same time I did. His eyes flashed. Was he still upset I'd landed this job with no qualifications? Or maybe he was amused I'd crash landed here at all, completely out of place.

I couldn't tell with him.

I kept my expression even and devoid of emotion.

Ha! As if. I totally blushed and looked away. How did his eyes pierce so intensely? It was like he could outline in a glance how much of a fraud I was.

And not just a fraud here at camp. When I'd first noticed the drop in my followers after my name made national news, the first major dent to my reputation, I'd assumed I would do as I always had—forge ahead and fix it. More content, better content, and reach more people. New people.

Meanwhile, the comments blew up. So many comments, on every platform. Rude, judgmental, scary. Supportive comments were mixed in, but mostly they were scary. Kristoff's fanbase had been *activated*.

That quickly, my online clout took a nosedive. Without followers, without my social proof, my platform would weaken. I could handle being a fraud at kids' camp, but a fraud in the online space I'd expended so much energy building—that hurt. Badly.

I risked losing everything I'd built as the Beauty Butterfly, with my lifeline being a clunky PC in a camp office out in the sticks.

I chanced a look at Lucas. He and an older woman—the camp nurse?—laughed together. What sort of thing made Lucas laugh?

"Miss Hudson, how did you get pink hair?"

The young voice called me back to reality. I'd already answered this question seven times today, but this girl didn't look familiar.

"A hair stylist did it," I answered.

"Can I do my hair pink?" she asked.

She'd look cute with pink hair with her little freckles and pinky cheeks. But once you went for the dye bottle, prepare to say bye bye to youthful, untreated hair. "You know what's even better? A wig. Then you can put on pink hair whenever you want, and take it off when you don't."

The kid rode that line of uncertainty, like she hadn't decided yet if I was full of it. "Do you have one?"

"No, but—" My hand did the thing where it moved toward the device I was far more dependent on than I'd ever realized. Ugh, this was the worst. Normally, I'd pull up a wig retailer and order what I needed in a matter of seconds.

I'd have to improvise. "Where's the craft closet?" I asked the table.

Twelve different answers came at me and there were only eight kids. I already had a few ideas.

Chapter 7

Lucas

OKAY, SO I'D BEEN watching her. Hudson. She seemed to command attention in any room she walked into. Here in the Mess, she looked anything but.

Except for those red splotches on her legs. Must be allergic to mosquito bites. I could get an armful and barely scratch, but some of the kids broke out in angry red bumps. I'd fetch her some bug spray. The good stuff we kept in a locked cabinet in the office.

Seeming to read my thoughts, or my stare, Rena, our staff nurse, nodded toward Hudson, who sat surrounded by campers. "What's with the new hire? She came here dressed for shopping at the mall."

Funny, when I first saw Hudson wearing that gauzy cape thing this morning, I figured her for a parent here to fetch her kid. A fancy parent for this side of the lake, but hey, we were grateful to stay open.

"I took her for a quick run by the old slasher cabin," I told Rena.

She swatted the air between us. "You're bad. I hope she laughed."

"She did not." Heh. Her face when I'd opened the door. The dirty mattress was a prop from our haunted forest camping weekend last year.

Rena, an experienced nurse with a couple decades on me, shook her head as she laughed silently. "Kids seem to like her."

Lucky for us if they did. I decided to keep the employment details to myself. First, that I'd allowed a friend-of-a-friend hire with minimal interviewing (okay, none). And second, that Twila ran circles around me to get what she wanted. Made me look bad.

Now, if I could only stop looking Hudson's way. She was no doubt freaked enough already from me yelling today. When did I become a guy who raised his voice? And grumbled about coffee pots?

Dangit—I still needed a new coffee maker. I should have left this morning to get one. But who knew what else Twila would get up to. She'd already hired someone with no skills. What next, selling the rest of the camp?

Which didn't sound half bad right now.

I glanced up. That pink hair kept catching my eye. Great, now Hudson noticed me looking at her. She looked positively bored looking back.

Geez, what a nick to the ego.

Returning her attention to the kids, her smile lit her face. She laughed, tipping back her head.

Like Rena said, so long as the kids liked her. Camp work or office work, she'd have to be it.

Good. Fine.

After Mess clean up, the counselors headed out with the kids to return to their cabins before tonight's activities. Giving me my cue to leave for the night. Something itched at me to get some space.

"Lucas?" Footsteps sounded on the path behind me. "Hey, Lucas."

I turned as Hudson approached. Her very presence and *pinkness* contrasted with the surrounding nature like a splash of bright paint against a neutral canvas. So much for space.

"Are you headed into town?" she asked, slightly breathless.

"I'm going home." I'd been staying late for weeks, even sleeping here in the owner's cabin, but tonight I wanted my own bed at my apartment. Maybe wind down with a documentary on the national parks.

"I was thinking of costume ideas." She tapped at her bottom lip as she spoke. A plump lip tinged with a shiny gloss. "Is there a wig shop in town?"

She couldn't be serious. "You want me to go to a wig shop?"

"A beauty supply store may suffice. Sometimes those sell hair extensions."

"I'm not buying you hair extensions."

Her eyes grew big. "Oh, they're not for me." She laughed. "Hardly. They're for the campers. I have some ideas."

"Absolutely not."

She paused. "Is that a no on the hair extensions or a no on my ideas?"

I fought a grin. Hard. I couldn't let her see me break. I was her boss, not some adoring fan. But she had a convincing air. I was already considering whether the local drugstore might offer what she wanted. They managed to stock a surprising variety of stuff no one needed couched between the everyday items we all used.

I nudged a loose rock with my boot. "I'm not coming back."

She blinked. "What? You're *quitting*?"

As if it were that simple to walk away. "No, I mean I'm going home for the night. In town. But I'm not coming back to camp. Not tonight."

Her shoulders eased, as if me leaving for good would be alarming to her rather than a welcome relief from irritation. "That makes sense. You're like Twila and don't live on site like the rest of us."

I bristled at the comparison to the exuberant office manager. "I stay here sometimes in the owners' cabin." Just not tonight. Not with...her around.

Because Hudson was incredibly distracting. With what she came in wearing today, I couldn't imagine what the woman slept in.

Nope. Inappropriate. That was a completely off-limits thought I would strike from memory. For good.

She certainly wouldn't be wearing that flowy thing over a silk nightgown. That would be ridiculous. But if not that then—

Stop imagining her in night clothes.

In front of me, Hudson appeared thoughtful, pressing those glossy lips together. "Right, because you run the camp but you don't own it. The owners, do they live nearby?"

I nodded. "I report to them. I'm just keeping the lights on."

"And good thing you are," she nearly bellowed. "Because of electricity, I mean. Having it is...good." Her cheeks deepened to a rosy blush. "I'm so very glad to have electricity and indoor plumbing. When you showed me that horrid shack, I didn't know what to expect."

Now my grin cracked through. "Sorry. Couldn't resist." Hopefully, she wouldn't rat me out to Marcy for my little prank.

Her eyes narrowed, but her smirk gave away her playful act. "I've got my eye on you, Mr. Russo."

With that, she spun on her heeled sandals and walked away.

I entered the camp office the next morning to techno music blasting through the office.

The door closed heavy behind me. "What is this, a dance club?"

Twila called over from the kitchenette. "It's our wake-up music."

"Wake the dead, more like," I grumbled to an audience of a potted fern. That was new too. And taking up a lot of space next to my office door.

Instead of Twila emerging from the kitchen, out came Hudson. She had on an oversized camp shirt and actual, functional shorts. Somehow, she still managed to look like a supermodel. Did supermodels still exist? Maybe she did supermodeling on the side from YouTubing.

"Morning, boss." She offered me a paper cup with a plastic lid. "Here."

I hesitated. "What's this? Other than the obvious."

"Twila brought it in from town." Hudson smiled. "For you. And she brought me a juice." She sipped from a glass bottle with square sides. The stuff was dark green and thick. Looked toxic.

Nodding to the green stuff, I asked, "How much did you pay for bottled swamp?"

Twila appeared. "It's very healthy." She zipped across the office with more energy than usual. And that was saying something. "Over here, Hudson. I want to show you our socials."

A second chair waited by Twila's desk.

"Hey, what's this? We need Hudson with the campers." These women would be the end of me. It was only eight-oh-five in the morning.

"No worries, Lucas," Hudson said. "Do you prefer Lucas? Or Mr. Russo?"

A grumble sounded in my throat. "Lucas is fine."

"Great, so the good news is we worked out a plan and a schedule." She showed me a spiral notebook. "I recreated one of my digital calendars last night and marked all available hours and where we need coverage. Maggie and I have our shifts noted. The free time during the day, I'll be in the office."

"Let me see." I should approve the schedule. Look it over and all that.

"Hudson is going to audit our social media," Twila announced.

I looked up from the schedule's scorching pink ink. "Uh—"

"Remember, she's a *literal* expert." Twila grinned. "We'll get our website fancied up and business will really boom."

I clenched the cup, realizing I had no idea if coffee or that green stuff lived inside. "Low key summer, remember? We don't have the resources to support more campers right now."

"More campers means more money means more staff!"

Twila was so dang proud.

Hudson looked between us, a calculating sense in her eyes. "We don't have to take any action yet. An audit is simply an examination of what exists so I can make a recommendation."

"I have actual paperwork that needs managing," I told them. "No need to audit anything. I'll tell you exactly what needs working on."

Twila and Hudson fell quiet. No, strike that. They were communicating silently. To each other. Through *looks*.

I wasn't cut out for this.

The camp was overrun by women. I meant this in the least sexist way possible, but I needed another guy out here. Just to...debrief. Maybe translate. Yeah, I definitely needed a translator. Hudson and Twila were now silently giggling and signaling things with their eyes.

I felt like a tool. No, a tool had a purpose. I was like that little metal IKEA Allen key that's useful to put your furniture together, but a needless contraption once you were done.

I set the cup down. "I'm headed to town."

"But you just got here," Twila said.

"Need that coffee maker." I opened and closed the door to sweet, sweet silence.

I returned to camp with a new-to-me coffeemaker from the thrift shop. The thing had stains in all the right places with a helpful note taped on top stating the appliance still worked. Perfect.

After parking, my phone lit with a text.

Marcy: *How's Hudson getting along?*

With everyone else, great.

Marcy: *You better keep your pranks to yourself. She's going through a rough time.*

Yeah, if rough meant limited shopping and relying on other people to bring her swamp juice. Besides, this was my job. I was a freaking professional.

Professional what...yeah, I didn't know. My expertise involved the outdoors. Not much else. But Hudson was Marcy's friend, for some unidentifiable reason, so I had to tell her something.

Me: *She's fine*

I gathered my stuff and exited the truck when the phone buzzed again.

Marcy: *That's it? Fine? I KNOW you've got an opinion. Don't try that fine thing with me. Make sure you look out for her, okay?*

How did I answer that? I didn't know, so I didn't. Marcy knew well enough I didn't text novels worth of explanation. Things were fine. Or they would be, because I'd make them.

Inside the camp office, things were not fine.

Three campers sat on the bench inside the door holding their stomachs. Rena entered from the hall leading to the nurse's station on the far end of the building.

"These girls have stomach aches from making their own home-made Junebug juice," Rena explained.

"Points for creativity." Maggie, standing by, barely broke a sweat. "But we don't know exactly what went into that 'juice.'"

"Let's go, girls." Rena and Maggie herded the campers to the nurse's room.

"Hudson, you're on," I said without looking at her or Twila huddled behind the computer.

"But the schedule—" Hudson began.

"It changes." I snapped my fingers. "In an instant. You'll have to come on today's hike."

She sat, motionless. "I'm sorry, I don't understand."

I put the coffeemaker in the kitchenette and swung by my office to unlock the secure cabinet. Took out a can of good bug spray from my personal stash and rejoined her in the main area of the office. "Maggie planned to come on today's hike with the campers. She'll need to stay with the sick girls in case any need to go home. You're coming with me."

She looked at me with a blank expression. "Come with you. On a hike."

I let out a slow breath and looked at Twila. "You want to explain?"

Twila finished typing. "Oh, Hudson, honey. It's for supervision. The teen girls go too, but we need another adult out there on the trails. You know, man leading little girls into the woods. Safety. Optics."

She nodded. "Right. Of course. That makes sense. Is my outfit okay?"

I almost bit back with a sarcastic comment, when I remembered Marcy's words. *She's had a rough time.* I had some sympathy for that, having been through a few rough months myself. Heck, things were still rough. Just because she didn't look it on the outside, didn't mean something wasn't hurting on the inside.

After all, someone as mismatched as an internet star working at a run-down camp had to mean she wasn't at the top of her game. Whatever that game was.

"Do you have better shoes?" I nodded toward her sandals. Open toe with all kinds of room for scratches and bites.

"I have some casual slide-ons—"

"English?"

"Sneakers. I have sneakers."

"That'll do. Oh, and this." I handed her the can of bug spray. "Put that on outside on the porch and bring back the can."

She stared at the label in horror. "This has chemicals in it." Her voice lowered. "*Restricted* chemicals."

"Best stuff on the market even if three states banned it." I nodded toward her legs. "Noticed yours were chewed up by the mosquitoes."

Her cheeks reddened. "I was hoping the bites weren't noticeable. Maggie gave me some lotion last night. Do I really need to put this stuff on?"

"Prefer to be eaten alive?"

Her skepticism turned to a pout. "Fine."

Kind of cute, but I'd never admit it.

Chapter 8

Hudson

THE GIRLS WERE ONTO their third camp song as we marched into the woods.

I pressed back my annoyance at leaving the office so abruptly. I hadn't yet gotten to access my social media on Twila's computer.

I'd meant to take a peek last night, hoping to get a blip of connectivity out at the cabin, but, well, I'd crashed pretty early. Despite the lumpy mattress on the top bunk. I was out cold by nine-forty-five.

The girls excitedly chattered ahead of me, each walking single file behind teen counselor Amy. Leading the pack, our fearless grump, Lucas.

Each step on the trail offered a new lump or rock to step over or around. I was used to paved paths and sidewalks. I'd heard of great trail walking in Southern California, but I'd spent most of my time filming videos indoors or trying to get noticed in the club scene.

If only all those L.A. clubbers could see me now, a complete sweat fest who could barely walk without stumbling. Was that a tree root, sticking right out of the ground? What a hazard!

No, I could do this. If all these girls could manage this trail, so could I.

Moreso, I refused to let Lucas see me struggle. He already thought I couldn't hack camp life.

A buzzing sounded in my ear followed by a light prick on my cheek. I slapped my own face. *Ow.*

"Are you okay Miss Hudson?" The group had stopped walking and the camper in front of me watched me with concern.

My palm served as a canvas for a mangled mosquito. "Ew. It bit my *face.*"

The camper rightfully scrunched her nose. "Gross. You'll get used to it."

I certainly would *not* get used to mosquito face bites. And no way would I shellack any more of my skin with that industrial grade mosquito repellent. It was bad enough I'd coated my legs with the stuff. I could only pray the toxins wouldn't seep too much deeper into my epidermis. *Come on organic body lotion. Protect that moisture barrier like a champion.*

"Alright, campers," Lucas announced as we gathered in a semi-circle in a wooded clearing. "Who here can tell me what this is?"

"A tree stump, *obviously,*" one girl drolled, sending the others into giggle fits.

"What kind of tree?" he asked.

She shrugged. "I dunno. They're all the same."

Lucas visibly winced, but shrugged it off with a smile. "Come a little closer, everybody. See these rings? Anybody know why those are here?"

A girl with black braids raised her hand. "It tells how old it is."

Lucas' eyes lit with excitement. "Yes. Nice job. These are growth rings. Trees start out small and grow larger, just like you and I do. Some rings are lighter in color for wood that grew early in the year, and darker for wood growing in later seasons."

While a few kids looked bored or distracted, most listened and asked more questions.

Lucas moved to another spot with a scraggly looking bush. He drew the campers in to tell them about the leaf shape and how to identify trees and shrubs by their leaves. He used scientific words couched in simple explanations. He cautioned to avoid eating any berries found in the wild until they learned to properly identify them. Many plants had medicinal or healing properties found by knowing their shape, texture, and color.

Normally, I'd consider this pretty dull myself, but he had my attention with the healing and medicinal stuff. Lucas had a way of talking about foliage like it was hot juicy gossip. Okay, maybe less hot and juicy, but his excitement made me care.

He positioned himself closer to the ground, in a one-knee kneel, holding a leaf upward.

"Ew!" A camper with an armful of friendship bracelets pointed at the leaf. "There's a *bug* on it."

"It's an inchworm," the braided hair girl stated. "They're cute."

"No, icky!" The bracelets girl shrieked and ran in circles. "Icky icky icky!"

A frenzy of squealing erupted. One little blond jumped onto the stump and screamed at the grass like it was hot lava.

Whew. "Dramatic."

Amy beside me must have heard. "Yeah. This happens at least twice a day when it comes to bugs."

Only the girl in braids seemed un-freaked by the leaf bug. Lucas appeared frustrated again, his face twitching as a real eardrum-piercer ripped through the air.

"Let me see." I walked toward him, the leaf, and the worm.

I hated worms. I'd been that girl the kids on the playground taunted with worm threats, once having one flung at me in retaliation. For what, I couldn't remember. But I'd been convinced the thing would build a nest in my hair. I could not be consoled by the teacher who insisted worms did not nest, and nothing lived in my hair except for hair follicles. Which sounded just as disgusting at the time.

I felt at a deep level why these girls shrieked. But if I shrieked with them, I'd give Lucas further proof I didn't belong here. I wouldn't let nature best me.

Besides, my whole brand revolved around butterflies. An insect. And those were beautiful.

I approached the leaf, closing in on Lucas' space. A teeny, lime green worm scrunched and flattened, scrunched and flattened. It *was* cute. Ish. "Isn't that the cutest? I can see little Wormy accessorizing with a pink or purple hat."

"A *hat?*" The girl in braids repeated. "That's dumb. It's a worm. They don't wear hats."

A few of the shriekers crept up behind me.

"Maybe sunglasses," I suggested. "It's sunny out."

A giggle sounded somewhere. "Let me see."

"Inchworms are technically caterpillars, not worms," Lucas said. "And most don't like sunlight, so those shades might come in handy." He winked at me.

A direct hit landed with that wink. I stepped aside to gather my wits. How was he suddenly the sexiest man I'd ever seen? The gentle kneel, the rolled-up plaid sleeve, the exposed forearm holding a leaf with such care.

Sexy, really, Hudson? Maybe *I* needed adult supervision. This was the least romantic place I could imagine. We were surrounded by children and a creepy crawly caterpillar. And I was covered in DEET.

We moved on from the clearing to a well-worn path. Lucas started a game of I-Spy: Leaf Edition—the actual name he said out loud—where the girls called out leaf shapes which he stopped to examine and identify.

Beside me at the back of the group, Amy sighed and looked at her watch. "I'm so ready for lunch."

"You hate it here, huh?"

She shrugged. "No. I've heard all this before. We're a weekly camp, so it's the same leaf stuff. Same crafts."

"Oh." I hadn't realized the campers switched out each week. The movies I'd seen made it seem like summer camp lasted the whole summer. "You do the same activities every week?"

She shrugged again. A go-to response, it seemed. "Mostly."

"What would you rather do?"

"Watch YouTube."

I nodded. "I hear that."

"*You* can do whatever you want. You can watch videos on your phone. Right now. Do you have a phone? Can I see it?"

Her eyes pleaded with desperation for content. Digital content, hit after entertaining hit. I knew that look well. Too well.

"Sorry, just got this." I pointed at the boxy two-way radio I'd begrudgingly accepted at the office. I hated the look of it, but it also reminded me of using a kid version of these radios with the neighbor girl whose yard backed up to mine. We thought we were so cool with our comms. When her stepdad bought her a cell phone, everything changed. She moved on to *cool girl with cell phone* status, while I remained phoneless another year. Little good that parental restriction did for me in the long run.

I was as addicted to online life as Amy. And here we were both stuck at this no WiFi camp.

Amy's shoulders slumped. "It was worth trying."

Her words repeated in my head. *Worth trying.*

I glanced ahead to Lucas. Three girls excitedly questioned him about a flowering bush along the path. He nodded, listening. He knelt beside the bush and summoned the group closer.

It was freaking adorable. Mr. Grump fully surrounded by chatty campers? I loved every second.

And funny. None of them seemed bothered by the lack of internet.

Maybe camp was more than a place to ride out my bad publicity. Maybe a phone-free existence was worth trying out.

As soon as the hike ended, the girls raced to their cabins with the counselors quick at their heels. I let out a sigh.

"They can drain you, huh?" Lucas said.

I'd let down my guard with my big sigh, not expecting he'd hear me. Or comment.

"They're...energetic." I smiled. "I'm—" I almost told him I wasn't used to being around this many kids, but that seemed like a misstep given how quickly I'd been hired. For a job with children. "Just adjusting."

"Thanks for your help with the caterpillar," he said.

Which may have been the weirdest thing anyone had ever said to me. And I'd once been invited to a dog show for a make-up consultation.

"No problem. I'm trying to...find my place."

He gave me a sidelong glance, which didn't make me feel uncomfortable so much as defensive.

"Look," I said before he could point out the obvious. "I know I'm not your first pick for the job. And I sense Twila colored outside the lines, so to speak, by getting me in the door so quickly. But I promise I'll do my best. I need to be here, in a place like this. Away from...stuff."

Instead of clapping back with a grouchy retort, he considered my words and nodded. "Sorry I came off harsh. I don't know what you're going through."

Now I did feel uncomfortable. "Did Marcy talk to you?"

"Marcy? No. Just a text. So, yeah. I guess."

Great. So he knew. Or did he? Marcy wouldn't blab my personal business to any old someone. But Lucas was family. Family went by different rules. At least Marcy's did—they were all so close.

Unlike my family. My older brother and sister worked in professional careers that could easily be named. They were each married with kids. I had nothing in common with them and they didn't understand me. I was their adorable little social butterfly and could never escape the label. So much so, I'd labeled myself that way and centered all my branding around it.

Lucas and I stood side by side at the edge of the wood, the awkwardness inching forward like that pesky little caterpillar.

"Marcy said," I started, when he said, "So, Marcy is your friend."

We both laughed. Awkwardly. Ouch, was this painful. He rubbed at the back of his neck and shifted his weight around. But he wasn't leaving.

I'd been in plenty of situations with socially uncomfortable people. My primary skill set involved shining in a social situation. Filling in conversational lulls and inviting quiet types to engage. I attempted another angle. "I imagine you're close with Marcy and her brothers."

"Oh, uh, yeah. We all lived down the street from each other like one big, messy Italian family. I'm the same age as her brother Matteo."

I'd heard so much about the Russo clan over the years but couldn't remember ever meeting Lucas. I would have remembered. "I wonder if we ever crossed paths? In college, Marcy and I hung out all the time—went to each other's houses over breaks. I've only met her brothers a few times though since they were out of the house and in college too." Wild. I should look through my old photos and try to find him. "There are four of us who were close in college. We sort of lost track of each other. Or, I did. Life stuff. But we've been back in touch and Marcy is the one who suggested I lay low—I mean, find a job here. Like a reset, of sorts."

"A reset? From what?" He seemed less uncomfortable now, and his softened gaze appeared curious about my reason for being here.

Okay, so he didn't know much. Lucas certainly didn't seem the type to follow hysterical media sources, so likely the *billionaire dumps influencer after federal raid* news never reached his eyeballs. Or ears. Maybe he was a radio guy. He seemed pretty low-tech.

Which left me in control of filling in details. Perfect. And if I knew anything about controlling a narrative, at least as an online presence, staying as close to the truth as possible made for a much less stressful existence. Online personas were all about embellishing and highlighting. Glossing over the ugly but staying true to your core self. "See, I'm addicted to the internet and wanted to be somewhere without it."

A lie, because I didn't want to be here at all, but at least I couched the reason in real things.

"Addicted? How does that happen? Do you mean like online shopping, you buy too much?"

"No. More like being online in general. Too long, too much." I waved a hand in the air. "Never mind. I only wanted to say I'm grateful to be here. It's so...organic." I snapped my fingers. "That's it. That's your angle. You have something here the slick camp across the lake doesn't. A naturally organic lifestyle camp."

He blinked at me.

"Just picture it." I moved fully in front of him so he wouldn't miss a word. "Companies right now are bending over backward to show how honest they are and how much integrity they have and how their products are natural or chemical-free or whatever fits. Your camp? This place is the most low-tech, home-grown experience I can think of for a modern kid." I held up a hand and ticked each item off. "No cell phones. No Wi-Fi. Camp songs and sharing time around the campfire. Ancient bunk beds with initials carved into them. A cafeteria straight out of 1985. Don't sleep on the nostalgia angle. You're marketing to parents, not the kids themselves."

His face scrunched. "Don't sleep?"

I was too excited to explain. "Amy hates it here and would rather watch YouTube, but you know who doesn't? Bianca. Her parents attended Camp Junebug and when she came herself as little Junebugger, she dreamed of the day she'd become a teen counselor. And now she is one, living her dream. She's perfect for a customer profile. We should interview her. I could interview her. I could do it right now."

I beamed at him. He reflected confusion. "How do you know any of this? You've been here two days."

"Bianca told me all of that yesterday. And about the rival camp with the evil son who ripped Camp Junebug in half. Not that the halves are anywhere *near* equal."

His mouth appeared to form several words but no sound emerged. Finally, he spoke. "I would take what Bianca says with a hefty grain of salt."

"Maggie made necessary corrections." I folded my arms. A few light bulbs flicked on in my brain. "Is this why you grumble around so much? You don't really want to be running this camp, that's clear, but here you are. Did you choose to stay to keep the dream alive?"

It was darn right poetic. And sweet. Very sweet, despite the hard set to his jaw. Speaking of, that jawline really was exquisite now that I could see it a little better. He'd trimmed the beard. He had sort of a younger-brother-to-Oscar-Isaac vibe happening that I wasn't at all mad at.

He blinked again, a lot, maybe trying to eye-force a response into existence. Introverts must have it hard.

"Hey." I laid a hand at his arm, an attempt at comfort. Bad move. His warm skin pulsed beneath my touch. It called for me to trail my fingers further in exploration. His breath hitched and I snapped my hand back. "I heard things have been difficult since the camp split. I don't know details, but if I can help in any way, that's what I'm suggesting. I'm good at social media. I can pitch your camp to the right target demographic—"

"No."

Right. Too strong, too fast. "I have a Communications degree with a Psych minor." I pulled out those credentials when I sensed people weren't taking me seriously. It never worked with my family who viewed everything I did as a cute thing I'd grow out of, but outside of them, I had a decent success rate. Plus, that charm factor. "With a solid marketing plan, we could boost this camp's enrollment—"

"I said no."

No was the first step in a business negotiation. "I can help you. I have online marketing experience."

He eased forward, his voice as firm as the sun-caked ground I stood on. "I don't need your help."

I would have let up, but something in his eyes hinted at conflicted emotions. "I don't believe you."

He laughed in one short burst. "You've been here less than forty-eight hours. Don't assume you know how to run a camp just because you don't like the brochure."

"There's a brochure? Because I'd like—"

"No."

"I wasn't suggesting—"

"Do the job you're being paid for." He abruptly turned and headed up the path toward the office.

"And what is that exactly?" I called after him. An actual job description would be nice. I could even help draft it to reel in these moving parts.

I was pretty sure I heard him growl. "Go find Maggie."

Chapter 9

Lucas

AFTER CHECKING OFF A list of maintenance tasks, I returned to the office mid-afternoon. Where I was supposed to be. For paperwork. Where I hated to be, every single day.

I woke up my office laptop and found myself typing a familiar website address. Why I did this to myself, I couldn't figure out. It never helped.

Images of rocky cliffs and hikers loaded with packs and gear filled the screen. Tents pitched in the woods. My dream wilderness expedition job with my dream organization.

Colorado. The Rocky Mountains. I imagined the freedom. The fresh air. The eager students ready to learn survival skills and test their limits. The rivers, the trails.

Lost in thought, the ringing phone from the front desk cut into my fantasy.

Reality: a stifling office with knotty pine walls. Framed camp awards two decades old, and plastic binders of camp material yellowing with age.

One measly summer. Just get through it.

Because I was a glutton for pain and punishment, I scanned the open job positions anyway. Every single one required a completed college degree. As if outdoor adventure demanded a stamp of approval from a musty classroom.

Without thinking, I searched Camp Junebug.

The website wasn't so bad, was it? All the necessary information appeared front and center. Address. Phone number. A photo of the lake where the big lodge across the water couldn't be seen. Or maybe the photo was so old the new lodge hadn't yet been built.

Funny, the new lodge was one of the features that drew me to the camp job in the first place, built with eco-friendly initiatives and some recycled and repurposed materials. Maybe not so funny since it was now off-limits.

I clicked around the website. The staff profiles page hadn't been updated since the split. Nothing existed there except for the camp phone number. Fine by me, I didn't want my face splashed across the internet.

I opened a new browser window and searched Camp Trail Blazers. Guitar rock burst through the speaker. I shot back in my roller chair, ramming into a box I didn't know existed.

"What..." The sound was coming from the website. I bashed the keypad, searching for the speaker icon to mute.

"Ooh, sounds like a party in there!" Twila called from the front of the office. Footsteps sounded and the voice grew closer. "I used to blast Whitesnake in my Chevette and cruise around town with my crew."

No response seemed adequate.

"I was a little wild in my early twenties," she went on. "That's how I found my Jim. We met in a heavy metal parking lot."

I had to move on from the mental image of Twila's hair as a 1980s pop metal fan. "It's the website for the Trail Blazers. Look at this."

She came around to view the screen. Images slid on their own. Close action shots of children posed like athletes. Trainers and counselors who belonged on TV selling sports drinks. A big fat button right at the top urging viewers to *Take the Trail*.

I hated it. Every bit of it.

Twila made a dismissive mouth noise. "Oh, they're all flash. Don't mind them. What's got you curious about their website, anyhow?"

Hudson. Though I wouldn't admit it. She'd seemed pretty excited about her ideas, even if I didn't understand them. "Figured I'd take a look," I said and left it at that.

"A look can't hurt. You know, when I showed Hudson our social media accounts, I thought she might run out of the building."

"We have social media accounts? No, wait. I knew that." A Facebook page. Possibly something else. I assumed Twila made the updates. That's what Hudson's whole audit thing was about. Sounded ridiculous.

Seeming to read my thoughts, an infuriating realization, Twila continued. "She only scratched the surface with her audit since she's had to be away from the office so much already. Once she has time to look, I think her advice will help."

Only we didn't need that sort of help. Sure, the camp didn't have any real direction other than to retain the sort of values it began with. Seemed fine enough to me. Any larger vision belonged to whoever took over after me. I'd only been asked—begged—to keep the camp afloat for another summer. Not to reinvent the place and package it with an organic seal of approval. Which sounded like a lot of paperwork, to be honest.

I sat deeper in the seat, glaring at the shiny Trail Blazers' images. "Now isn't the right time to go bananas with advertising. We don't have what it takes to follow through."

Twila hovered, oddly quiet.

Too quiet. "What?"

"You underestimate yourself."

I adjusted in the chair and the worn leather squeaked. "I wasn't asking for your opinion on my abilities."

She nodded and left the room.

Dangit. I'd hurt her feelings. She simply didn't grasp the work needed to get this camp where it deserved to be. And if I committed to that plan, well, then I'd be stuck. I'd never see Colorado and I knew it.

I left my office to apologize, only her phone rang. She answered on the first ring.

Twila was right. I underestimated myself. *In this job.* My confidence was in my skills outdoors. Where I wanted to be. Where I belonged.

The next day, I made rounds to the cabins while the girls worked through their activities. I fixed sink leaks and replaced burnt light bulbs. Anything more severely broken went on a list to repair later or hire out.

Emerging from the last empty cabin, I headed toward the central outdoor activity space. And stopped in my tracks.

Bubbly pop music blared from a portable stereo in the rain shelter. Girls lined up in the grass in two rows facing each other. A little girl strutted—that was the only word I could think of—across the grass between them. A huge straw hat nearly covered her eyes. She had on a feather boa and layers of pink clothes. She paused to open a hot pink waist pack, revealing a mini water bottle and a travel size sunscreen. At least she came prepared.

"Work it!" a camper shouted as she danced to the synthetic beat.

At the head of the group stood Hudson, wearing an equally obnoxious assortment of scarves and crafted yarn accessories, clapping enthusiastically along with the campers and counselors.

The next girl to strut wore a pink wig.

"Not my business." I scouted for a route to the office least likely to attract attention. Maybe I could circle through the woods—

"Lucas! Come join us!"

Too late to run.

But I was fast. I worked out. I lifted heavy things.

I began to turn away, when the voice beckoned again. Hudson waved me over as if we'd planned to meet and I was simply late showing up.

"Mr. Lucas!"

"Luuu-cass!"

Now the campers summoned me, waving and making a fuss.

I kept a wide berth and landed near Hudson. "So, uh, what's all this?"

"Runway show." She looked away from me to the next camper walking the grass. A scarf wrapped around the girl's hair and she had more scarves tied around her waist and at her neck. "Way to work those scarves. Woohoo!"

I rubbed a hand across my face. "You think a fashion show counts as a sanctioned camp activity?"

She flinched. Maybe it was the word *sanctioned* that ruffled her. "Actually, the girls came up with the idea themselves. Next is Dance Club. The girls have been learning dance moves and there's a disco floor in progress with colored chalk in the rain shelter."

"That's a thing? We let the kids run the camp now?" I apparently said that too loud because one of the teens glared at me.

"Yes, it is," the teen counselor insisted. "The last full day of the camp week, the girls run their own group activity. This won in the vote at Campfire last night."

"That's where all the big decisions are made," Hudson stated. "Nightly Campfire." She bumped fists with the counselor.

Okay, this was too much. The woman hadn't even been here a week and she felt the need to inform *me* where the decisions were made.

"You look mad," Hudson said in a lowered voice.

I grumbled. "I'm not mad."

"No, I think you're mad." She chewed at her lip, which made my eye twitch for some reason. "Obviously, I meant the campers' decisions are made at the campfire. Not that they are running the camp."

I let out a breath. "It's fine. I overreacted. But look, I hate to be a stick in the mud, but isn't that sort of the point of summer camp—playing around with sticks and mud? Not dressing up in pretend fancy outfits playing out some commercial clothing industry nonsense?"

"We're multi-faceted," one of the teens countered, and with a good wallop of attitude. "I happen to like playing in mud *and* wearing stylish clothes. Both are valid."

"Don't box us in," a camper with yellow hair in pigtails sassed back.

My socks were older than this kid.

I threw out both hands in surrender. "I'm out of my element. You all go on with your fashion show."

The pigtails girl did the oddest thing. She curled her finger at me, beckoning me closer.

Frozen like a deer facing a roadkill death sentence, I looked at Hudson. *Help.*

She caught my eye, smirked, and turned to the girl. "What do you want to tell Mr. Lucas, Angelica?"

The little girl continued to curl her finger at me. No other options available, I leaned forward and knelt to her level.

"Do you think Miss Hudson is pretty?" the girl whisper-shouted at me.

Every living thing in a twenty-foot radius had to have heard. Including Miss Hudson herself.

When I'd taken this job, a hefty helping of humility came as a side dish, having to play second fiddle to the glossy camp across the lake. But I hadn't counted on total and complete humiliation at the hands of a nine-year-old.

The campers waited. At great cost, I looked at Hudson. She returned a neutral expression I couldn't read. Maybe she hadn't heard the sonic whisper after all. Maybe I could duck out and hide in my truck. Forever.

Hudson's mouth quirked. "Well?"

I laughed, trying to play along. That's what this all was anyway, play. "Of course." I grinned like an idiot and played my part. Sure, sure. I'd be the crumudgeony wilderness guy smitten with the sparkly fashion diva. Cute, sure. Whatever.

The girls squealed in delight.

A knowing glint shone from Hudson's eyes. Like she knew this wasn't play at all.

Oh, boy was I in trouble.

Chapter 10

Hudson

I SKIPPED CAFETERIA DINNER with the campers to snag some office time. First, I checked my phones, real and burner, back at the cabin. Unfortunately, no "it's over, come back to civilization!" text from the attorney or the federal agent. Plenty of missed calls from unknown numbers. A couple of spam messages including one about a key and a locked account I deleted based on the preview text. Like I'd fall for some cheap and obvious *give me your account number* scam.

Oh, and a text from my mom.

Mom: *My friend has an open administrative assistant position at her real estate company. Now that you're done playing celebrity, call me and we'll get you an interview!*

Ugh. Way to kick a girl when she was down, Mom. No, *how are you?* just dig right in at my failure "playing" at my career.

My family had never taken my interests seriously. They all seemed to be waiting on me to outgrow whatever they viewed as my current phase. To them, I was the pretty, social girl who needed to fail out of her ideas before settling in to some conventional job they could easily explain at dinner parties.

My parents were big fans of the dinner party brag. My sister, an HR director at a respected company, had two kids who looked just like she and her husband. My brother, a business analyst for a tech company, had adopted a son with his partner. Practically sainthood.

Which left me. My parents loved to bring up how I'd been titled "Prettiest Baby" at some county fair contest. Firstly, Prettiest Baby was a pretty gross title to award a being who couldn't control what went in or out of them. But it primed me for my next title, Prettiest Toddler. Same county fair two years later. Mom had designs on pushing me through the local pageant circuit. Only tantrums and a general distaste for following any direction from adults soured those chances quickly. To this day, I *loathed* ruffles.

They'd registered me for child acting classes. Dance lessons. Modeling gigs. Nope, nope, nope. I thrived on attention, but always on my terms. None of those boundary-filled activities involved anything related to *my terms*.

So they gave up on molding me. They dubbed me their little social butterfly and didn't expect much else. My creative interests involved hosting stage productions with toys for the neighbor kids. I played around with video on an old camcorder. Once I discovered YouTube, my world changed forever.

Guilt pressed in that I hadn't let my family know I'd returned to Michigan. I would, in time. Right now, the fewer people who knew my location, the safer I felt.

Twila had taken off for the day, and as promised, left me the computer's password: *ProfessorPeanutButter!* It broke the second golden rule of passwords, using a pet's name (the first being using the word *password)*. She'd left it for me on a sticky note with the added disclaimer: *Don't share with anyone!*

What mattered was it worked. I was in. Time for damage control.

I pulled up YouTube, where the most cesspool and bottom feeder-driven comments lived. As expected, more downvotes than usual appeared on my recent videos. Way more. Videos that hadn't had much new engagement in months now offered new comments. I tended to see familiar usernames posting, but these new comments came from unfamiliar names. The general sentiment being I was a hack, a broke girl boss, unoriginal, ugly, fake, talentless.

Yikes.

Then I found the descriptions about my face and body that devolved from critical to cruel.

My throat tightened. A heavy sensation hit my stomach as I sank farther into the chair. The worst comments rewound again and again in my head.

Criticism came with the territory of putting myself online. I was used to it. The influencers I knew said to keep doing your thing and move on. Haters were unhappy with their lives and took out their frustration on public figures because they couldn't fight back. Or wouldn't.

I clicked on another video finding more of the same. The pit in my stomach grew solid. My bones filled with heavy dread. I kept clicking, kept reading.

I couldn't stop. This was like some troll-infested merry-go-round I couldn't pull myself off of.

What if they're right? I'm a fraud. A hack. Ugly. A loser.

The insults cycled through my mind. Each new round an attack.

A crackling noise outside snapped my focus from the screen. I shot up, moving to the window. Nothing. Nobody. A branch lay in the grass in front of the office.

My heart beat fast. I wasn't getting anywhere with damage control to my brand. More like *I* was damaged after reading how much these trolls hated me.

Forget YouTube for now, I'd check Instagram. People could be mean there, but overall, I viewed the app as my happy place. The organic beauty community made efforts to support each other. I logged in with my fake, unknown to anyone account on the desktop computer. My content looked pretty and my videos had a streamlined look I'd worked hard to create.

I flinched noticing how long it had been since my last post. Everyone would forget about me without any new content.

What would I even post about? Toxic mosquito repellent? Hmm, maybe a natural repellent existed I could explore.

Only the very thought of coming up with new content exhausted me.

Back to scrolling. The comments on Instagram wildly speculated about my life.

I heard she's in federal custody.

Maybe she's in witness protection.

Witness to what? Bro crime?

She could at least give us an update on the Sheek moisturizer combo she promoted. Is the 30% off deal still valid?

Never mind I hadn't been named the official spokesperson when I'd mentioned that deal. And I had no control over discounts.

I added a comment from the lurker account to check the Sheek website for sale updates. Anything more and I'd go too far and raise suspicion.

I needed to log into my real account and check my DMs. I regularly communicated with the brands I worked with by direct message. Just because the Sheek deal fell through didn't mean I couldn't look for another opportunity.

I logged out of the lurker account, and into my real one. Shoot—two factor authentication required. The account didn't recognize Twila's computer as a trusted device. My phone where the code was sent—back in the cabin. Of all times to not have my phone.

A growing sense of panic pressed against my chest. Dread filled everything else.

The office door flew open.

"Yee!" I shot up from the chair. Lucas. Lucas was here.

He paused in the doorway. "What are you doing here?"

I scrambled to shut down the computer. "I was just leaving." A chill hit my body. Could be from the open door, or the sick feeling overtaking my body.

"You shouldn't be in here after hours." He folded his arms, then unfolded them, as if uncertain.

"I...I'm sorry. Twila said it was fine but—" Twila was not my boss. "Sorry. I'm leaving."

I grabbed my stuff. My stuff being a water bottle and a two-way radio. Pathetic.

Lucas moved aside to let me out. "Hudson, wait, I'm sorry. I didn't expect to see you here."

I opened the screen door. "Yeah. That's beginning to seem like a pattern."

At the cabin, silence greeted me. It should have been sweet and blissful. Instead, the stillness drained the last of my confidence.

I was alone. At a camp out in the sticks with no Wi-Fi and a shower with weak water pressure. Yes, I'd been grateful for indoor plumbing, but reality cut deep.

I cried. I made it to the bedroom and dug out my real phone. The weight of it felt foreign in my grasp. Every part of me felt off kilter, maladjusted, broken.

The cabin's door opened. "Yoohoo!" Maggie called from the front room. "Mail call!"

I wiped at my face and tossed the phone onto my top bunk.

I sensed Maggie's presence filling the door frame. "You've got mail. In case you weren't sure what mail call meant."

I sniffled and kept my back to her. "Thanks."

Without further comment, her footsteps retreated. I turned, finding an envelope on the dresser. A handwritten address to me on the front. The return address: Marcy.

I ripped open the envelope and stifled a laugh. An honest-to-goodness letter written on stationary. Little cartoon animals wearing shorts and T-shirts bordered the bottom. Like they were at summer camp.

Dear H [full name redacted for security],

I can't remember the last letter I wrote apart from a holiday card. It's kind of fun! I found this old stationary from when I was kid and thought you'd like some mail. I wanted you to get a letter your first few days, so I'm writing this right after you left. You literally just left my apartment. So, nothing new has happened since you air dropped back into our lives. For which I'm grateful. I'm sorry you're in the space you are right now, but so glad you came to us for help.

Hope the bugs aren't too bad. Let me know how it's going, and what you think of Lucas!

Love,

Ya Girl,

Marcy

The tears came again, only the hard pit in my gut eroded. This little note captured enough of my old life to grasp onto. More than visiting my social accounts, which I assumed would give me a sense of control rather than spiral me into despair.

I grabbed my phone. A half bar of connectivity. I'd need to venture closer to the office for better service.

After cleaning up in the bathroom, I tiptoed out of the cabin. The campers would be involved in their after dinner activities for a while yet, which I'd been let off the hook from tonight. I called Marcy the second the connectivity inched higher.

She answered on the second ring. "What are you doing using that phone? Isn't it contraband? Did you get my letter?"

I laughed, though it came out unsteady. "Thank you for the letter."

"Oh, good. How's it been?"

My body buzzed from absorbing all those horrible online comments. "I checked some of my accounts." Leaning against a tree within site of the camp office, I told her what I found.

She listened, never once interrupting.

"So..." I trailed off, not sure what I wanted from her as a response. Again, silence. Was this thing even on? I checked the connectivity. Seemed viable. "Are you there?"

Her voice came with a little static. "Yes, I'm here. I cut out for a second. There was a lot of swearing on my end. It's better you didn't hear."

Ah. At least she understood.

"I can't believe people can be so heartless and unkind to someone they don't know. I'm so sorry, Hudson."

I nodded, though she obviously couldn't see. "It was stupid of me to check. I don't know what I was thinking."

"How about maybe you'd find some support from your fans? That would be reasonable. It sounds like the trolls are hard at work tearing you down instead of making their own content." She muttered what sounded like threats. "Sorry. I am *riled* up."

"Thanks. Not that you're riled up, but that you care enough to be." I pressed my lips together, breathing in deeply so more tears wouldn't invade our conversation. I didn't know how long the connection would hang on. "It makes me feel less alone."

"I'm sorry you're going through this. It's reminding me how much we all need each other. I've been thinking—"

"Me too!"

"That we need a more solid plan to support each other?"

"Yes, exactly. A *Golden Girls* scenario."

"Okay, you lost me. What do Dorothy and Rose have to do with this?"

"Hello, and Blanche and Sophia. Four of them, four of us. We should all move in together!"

Either the connection flaked out again, or my idea wasn't so brilliant.

"Yeah, I don't know about that," Marcy said. "Jillian's going to marry that boy and Noah lives in Chicago."

"Jillian and her ex—they're moving that fast?" And while I knew Noah lived in Chicago, I guess, well, I hadn't thought through my plan.

"Yes, Jillian and her man are moving fast." Marcy filled me in on more details. How hadn't that come up at the sleepover?

Oh right. They'd been focused on me. "We need a regular meeting schedule. We need a name too. A girl gang name."

"Okay, but maybe we don't call it a girl gang," she said. "A crew, maybe. I don't know. And hey, you can call me any time. Have you used that burner phone yet?"

"No. It makes me feel like a criminal."

"Plenty of people use gas station phones who aren't criminals."

"Like who?"

"Maybe like, a senior citizen who doesn't need a whole monthly plan. Or for a child, where the parent won't pony up for a phone with all the frills. I bet my cousin has a phone like yours. How is Lucas, anyhow? He won't text me more than a word at a time."

I laughed. "Yeah, that sounds about right. It's how he talks too. I think his favorite word is no."

She groaned. "I promise he's a good guy. I mean, I know he's family so we can't get rid of him, but we actively like Lucas. He's doing a good thing out there."

"The camp split is a sensitive topic around here. I got most of my intel from the teen counselors."

"Mmm, well, there's definitely more to the story than I know too," Marcy said. "I know Lucas gets down on himself sometimes for reasons that are stupid and also that he's doing the responsible thing by staying at that camp when others bailed."

"I gathered he'd made some kind of big move. A tough guy like him running a camp for girls? It's sweet, isn't it?"

"Yes," Marcy agreed with gusto. "That's exactly what I told my brothers. They teased him to no end. Sent him boxes of Girl Scout cookies when they found out he took the job. They thought they were being funny."

"How did Lucas take it?"

"He responded with a joke in our text thread, but I told my brothers he might be masking. They told me to stuff it with my therapy terms. I told them *they* needed therapy. Anyway, my brothers texted him that they have his back, and they do. They all tease each other, but they're blood and they don't take that lightly."

Marcy had known Lucas through every stage of his life. What had he been like as a teenager? Or in college? Who did he date? Probably nobody with pink hair.

Not that it was any of my business.

I paced toward the office to keep the connection solid. I told Marcy about the camper fashion show and the little girl who asked Lucas if he thought I was pretty.

Marcy howled. "That is gold. Pure gold!"

I laughed, feeling like old times hearing her laugh so hard. "I know, what a chump."

A growl sounded within range. My heart sank and I found myself wishing the sound came from a wild animal and not my boss.

Chapter 11

Lucas

GREAT. JUST GREAT. HUDSON was laughing at me. No doubt talking to some famous friend.

"Take care, Marcy." Hudson ended her call, looking directly at me.

Even more great. Now Marcy knew a camper got one over on me, so the rest of my cousins would hear the delicious details soon enough. Best prepare for another onslaught of cookies.

"Hey," Hudson smiled big, too big, my direction, as if she hadn't been caught laughing about me. She took a few tentative steps up the dirt path toward the office front porch where I stood. "How are you?"

I was that guy who wouldn't let it pass. I left the porch to join her on the path. "Telling Marcy how terrible I am as a camp director?"

Her smile instantly disappeared. "I would never do that. You're not a terrible camp director."

Of course she'd say that. She wanted to keep her job. Now if I could figure out *why*.

"We were laughing at the sweetness of your response to Angelica's theatrics at the runway show," she said.

My cheeks felt like a match lit against my skin. "I played along. Awkwardly, I'm sure." Like right now.

"I liked that part best." She grinned. "It was sweet."

I grumbled. *Sweet* was not a word I'd use to describe myself. It sure wasn't going on my resume. "Okay. Why aren't you with the campers?"

She seemed to take a second to pivot. "I worked out time away tonight to take care of some things. It's why I was in the office earlier. Again, totally sorry. I didn't know I wasn't allowed in there after business hours."

I waved off the apology. "No, that's on me. You're allowed in the office whenever you need." The timing meant she'd missed dinner in the Mess. "Did you eat?"

She played with a strand of that pink hair. "Maggie's bringing me food. We've got the little fridge and a microwave in the cabin."

She didn't seem like the kind of person who thrived on leftover cafeteria food. In fact, every time I'd seen her in the Mess, she stood out like she was photoshopped in. Not because of the pink hair. It was her whole *everything*. She didn't belong here.

No—not that she didn't belong. More like, she wasn't like anyone else here.

"I'm headed into town if..." I coughed. "I could, uh, pick up some food. For you."

She raised a sculpted brow. "Food but no wigs?"

A laugh came out of me. "I'd have to be heavily convinced to buy fake hair."

She rolled her eyes. "Sure, sure. Too cool for wig shopping. I get it." She leaned a hand against the outer railing of the office porch. "Thanks for the food offer, but it wouldn't make sense to come all the way back to camp."

I scratched at my neck. Warm, like my face. "It's not a bother. Besides, I have extra stuff here at the owner's suite for when I stay."

Her eyes lit up. "You said it was the owner's cabin. Now you're calling it a suite?"

I laughed, which caused her to flinch. I guess I didn't do that often. "It's technically a cabin. Alan and Alice, they would call it that—the owner's suite. It's a cabin with a full kitchen, living space, and a bedroom. It's not too much bigger than where you're staying with Maggie."

Her shoulders slumped a little, which made me laugh to myself. She was grasping for any hint of luxury in this well-worn camp. "It's no big deal if you'd like me to bring you food," I said. "Just tell me what you want."

Her own cheeks colored. I'd say they matched the shade of mine, but her skin was perfect. Mine was bearded.

"What I want..." she trailed off.

A thick and weighted sensation hung in the air between us. I desperately wanted to know what she wanted. And it had nothing to do with food from town.

Shoot. Maybe she could sense my thoughts focused on something other than food from town. "I didn't mean anything weird by that," I told her. "I meant like, hamburger or sub sandwich."

She snickered. "Yeah, I got that. I guess I'm in a more contemplative head space right now." She straightened, as if gathering herself together. "I'm going to go back to my cabin. It's been a long day."

"Okay." The day had felt long for me too, but with brighter moments I found myself enjoying. Brighter tinged with pink.

She tugged at her hair again, then took off toward the heart of camp.

I replayed her comment about me being sweet. It didn't fit, but that didn't mean I found the comment unwelcome.

Fridays were always hectic. As a weekly overnight camp, that meant parent pick-ups beginning mid-afternoon.

And parents who visited the office for all sorts of unnecessary reasons. Their visits kept Twila and me glued to our desks for the afternoon. While Twila thrived, offering parents and guardians doughnuts and lemonade as they waited or poked around un-prompted in the camp office, I merely survived. And not in the way I preferred, which was outdoors with a simple pack and a weekend free of obligation.

One of those parents sat in front of me now, in my office, yammering about score sheets.

I cracked my knuckles, causing the woman to flinch. "Camp Junebug doesn't use score sheets."

She appeared reasonable, dressed in a yellow top and jeans, but the words coming from her mouth might as well have been alien. "What do you have that we can show the school about her accom-plishments? The kids are graded on their summer curricula." She waved a piece of folded construction paper covered in stickers and marker drawings. "*This* does not count."

I couldn't believe I had to say these words after she had regis-tered, paid, and sent her child to live here for a week. "This is a summer camp. We are not a school with grades."

I then regurgitated the paragraph on the website that stated exactly what the camp entailed. Camp Junebug was a traditional summer camp with cabins and crafts and nature trips in the woods. Light structure with time to explore, safely, under supervision.

She interrupted me. "Camp Trail Blazers has a full report-out waiting for each parent. There's a syllabus with the training pro-gram mapped out—"

"I'm going to stop you right there." Interrupter, meet your match. I stood. "The Trail Blazers have their own agenda and process. Camp Junebug is a children's summer camp. That's it."

The woman appeared non-plussed with my response. In fact, she fumed with disgust. She stood herself. "We need to show our private academy proof of an enriching educational experience. I demand you score my child!"

I grabbed the nearest scrap of paper and a pen. I scribbled what she wanted and handed it to her. "Here. A plus."

If the threat *Go directly to your room without dinner* could be personified, it was this woman, right now. Her cheeks bloomed red and her eyes bulged like something out of a cartoon. I hadn't seen eyes that scary since my cousin Matteo suffered a severe allergic reaction to prairie grass during our ninth-grade class field trip. Poor guy rubbed his eyes and the eyeballs swelled past the socket.

The furious woman grew very still other than a slight quiver in her jaw. "This is *unacceptable*. I want to talk to your supervisor. *Immediately*."

So much fury had to be bad for the blood pressure. I'd suggest a walk in the woods, but I wanted this lady off the property.

I grinned. "Oh, the camp owner would love to discuss the merit of grading a child's camp activity. Old Alan will talk your ear off on that one. I'll get you his home number. That speech you interrupted? He wrote that. It's on our website for a reason."

Red-faced and now offering a verbal assault worthy of a ranting sailor, the woman stomped out. She paused by the table between my office and Twila's desk, touched no fewer than three doughnuts before choosing a maple glazed, sniffed it, then tossed it back on the tray. She grabbed what looked like a sample-sized container from a bowl and left.

"Ooh, she was one for the books!" Twila cooed with near glee. "The helicopter types crack me up. My book club loves when I bring them unhinged parent stories."

"Is that...normal?" Hudson emerged from the kitchenette. She hovered at the entryway as if testing the room for lingering fumes.

"I didn't know you were here." My heart hit my chest loud enough for the sound to bounce off the walls. I couldn't be sure whether the disgruntled mom caused it or, well, somebody else. For whatever reason.

"No," I said as Twila answered, "Oh sometimes. There's always a few."

"There are?" I blurted. "Why didn't you warn me?" Information I could have used when I'd agreed to this job. Vital data.

"It's only a scant few," Twila said. "Oh Hudson, dear. You look shook."

She had her arms wrapped around herself as if she were cold. She wasn't smiling like Twila. She did look shaken. "Shouldn't you be with the campers?" Not sure why my concern came out that way, but it was out and I couldn't take it back.

"There's only a few left," she answered blankly. "Maggie sent me here."

Huh. Across the room, Twila stared laser beams at me and mouthed something. I shook my head, not understanding. Twila focused her beams on Hudson, then on me again. Hudson continued to look dazed.

"Are you okay?" I asked Hudson. "Here, sit down."

She blinked, seeming to snap out of her trance to sit in a chair. "That woman bullied you, and you dished it right back. You held your own." She looked at me with near fascination. Near because I couldn't imagine she was fascinated. "Is that true about the camp owner? How they view the camp?"

I nodded. "It's not a radical concept. It's just a summer camp. I don't get this whole grading thing."

"Feedback is everything," Hudson responded, more in her usual tone than the detached state she'd been in. "People love feedback. They also hate it, but they crave it. It's the world we live in."

"We're not *grading* campers." No way, never. "The owner doesn't want it and I sure as heck will not be forcing some invented curriculum or criteria on anybody. Counselors, kids, nobody."

Hudson smiled. "Vision. *That's* vision."

Twila slow clapped. "A beautiful vision indeed."

I pointed at Twila. "No." I looked at Hudson. "It's not my vision. I'm just here to keep the lights on."

It was my usual line. I filled the position to keep the proverbial lights on at camp. But hearing it out of my own mouth today, I sounded...uncaring.

I'd taken the position, rooting for the old ways of Camp Junebug, because it made the most short-term sense. Short being the key word I couldn't lose sight of.

A few ranting parents I could handle. Twila, I could mostly handle. It was only for one summer.

"I understand the camp a little better now," Hudson said. "The grassroots angle can be highlighted in the marketing—hear me out." She held up a finger, already knowing my objections came pre-loaded. "You want to get the right families here. Not ones who are disappointed they aren't receiving report cards and educational agendas."

"Sure," I said. "Problem is, they pay. And somebody's got to pay to keep this place running."

The office door opened and a man came in with a little girl in tow, carrying her bag and a sack full of camp crafts. Twila's attention now diverted, Hudson stood again and approached me.

"I want to know more about this Trail Blazers camp," she told me.

I started to say no, but figured she'd press. "I have no interest in talking about their camp."

She looked past me to my office. "If I could understand what they're all about, to contrast it from what you don't want Camp

Junebug to be, that can help sharpen the—" she paused. "Snapshot that's portrayed to the public."

I bristled. She didn't say the word marketing, though she said everything around it. But she had a point. If our website offered more information, maybe these parents who wanted a different experience than what we offered would bypass Camp Junebug altogether. Save us all some grief.

But I didn't want Hudson's help. If I took it, that meant investing more in the camp. Not simply *keeping the lights on*. I didn't have it in me to invest more than I already had.

I'd only ever intended to work at Camp Junebug two summers, tops. Earn my camp leadership experience, get my recommendation, and move on to the work that excited me in Colorado.

Only I'd been played. Burned. By the person I believed I could trust. The person who'd brought me into camp, before the split, promising me a recommendation using his connections which extended to programs across the country. Until he abandoned that plan for his own agenda.

I was done trusting. I could only depend on myself.

"You can look at the Trail Blazers' website yourself," I responded. Except for that thing she told me about avoiding the internet. "You said you had that internet addiction thing. You were in here yesterday on Twila's computer." I lowered my voice. "You're not out of bounds on some ten-step program, are you?"

She had grace enough to look a little ashamed. What was I talking about—Hudson was all grace. But she did look a smidge guilty.

"I think it's twelve steps—not that I'm in a program." She smoothed her already smooth hair. "I had Twila's permission. It was a mistake, though. Nothing good came of it."

"Oh." I wasn't sure what that meant, but it wasn't my business. If she'd asked for my help, that would be different. She hadn't.

"Maybe I'll tell you about the Trail Blazers someday over a cold beer."

Her reaction was about what I expected. A little surprised tinged with disgust. She probably sipped martinis by hotel pools while I preferred the dusty bar in town.

One of the college-aged counselors came in. Becky, maybe. I needed to get better with names. "Everyone's out," she announced. "Is it okay for us to leave?"

"Did Maggie say you could go?" I asked.

She nodded. "You can radio her to confirm."

"Naw, go ahead."

The woman left nothing but a dust cloud and the door swinging shut behind her.

"They have a schedule worked out," I told Hudson. "Some leave for the weekend, and the teens often cycle out, only here for a few weeks at a time. I imagine Maggie gave you the rundown."

Twila buzzed around the office cleaning up. She approached the doughnut box.

I grabbed the trash bin and pointed inside. "Pitch 'em."

She huffed. "They're perfectly good doughnuts."

"They're compromised. By the angry parent."

Twila did as told and I cinched the trash bag to take on my way out. I paused by the table. "Are those lotion samples?"

Hudson tucked hair behind her ear. "I brought the last of my stash. I figured parents might want them as a freebie."

"Well, that was...kind of you." I nodded to Twila. "Put them away until next week."

Hudson lingered. She had a calculating look about her which couldn't be good. More marketing ideas, probably. Or she wanted weird stuff from town.

"Uh, you can go too." In case she wanted permission. This boss thing took getting used to. "The next campers arrive Sunday afternoon."

She kept doing that lingering thing when Maggie burst in. "Who's up for a trip into town? I need a burger and a stiff drink. Drinks on me."

Twila danced in place. "Happy hour!"

Hudson whirled toward me, practically glowing. Not a bad look. "Sounds perfect." She plucked me by the arm. Her warm, delicate hands encircled my forearm sending heat hurdling through my veins. "Lucas, you're coming with us."

Chapter 12

Hudson

A TRIP TO TOWN. With people. And places to be seen, heard, noticed.

I hadn't left camp since I'd been abandoned, er, dropped off. I couldn't remember the last time I'd stayed put in one place for days on end without so much as quickie trip to a corner Walgreens. The perennial social butterfly had essentially been caged. These wings were desperate for flight.

Thankfully, town was a nowhere blip on the map, so I could continue my lay-low lifestyle.

As a precaution, I pulled my hair up and tucked it beneath one of Maggie's caps. A cute denim ball cap with nary a brand logo or sports team stitched on the front. Average, forgettable. I tossed on a Camp Junebug T-shirt a size above what I'd typically wear.

And a little fresh lipstick. I wasn't a peasant.

We ended up at a pub-style joint where old-timey framed photos and wacky tacked-on things covered every inch of wall space. Lots of mounted fish and boat oars. The happy hour specials landed in front of us on a sheet of bright green paper with grease spots dotting the edges.

Pure energy shot through my veins. Chattering voices filled the bar area with high-top tables. Many of the booths filled with families and a few with groups of teenagers. This wasn't exactly a place anybody went to be *seen*, unlike my rotating lists in L.A. and Nashville. And yet I was grateful. I considered any social event a plus if it didn't involve a plastic cafeteria tray or banned bug spray.

"We'll have the Nacho Megaboat," Maggie recited to the server without glancing at the menu.

"This is a fishing town," Twila explained. "Everything around here has a boat theme. Oh, and whatever you get, don't get the chili here. Trust me."

I couldn't stop the face I made. "Noted."

"Shots all around?" Maggie offered, looking at each of us. Twila, the college counselor Jasmine, and the camp cafeteria staff took her up on it. Basically, everyone but me and Lucas, who sat across from me at the end of the table.

"Local beer on tap for me," Lucas said to the server.

The margarita tempted me, though the size was enormous. I aimed to walk out of here in a straight line. I decided to switch it up. "Same."

Lucas glanced sidelong at me as our server moved on. "Didn't figure you for a craft beer drinker."

Truth: I didn't drink much beer, but I liked supporting small creators and that could easily stretch to local beer brewers. "There's a lot you don't know about me."

I could have sworn his cheeks colored. That little patch of skin above his beard. Was it smooth or rough?

"I know next to nothing about you." He grunted. "Which is a problem since I supposedly hired you."

I flitted my hand in the air. "Are you still on about that? Look, Marcy got me in, and Twila did the dirty work. You don't have to beat yourself up about it."

A warning flashed in his eyes. I'd gone too far. The man was my boss after all. But instead of growling, he grinned. "You're probably right. Marcy doesn't trust just anyone. And you passed the background check."

Twila angled toward us from the opposite end of the table. "Are you getting Mr. Grumpy to talk, Hudson?"

"I can't believe he's even out with us," Maggie said.

"Hey," Lucas shot back. "I'm *right here*."

She slapped a hand against the table. "We know. It's a miracle."

He made some grumbly sounds, working that defined jaw. His beard was closely trimmed. He didn't seem the type to use beard oil, but he was rather impeccably groomed now compared to the first day we met. Did he ever use any high-end products?

Across from me, Lucas tapped a finger against the worn wood table to a beat only he could hear. He didn't seem particularly nervous or irritated, just thinking to himself.

Once drinks arrived, I threw a few softball questions his way to get him comfortable. After all, it sounded like he rarely—if ever—took up the happy hour offer. Lucas answered easily enough but didn't seem fully engaged.

Right. It wasn't as if we had any of the same interests. We might not even exist on the same planet.

I slid my phone from my purse. Yes! A decent connection now that we were outside of the woods. I needed a quick peek at some accounts. Except didn't I tell Lucas I had a thing about staying offline?

"Excuse me." I shot him a smile—as if he cared to look up from his beer—and dashed off to the ladies room.

No shame in a quick scan while I did my business.

New comments appeared in the posts I'd made weeks ago. Speculation on what happened to me. One hopeful theory suggested I was slinking around with that former SNL guy who dated everybody on the rebound. Ha!

An image of Lucas staring into his beer flashed in my mind. I'd sort of ditched him out there, hadn't I?

I slipped the phone into my purse and washed up at the sink. I removed my hat and shook out my hair for an overall scan of my face and make-up. A quick lipstick refresh and a spritz of facial mist and I was ready to go.

The main bathroom door opened and two chattering women entered. They parked themselves in front of the mirror beside me.

"Ooh, that's a great lipstick color," one of them remarked. "What kind is it?"

On instinct, I reached into my purse. "I have samples. Would you like one?" I handed over two Sheek branded mini tubes of lipstick individually sealed in their own packaging. "I'm not selling anything. I have them because of a...thing I did." I shrugged.

"That's so sweet. Thank you." The woman appeared close to my age with impressively sculpted brows. Sporty clothes, kind of like me, but brand name, unlike me.

I smashed the hat on and left the bathroom feeling energized. I loved giving things away. That was the slice of my influencer life I enjoyed most. Connecting with people with products they might not have found without me.

At the table, I sat at my spot across from Lucas. "Tell me about the other camp."

The rest of the table appeared fully engrossed in a discussion on conspiracy theories tied to Taylor Swift's latest album, so we were in the clear.

Lucas shook his head, but a faint smile appeared. "You're persistent. Probably waited until I had a few drinks in me." Looking at his frosty glass, he glowered. "Wait, *is* that what you did?"

I tossed out a playful smile. "Maybe. Hey, I went all in for the full camp experience and I'm drinking your beer choice. It smells like stinky socks and doesn't taste much better."

"Why are you drinking it if you don't like it?"

I shrugged. "I figured it's more of an acquired taste." Like some other things I'd been exposed to this week. Possibly including the person sitting across from me. "I'm experiencing so many other new things, why not expand my horizons to craft beer?"

"You're trying to butter me up." He sighed. "It's working. Okay. What do you want to know?"

Thank you butter and a bit of patience. "How did you end up running a girl's summer camp?"

His jaw ticked, just the slightest movement, and something stirred deep inside me. He had that rugged tough exterior, but I'd seen him talk with passion about shrubbery. To children. A compassionate gentleness lurked beneath the sandpaper he presented to the world.

"I was hired as a guide, before the split," he said. "Pretty much everything about the state of things can be defined because of the split."

I already had the dirt from Bianca about the owner's evil son breaking the camp in two. But not how Lucas ended up carrying the weight of the old camp. "Why not stay with them? Or leave for something else? It seems like you're, well, more than a little miserable."

His eyes cast downward. "That obvious, huh?" He tipped back his glass and took a beat before answering. "I hope the kids don't notice. Not that they care what I'm doing. It's not their fault."

Not exactly an answer, but it showed me he cared how his grump waves might affect those around him. Twila seemed impenetrable.

He tapped the side of his pint glass. "He was my friend—Brycen. The guy who runs the other camp."

Hmmm. I sat on my hands, willing myself not to stop his flow. He seemed to do better with a little space to speak.

"He's the one who got me the job," Lucas went on. "I met him on a weekend survival training course, and when he told me he ran a camp with his family, I signed on. He had all these connections through his family. People they'd hired over the years to do wilderness trips and things. We had a plan. After a couple years at camp, then he'd get me into, well, where I wanted to be. I needed experience in a camp setting to build the right job experience."

I nodded. "Wow, fascinating."

His gaze shot toward me and I realized he may have thought I was pandering. "No, it's actually fascinating. I had no idea a job hierarchy existed for wilderness guidance. Okay honestly, I only know about summer camp from that old movie with the estranged twins who set up their divorced parents and conspired about it at camp."

"*The Parent Trap.*"

I grinned. "You've seen *The Parent Trap?*"

"I was a kid once too, you know."

And had he been this much a grouch? Or had he been carefree? A dreamer, like me, but with dreams of forest brush and tree bark instead of world domination by video streaming?

I'd had so many dreams and ideas as a kid, I could never pick one thing. Beauty tutorials came easily to me, and got high views if they were done well, so I kept on making them. I'd done so many, and connected with so many people about skincare and wellness, it became all I did. Other than my usual side hustles to stay afloat.

"So this guy, Brycen," I continued. "He was your friend. He helped you with a plan. But something happened and it blew up."

Lucas grunted. At least I hadn't heard any words resembling English. Or Italian, in case he was bilingual.

"Money," Lucas finally stated. "It always comes down to money for some people. Maybe all people. He met some investor types and saw dollar signs. That's when—" He stopped and his attention shifted.

A commotion of happy voices grew louder behind me. This town really kicked into gear on a Friday. I turned to see what caught his eye. A group of adults in pricey athletic gear and outdoorsy type clothes gathered at the front of the restaurant, waiting to be seated. Attractive adults. Fit, confident, loud and—oh. Oh no.

I whipped around. Lucas' hands balled into fists. At the other end of the table, our coworkers exchanged glances between each other, then to the loud group, then to Lucas.

"Well, look who it is," a male voice boomed from behind me. "Our old friends at little Camp Junebug."

Lucas' jaw went to steel. His eyes hinted at a warning as he looked up and made contact. "Hello, Brycen."

Chapter 13

Lucas

"Why the grim face?" Brycen's presence shadowed across our end of the table. "Enrollment should be up for Ole Junebug. We sent a few campers your way after our waiting list maxed out. You know, as a last resort."

Brycen may have lacked a couple of inches in height to meet mine, but his ego sure made up the difference. "Must have been your cast-offs who left fuming after demanding report cards." I couldn't help shake my head again at the ridiculous request.

"We give the parents what they want." Brycen shrugged. His sandy hair grazed his shoulders. He must let loose after five. Better than that goofy manbun thing he usually wore. He looked past me to others at the table. "I see you're with your ragamuffin crew. Charming."

"Do you kiss your mother with that mouth?" Twila countered with a sharp tone. "Calling us *ragamuffins*." She turned up her nose, then shifted so her back turned toward Brycen.

"Always had a mouth on her," Brycen grumbled.

"Watch it." Me defending Twila. That was new.

Brycen ran a hand through his hair. Behind him I swore one of his coworkers swooned. A lot of new faces with him I didn't recognize. Young and looking like models for an outdoor clothing catalog.

"Our table's ready," a tall blond woman cooed at him. Her hand trailed Brycen's bicep.

He glanced at her. "Yeah, babe, give me a minute."

Across from me, Hudson made a sound. A delicate growl. *Hudson*. Who knew what she thought right now. I could hardly put words together while this dude hovered over us like a menace.

"The Summer Trail Games," Brycen said, as if that meant something to me. "Staff teams competing in games and activities. A little friendly fun and competition. How about your camp versus ours."

Yeah right. Like I'd ever—

"We'll do it." Hudson tilted her head a mere fraction toward Brycen, her eyes shadowed beneath her cap.

"No," I started, when Hudson reached a hand to mine and pressed firm.

"Yes. We'll do it." Her voice came solid and strong.

Brycen's thin lips revealed a toothy smile. "I like her spirit." He pressed his hands together in some kind of gentle prayer pose and bowed his head. "We'll be in touch."

And he was off.

I jerked my hand back. "Why did you agree to that?"

"What'd he say?" Maggie asked from several seats away. She scowled toward the departing group. One of her friends had crossed over to the Trail Blazers and she was still caught up about it.

"He challenged us to a competition," Hudson answered. "Camp versus camp."

Jasmine's lip curled. "He's so arrogant."

"She told him yes," I said to the others. A death sentence. Besides, if I had to see him do that stupid bow again, I'd blow all my gaskets. Every last one. I couldn't believe I ever saw him as cool.

Maggie winced. "I don't know about this."

Jasmine folded her arms. Twila rolled her eyes. The cafeteria staff murmured to each other. Pocket Pete, nodded toward me. "When do we start training?"

After another round or two of beers, where the conversation turned to strategizing against the Trail Blazers, we decided to call it a night.

I was deemed too inebriated to drive.

"You're coming back to camp with us," Hudson declared. She seemed far too sober for how long we'd been drinking. Then again, I'd only seen her drink the one beer. Hours ago.

"I drank water the rest of the night," she told me, as if I'd pondered my thoughts out loud.

Had I? This whole challenge deal from Brysen had me out of sorts. Worse, our Junebug staff believed they stood a chance against the other camp.

I headed out of the restaurant with the group. We'd already seen the Trail Blazers leave ahead of us a good thirty minutes ago.

Hudson held her open palm out. "Keys."

"Fine." I handed her my keys. "You know how to drive a truck?"

Her soft fingers grazed mine as she took the keys. Her touch didn't linger. Not to say I wanted it to linger. Nope. I was just a little brain fuzzed right now. Those craft beers had a higher alcohol by volume than the watered-down types I picked up at the store.

"Like I said, there's a lot you don't know about me," she said breezily.

A few snickers sounded behind us as Hudson yanked open the driver's side door of my truck. "Hey, give her a break," I said to whoever was laughing.

Pocket spoke up. "We're not laughing at her, Boss." He looked at me grinning. "See you Sunday."

He only called me Boss when he wanted to stick it to me. Stick what? Man, this brain fuzz didn't help. I couldn't remember the last time I'd felt like this, though my cousins had been involved.

I climbed into the passenger seat of my own truck and tried not to feel like a child. I glanced to Hudson. She fumbled with the seat adjustments and slowly inched closer to the steering wheel.

"Here." I turned the ignition for her as she belted in.

"I figured you'd put up more of a fight," she said.

"I told you, I don't want anything to do with the other camp."

"I meant about driving you home."

Oh. "Well, I drank too much. It's not safe."

She looked me over. "Don't make fun of me, but I've never driven a truck before."

"I thought you—" Never mind. She said I didn't know much about her and well, we sure were learning. "What are you used to driving?"

"A Honda Fit. I'm not even sure what I'll do with it now that I'm, I mean, it's back in L.A." She tapped at her closed lips. "You think I could lease it out? Do people do that? Like they sublease apartments?"

I scrubbed a hand against my beard. "Just take it slow. We aren't far from camp."

"Sure, right."

She was nervous, I could tell. Maybe keep her talking? "Why are you here instead of L.A.?"

Her eyes widened. She blinked, then her face changed like she'd only accidentally reacted. "My um, my family—I grew up here. Friends and school. I'm here visiting. Well, between jobs more like."

We still hadn't left the parking lot. "Look, just shift to drive and go slow."

Hudson returned us to camp in one piece. I'd had to provide directions since she didn't remember which way we'd driven to the restaurant, but other than that, smooth sailing.

And I didn't mind so much being driven around by a pretty woman. It'd been some real time since I'd been on a date. No, this wasn't a date. I shouldn't even go there in my head.

We parked in the office lot beside Maggie's car. She and the counselors had disappeared by now to do whatever they did on weekends. Not my business.

I pocketed my keys and headed toward the owner's cabin.

"I want to see the other camp," Hudson said.

I faced where she stood on the sidewalk leading to the office. Two light posts in the parking lot illuminated her soft skin. I knew it was soft because she'd touched my hand. "You'll get to when we're summoned for those preposterous camp games."

She approached closer. "I mean now. Tonight. Can't we cross the camp boundary line and go over there?"

"Yeah, and do what? TP the lodge?"

She smiled with way too much mischief. "*That* sounds fun."

Sure, except for the cost of the toilet paper. A real budget buster. "No."

"What's stopping you from going over there? A measly little fence? A tree with a Keep Out sign?"

I knew exactly what kept me out. It started with a B and ended with I didn't care.

She poked me in the arm. An actual poke, like from a camper to get my attention. "The Trail Blazers went to a second location. I overheard them when they walked by our table leaving the restaurant. They're going to a club in some other town. That means there's minimal staff on site."

I could barely keep up. "And? What are you interested in over there? It's a fancy camp. That's it."

"We should know what we're up against. And I'm nosy. According to a personality inventory, I'm a high input learner or something like that. I gather data. It's why I'm—was—online so much. I want to see the camp for myself before the actual competition."

"We're only *up against* anything because you agreed to it."

She at least looked a little sorry. Good.

"I know. I couldn't stand hearing Evil Son talk smack about Camp Junebug. *I see you've got your ragamuffins,*" she lowered her voice to sound like a dopey guy. "*Babe, give me a minute. Babe, check out my hot bod. Babe. Look, Babe. Check out these guns.*" She flexed her arms, continuing the charade.

I burst out laughing.

Hudson smiled. "I've never heard you laugh. Not like that."

"Yeah, well, not a lot is funny lately."

She studied me. "I like your laugh."

Hoo boy. Her continued stare made me want to dive into a hole. I wasn't much for attention, and right now, she focused all of hers on me.

I should have been flattered, but I wasn't good at this sort of thing. Especially with someone like her, wearing designer clothes and with interests I couldn't repeat back if someone asked me. She was completely different than anyone I'd ever spent time with. In any capacity, in any environment.

I didn't have a clue how to relate to her.

"I'm calling it a night," I said.

She started down the path toward the cabins. "Suit yourself. I'm going to the other camp."

"*No.* You can't go over there."

"Why? They don't know me. Besides, I'll stay hidden."

She kept walking. I caught up to her on the path. "No."

"That's not a reason. Is it because it's *trespassing?*" She said it like a taunt. Like a dare.

"It's dark. You'll get lost in the woods."

"Then be my wilderness guide."

Bullseye. How did she manage to hit right where it mattered?

After a full week managing a children's camp and a night out drinking, a man had only so much restraint. After all, I was born to guide.

Chapter 14

Hudson

WE DIDN'T SO MUCH creep through the woods as walk fully upright with flashlights. Still, I breathed in sweet victory. I'd convinced Lucas to lead me to the other camp.

A meager fence with a sign noting the camp boundary met us at the property line. Taller than me, but a simple chain link I'd climbed dozens of times as a kid. I moved forward.

"You can't climb that, Hudson," Lucas said, ever the stickler for rules.

I should have brought Maggie. Or Bianca. I bet Bianca would have been up for a little nighttime fence climbing. "If I can manage an advanced barre class on four hours sleep, you bet I can do this."

"I don't know what that means."

Ugh, men. "Is there another place to cross?"

"The road, at the main entrance."

Fat chance. "Then why did you take me through the woods?"

"Figured you'd come to your senses once we reached the boundary."

My senses—ha! Normally, my senses would direct me to a deep dive on the camp's social media accounts, followed by a closer look into the online presence of the people who ran it. Brycen had to be a gold mine of data. I knew his type. I'd bet the entire line of Sunday Riley's skincare regimen he had an Instagram less than a couple years old, completely re-crafted to his current persona, with a dead account lurking somewhere hiding all sorts of secrets.

But for some reason, holing up in the camp office late on a Friday night under the low-glow flicker of Twila's aging desktop didn't appeal. Neither did fighting for connectivity in my bunk. I'd accidentally scraped my knuckles against the rough ceiling more times than I cared to count.

Nope. I wanted the real deal. A sneak peek at the rival camp with my own eyes. A little adventure.

I tucked the flashlight into my back pocket with the light pointing up. I started my climb.

"Hudson," he warned.

"I'm not a camper. You can't tell me what to do." I swung a leg over the fence.

"I'm your boss."

Okay, sure. He could fire me. But then the adult-to-camper ratio would be jeopardized, and a full load of campers were enrolled the coming week.

The fence shifted, absorbing new weight. Lucas was climbing.

I beamed at him—my smile, not the flashlight.

He joined me on the other side. "This is a bad idea."

"So is microdermabrasion the day before a public event. Sometimes you take the risk."

He trudged alongside me. "I sound like a broken record, but yet again, I have no idea what that means."

Darkness permeated the path. Every step involved scouting for rocks or tree roots poking out of the dirt. I stumbled and a strong arm caught me. "Careful."

I tried to see his face through the dark, but he moved ahead of me. "Follow where I walk."

Only our breathing and footsteps sounded for the next few minutes until a clearing came into view.

"Activity area." Lucas stopped, his voice close. "Ropes course. See?" He shined his flashlight into the branches where a wooden bridge crossed the air between large trees. Various ropes stretched across the clearing. A wooden structure the size of a park's playground equipment featured more ladders and ropes.

"Is it like *Survivor*?" I'd seen enough episodes of the reality to show to know they did obstacle courses involving ropes and bridges. "Ooh, do you think we'll do giant puzzles on a beach?"

"I don't know what they have over here anymore."

"Ah. Good thing we're on this mission."

A grumble emitted from Lucas. I took that as a cue to move on.

The path widened past the ropes course with trees further cut back. Ahead, a large building loomed. An indoor facility of some type.

A sign reading *Training Center* was posted in front of the building. A paved walkway leading from its front door headed the other direction, uphill. Lights posted above the door lit the entrance. I kept to the shadows. "This sure puts our rain shelter to shame."

"*Our* rain shelter?" Lucas glanced at me.

"What? I've assimilated into camp life, haven't I?"

A low grunt was my only response.

"What's that up there, beyond the trees?" I asked.

"The lodgings."

I squinted through the dark. "Those look like apartments. It's two stories."

"They're closer to dorms than cabins."

The facilities at Camp Junebug were definitely of the cabin variety and definitely built before the millennium, unlike this modern structure. "Let's take a closer look."

Lucas sighed but didn't argue. We took the long way around the Training Center, away from the lights, and approached the lodgings from the back. Small pine trees nestled in groups around the buildings in contrast to the scraggly mass of trees and bushes at Camp Junebug. This landscaping looked professional.

We crept closer. A dim light shown in the window of one room.

Lucas crouched beside me. "Have you seen enough?"

A thrill rushed through. "I want to see the big lodge."

He covered his face with his palm. A shame. I liked that face. I was growing to like it even when he was exasperated by me. "Come on, where's your sense of adventure?"

He pulled his hand away. A determined look bore into me. "Don't tell *me* about adventure. I'm the one trained in survival skills."

"Like backpacking in the woods?"

"I've hiked challenging terrain with elevation changes. I've done week long excursions in difficult climate. I've spent a week alone in northern Wisconsin."

Impressive, though I had no interest in doing any of those things. "I can't imagine any of this intimidates you. Two story dorms and training facilities aren't needed for true survival." Cheap bait, but I couldn't help it. He could have turned away at any time and hadn't.

"I'm not intimidated. I don't want to get caught."

It was doubtless viewed as unprofessional for a camp director to lurk in the dark on a competitor's property, but honestly, I hadn't had this much fun in a long time. "So, let's not get caught."

I moved ahead to the next grouping of trees, angling to see up the incline toward the big lodge.

Lucas followed. "Turn off your torch."

"Torch?"

"The flashlight."

I clicked it off and hunkered down. "The last time I sneaked around at night like this was with my college friends," I whispered to him. "We used to dumpster dive behind an outlet mall. Your very own cousin Marcy played lookout."

"You? Dove into a dumpster?"

"Usually, I stood and looked through the top layer in the dumpster. Only the adventurous—that would be Noah—physically entered the dumpster."

"No offense, but you seem like you can afford to buy things instead of dig through trash."

"It's incredible what's considered 'trash.' Once we found an open box of brand name tank tops sealed in individual plastic wrapping. What reason is there to pitch brand new clothes into the trash?"

"Maybe it was a mistake."

"Their loss, our gain. We outfitted the fifth floor of our dorm with free tanks. We were like the Robin Hood of fashion. Sneaking with a mission."

"More like stealing." Lucas huffed out a breath. "I wouldn't exactly call that noble."

We kept going to that outlet mall until security chased us off. Our last time there, a padlock secured the dumpster.

Yes, we'd risked getting in trouble, but something felt really good about taking commercial excess and giving it away. Maybe we would have been more like Robin Hood if we'd donated the clothes to a shelter instead of our dormmates. We may have called ourselves broke college students, but we were attending a university many people didn't have access to because of the cost.

Something deeper pinged at me, a concept I couldn't fully grasp. The thrill of the find fulfilled one part, but the joy of giving things away was what resonated. It was one of those moments I wouldn't forget.

"Earth to Hudson." Lucas cut into my thoughts. "Someone's out there. We need to go."

I glanced every direction. "I didn't hear anything."

"You're off in la-la land." He took me by the arm and pulled us down the hill toward the Training Center. My foot made contact with a stick, resulting in a snap.

"Who's there?" a voice called out. A guy, likely a camp staffer. Footsteps grew louder. Nearer.

Lucas' grip tightened. He made a zipping motion across his lips. We were close, so close his breath tickled my neck. My heart drummed. He could probably make out the beat, it hit so loud.

The outline of his face came into focus. Determined, steady, annoyed.

This was so much better than scouring the internet.

The footsteps retreated. We were safe.

Lucas relaxed beside me. "We're leaving. Now."

I wasn't ready. "We need to leave our mark. Show them we were here." If I couldn't make my own mark out there in the beauty world for the time being, at least I could do it for our camp.

Forget waiting on Lucas, he'd only say no. I dashed toward the next group of trees, keeping my flashlight off and watching each step. *Aha.* The lodge, within site. Our final destination.

A quick peek behind found Lucas waving me toward him. Nope. Onward.

I scanned the area again. No sign of human life. The lone staffer appeared to have returned to the dorm.

I crossed the next length of open land at a quick walk. Running was too suspicious. Finally, I reached the massive lodge where the covered porch extended fully across the rear side of the building facing the lake. Stairs opened up at the end in front of me. I crouched in the shadows.

A scuffle sounded behind me. Lucas. "I can't believe you. What's this about making a mark?"

"I swiped a Sharpie from the craft bin. I want to draw a junebug somewhere."

"You want to deface private property."

Sure, if you put it that way. "Yes."

I scooted toward the stairs, uncapped the marker, and started drawing on the wooden step.

Lucas peered over my shoulder. "That's a lady bug."

Okay, well, I guess I didn't know what a junebug actually looked like. "Good enough for me." If I'd had my phone, I'd have snapped a selfie. Instead, I took in the moment, breathed the fresh air, and smiled at my partner in crime. Agent Mulder would be so happy I was out here living life.

Lucas growled.

I grinned. "See? Wasn't this fun?"

"So we meet again," a voice reached to us through the night. A male voice, elevated, standing over us at the top of the stairs.

My eyes fell shut. Lucas would never forgive me for this.

Chapter 15

Lucas

I spent Saturday morning holed up in my apartment trying to forget everything from the past twenty-four hours. The TV blared, but I ignored it. I could be doing half a dozen things—laundry, dishes, purchasing one-way tickets to a town where no one knew me.

Brycen's haughty tone cut through my thoughts for the millionth time. "Never figured you for one to sneak onto our grounds," he'd said to me. "If you wanted back in, you could have asked."

Wild dogs couldn't drag a request out of me that had anything to do with him or that camp.

And yet, there I'd been, crouched in the shadows in the one place I'd sworn I'd never step foot in.

Total humiliation.

I knew Hudson felt bad because she'd grown quiet. Real quiet. Before she could come up with some terrible excuse for our trespassing, I'd blurted out we were leaving. And then we did.

We headed back to the trail, when Brycen called after us, suggesting we leave through the front entrance. He even offered us a ride to our camp. Hudson, whether to save her pride or her hide, kept mum and kept on walking.

I looked like an idiot. I'd already felt like one for taking on this camp director job. Now I'd sealed the deal by making a fool of myself in front of the single person I cared to impress. It was stupid to care, but clearly, I did.

My phone buzzed. I grabbed it from the coffee table next to me on the couch. Number unknown. Nope.

I switched over to an app on my phone for a local outdoors meet-up group. Maybe they were up to something this afternoon. My cousins joked about me having a flip phone, but I had a smart phone. Older model, but it connected online. Jerks.

A call came in again. This time a known number. A known number I couldn't ignore. I answered. "Marcy."

"Hey, stranger," she said brightly. "Thanks for picking up."

"Mmhmm."

She sighed. "Is that all I get? How are you? How is Hudson? I can't believe you're leaving me hanging with no updates."

"There's nothing to update. Your friend is still employed. Despite all odds."

"What does that mean?"

Where did I begin? "You don't want to know."

"Now I definitely *need* to know."

I could practically hear her smile over the line. "No."

"You can't tell me no," she said. "Maybe you can get away with that with other people, but not me. Look, Hudson is dealing with a lot right now. Is she okay? It's driving me wild that she can't use her phone."

"I caught her talking on her phone. To *you*." And they'd been talking about me. Embarrassing.

"Well yeah, but it's only for emergencies."

Why did this conversation seem like crucial details were being left out? "Why does she have to stay off the internet?"

"She told you that?"

"Look, something bigger is afoot and I don't like not knowing."

She snickered. "*Afoot.* You're so nerdy sometimes. As for Hudson, it's up to her to tell you what she's comfortable with. But let's just say it's a matter of safety."

I sat up. "Safety? What does that mean? What is she hiding from?"

"I didn't say she was hiding," she answered quickly. Too quickly.

I rubbed my hand across my beard, still not used to having less of it after a hefty trim the other day. For no real reason. "If there's something—or someone—dangerous she's hiding from, that puts our kids at risk."

"It's not like that." She paused. "I don't think he'd look for her. That would mean leaving his precious L.A. bougie bubble."

Okay, now I could see how the Marcy-Hudson friendship existed. I didn't understand half of what she'd just said. But she'd said *he*. "So she has an ex."

"Yeah." A long beat of silence followed. "And he's a creep. But he wouldn't follow her. Besides, she's been laying low. Girl gave up all her online accounts."

To stay away from this dude? "Be straight with me. Is the camp at risk?"

Light sounds of kitchen noises came across from the other end. "Well, I never actually considered that. Her agent suggested the lay low thing as a precaution."

Agent...so YouTubers had talent agents? Twila said she had something like a million followers. Probably staying out of sight from an ex meant less online time which translated to less money...Okay, dots were connecting.

"Marcy. This is serious. I'm responsible for the camp. For the kids. The parents trust us with their children's lives. They trust the Camp Junebug name. The owners, they put me in charge because they trust *me*."

"Wow. That's the most passion I've heard from you about the camp. And here I thought you were riding out your time until you took off to Alaska or wherever."

"*Colorado*." A low sound emitted from my throat. "I'm just saying, there's trust involved. What aren't you telling me about Hudson?"

"If you were online like the rest of us you wouldn't have to ask."

Back to this again—razzing on me for being a digital hermit. "I'm part of a chat forum for my outdoor meet-up group." Even I could tell I only proved her point.

It hadn't occurred to me to search Hudson's name. After this conversation, I almost dreaded what I'd find.

"Promise me you'll show her a little grace, okay?" Marcy said. "Everyone deserves a second chance. She's sort of figuring things out. I'm hoping camp life shocks her system enough for some major self-reflection. Not that I should talk—I'm working a job I hate and constantly trying to keep this family from tearing each other apart."

"What's going on with the family?" I hadn't heard any drama. Figured. I was usually the last to hear any drama.

"Oh the usual. With Papá recovering from surgery, Mamá's in full micromanage mode, focused on her lone daughter, yours truly, in particular. Now I'm the one planning the family reunion."

A big undertaking in our family. It was one of my favorite celebrations. Outdoor games, grilled food, boxes of fireworks bought from our favorite joint over the Indiana border. "Your Mamá usually handles those plans, right?"

"Despite her micromanaging, she can't focus on large tasks right now. I took it on myself. Only she tells me everything I'm doing is wrong." She sighed again. "Thanks for asking how I'm coping, by the way."

I hadn't asked. Oh, right. Point taken. "Sorry. I'm not good at that part."

"I know, but a gal can hope. You're good for a listen, so I appreciate that at least. Look, I'd like to visit camp and check in. It'd be good to see you and Hudson both."

You and Hudson, as if we were paired together. Hudson's determined smile flashed in my head. She'd climbed that boundary fence as if it was nothing. Maybe the sexiest thing I'd seen her do. No, the sexiest thing I'd ever seen a woman do. And in front of me in the woods. At night. Was she trying to drive me crazy?

"How about the weekend of the fourth?" Marcy suggested. "I'll bring firecrackers and sparklers."

"Yeah, sure. Hudson would appreciate it."

"But not you, because you're too cool."

"Shut up."

She snickered. "Love you too, cousin. Take care." Marcy ended the call.

A notification popped up from the meet-up group. I bypassed it and went to YouTube. What was Hudson's last name? I visualized the payroll paperwork. Hawley. Hudson Hawley.

In one search, her face appeared on the screen. The main video featured on her profile showed her with longer hair streaked with light purple against dark blond. Her same bright eyes and smile made her instantly recognizable.

I scanned the featured video titles and images. All make-up and face stuff. Yeah, she'd said as much. I watched a couple minutes of the first video. She came across energetic without seeming like she tried too hard. Almost like she was talking to a friend instead of recording a video for an audience.

Another video showed her in a plain T-shirt with green goo on her face. So she drank swamp stuff and put it on her skin. She wiped off the goo with a cloth, leaving fresh pink cheeks.

My breath slowed. She was beautiful. No make-up, no trendy outfit. Not the least bit insecure as she talked about her pores or whatever.

No wonder she had so many fans. I'd spent the last ten minutes watching her and I didn't care about any of these products.

But why was she hiding? What kept her off the internet if she had all these fans?

I took my search to the main browser and put in her name. A different set of links resulted.

Beauty Influencer Allegedly Destroys Billionaire's Empire

Billionaire's Girlboss Girlfriend Cleared of Embezzlement Accusation

YouTuber Caught in Financial Scandal: Krom's Empire Shifts Blame

Krom...No, it couldn't be. Kristoff Krom? Hudson was connected to Kristoff Krom?

I clicked on the link from the most reputable news source of the bunch and read on. Brycen idolized Krom. He used to talk about Krom and his business ventures. A self-made investor who'd taken the business world by storm. A ladies man with a cocky attitude. Millions of online followers and all that.

"*Krom* is Hudson's ex?" I said it out loud, to myself.

And he was dangerous?

I kept reading. She'd signed on as a spokesperson for some mega makeup company Krom invested in. The deal fell apart when Krom's offices were raided. Accusations of money laundering. Something about a breakup video.

Despite my better judgment, I clicked on the linked video.

Krom, with dark, longish slicked back hair, wore a crisp dress shirt and sat behind a monster desk with his company logo above it. A second frame within the video showed Hudson without the usual stuff on her eyes and lips. Natural.

It didn't take long to realize this was intended as a private chat. Hudson's face morphed into shock, horror, sadness, as Krom steamrolled over her, accusing her of ratting him out and destroying his business.

A quick scan of the comments section of the video turned my stomach. I clicked off the phone. Stared at the wall to clear my head.

If I'd learned anything in life, it was guys like Krom bounced back. Setbacks were simply that, not career-ending. The money and power kept them going. Guys like Krom, and his wannabe proteges like Brycen, stayed at the top because money and power were all they cared about.

The rest of us? We were left somewhere in the dust.

Which was exactly what happened to Hudson. And now she was riding out the consequences at my camp.

Chapter 16

Hudson

THE CAMP OFFICE OFFERED everything I needed to stay busy. Coffee and snacks, air conditioning beyond an aging window unit, and of course, the internet. This time, I promised myself I wouldn't spiral into misery.

Lucas was confirmed off-grounds for the weekend. After the stunt I'd pulled dragging him to the Trail Blazers' camp last night, only to be caught, focusing on camp business might be my only chance at redemption.

I really hadn't expected to be caught. The Trail Blazers were supposed to be out two towns away. Though, now I knew Brycen wasn't a late-night partier. That knowledge might come in handy.

Poor Lucas. The sheer humiliation on his face told me he and Brycen's rivalry ran deep. And I'd been part of serving up that latest dose.

In ten minutes, I updated Twila's batch of Excel spreadsheets she'd confessed she was behind in. I wasn't entirely sure what she did all day, though online shopping appeared to take up a substantial chunk. It looked like she sold products too based on a separate spreadsheet containing links to bookmarked Ebay listings of porcelain figurines.

I looked over Twila's task list and checked off three more things. I'd temped in enough offices to know my way around boring spreadsheets. Besides, I didn't completely hate spreadsheets. Something about sorting the data into neat columns and color coding seemed mildly creative.

I moved on to researching camp accounts. I reviewed dozens of camp websites and their corresponding social media. Camp Junebug barely had an online presence, and while I understood Lucas didn't want to bankroll some major PR campaign when they couldn't hire more staff, I had to do *something*. It was like overhearing someone say they only washed their face with water and wondered why their skin broke out. As if I could stay silent under such dire circumstances.

I made notes and a branding file that I stored on Twila's computer. Colors, fonts, ideas for content. They could run with it. Or I could give them a head start. What else did I have to do?

Yes, that would keep me busy. I could explore the grounds further and snap a bunch of stills and background video as a base to overly text later. I glanced at the digital clock in the lower corner of the screen. It was barely noon. I had a whole afternoon to fill.

I clicked open a new browser window and ordered two new pairs of shorts, more socks, and a couple tank tops from a site running a big sale. I'd decided to take Twila up on her offer to store some of my less camp appropriate things in the main office to save space at the cabin. Heels, open toed sandals, dresses, and a bag of jewelry.

Okay, that took a whole fifteen minutes. What else could I do? I opened another website tab to lurk on my social media accounts. Some fans demanded new content. Others worried for my well being, despite the posted approved statement. Many seemed sympathetic to my needing time away from social media.

I'd always prided myself on being genuine with my online content. If I posted now about skincare like nothing was amiss in my life, it would feel dishonest. I wasn't sure what to say other than the statement.

No, that was a cop out. I was scared.

But what if my lurker account offered a little secondhand info? Like Jillian had suggested doing for me, but I'd refused as a natural control freak. A message supposedly passed along by a trusted friend source that things were cool, or at least, not currently smoking.

What was the harm? I just had to be careful.

I clicked through the last few Instagram posts I'd made. The itch to delete the troll comments came strong. But if I deleted them, they'd know I'd been monitoring. At least leaving the bad comments allowed my supporters the chance to defend me. And many were.

The lurker account used a flower for a profile pic along with a generic bio: *20-something skincare dork.* All posts locked as private.

I hit the comment button on my own most recent post.

Heard from a friend of one of Hudson's friends she is taking needed time to regroup and refresh. She wishes everyone peace and great skin in the meantime.

There. That sounded like something I might say that I hadn't ever said before. Like a message filtered through several people. Maybe a few fans would see it and know I was at least not hanging off the side of a cliff.

I switched to YouTube, where the comments remained a nightmarish apocalypse. Nope, no spiraling for me today. I closed that window and found myself typing my own name in the browser search bar. The latest trash blogs continued to blame me for Kristoff's downfall. One tabloid boasted he'd been spotted at an L.A. hot spot with a new lady on his arm. *Okay fine. You bait, I click.* The article clearly evaded spellcheck or any hint of editing, but I scanned through until I reached the accompanying photo.

Kristoff wore his typically messy but posh look: expensive clothes that appeared to have been simply tossed on at the last minute.

And there she was. A gorgeous woman somewhere in the Kardashian prototype. Glossy black hair, flawless airbrushed skin, and heavy makeup. She wore a bodycon dress illuminating her curves. She looked like she owned the world.

I sank into the chair. I'd been that woman. Briefly, but I'd been her.

So what?

I did a double take, looking around the empty room. My own inner voice had a real mouth on her.

So what? Being *that woman* had been *#Goals*. Every woman wanted to hold on to the arm of a billionaire like Kristoff.

No, they don't.

"Yeesh, inner voice. Why don't you tell me what you really think?" I was clearly losing it out here in the woods.

I looked at the tabloid photo again. The woman exuded carefully crafted beauty. The kind of beauty stamped with wealth and possibility. She looked like a billionaire's girlfriend.

A small plastic mirror tacked onto the frame of Twila's computer monitor displayed my reflection. I looked like a pink-haired kid playing dress up.

If I was honest with myself, I would admit that life with Kristoff always felt pretend. Maybe my mom had it right. I'd been *playing celebrity*. And now celebrity playtime was over. It had only been a role I played to gain what I wanted.

What I wanted. Then, not now. What did I want *now*?

The outer office door blew open. "What are you doing?" Lucas demanded.

My hand flew to my chest as my heart recovered from the interruption. Well, almost. It had a strange beat whenever Lucas came around. "You said I was allowed to use the office. So I'm using it."

"Right. That's fine." He blinked. "I...come in sometimes on weekends."

"Okay." I looked at him.

He looked at me.

I looked some more. He had on another heather gray shirt paired with cargo pants. He seemed like the kind of guy who would put useful things into those pockets.

He remained standing in the doorway, shifting his gaze everywhere but me. Last we'd spoken, I'd slinked away to my cabin after presenting him to his mortal enemy, caught unaware.

"Lucas, I'm so sorry." I'd said it at least thirty times on the way back to our camp the other night, but he deserved to hear it again. "It's my fault we were caught. If I hadn't been so intent on making a mark on their territory, we could have gotten out in time."

One side of his mouth seemed to involuntarily quirk up. Involuntary, because he tugged it down again. "You know, I'll tell you something about Brycen. He gets paranoid."

"Oh?"

"Now he's on edge. We went on the offense and I know it bugs him." He let the mouth quirk fully now. "I wish we'd left earlier, but at least we know we got to him."

"Oh, well, so long as we got to him, I guess that's good news." And Lucas' irritation at me seemed to have lessened.

"Now we need an action plan for the games. To show them what we're made of."

"The games..."

"The Summer Trail Games. You know, the games *you* got us into."

I bit my lip. "Yeah. Sorry. That Brycen guy irritated me so much. He was being such a jerk." *To you.* And I didn't like it one bit.

He scrubbed a hand against his jawline. A shiver went through me. I could almost feel the light pressure of his beard against my fingers.

Lucas appeared oblivious to my gawking. "I've got an idea for the games."

Guilt hit. Knowing he had to plan for a competition I volunteered us for, when he had actual priorities like running a camp, made me want to sink into quicksand.

He sat in a folding chair along the front wall near the door. "Don't you want to hear the idea?"

I was mainly glad he'd spoken words instead of grunts. "Sure."

"My meet-up group has a few folks who love outdoor competition. We could add them to the camp roster."

"But we can't hire any—" It clicked into place. "Right. The Trail Blazers wouldn't know they aren't our actual staff."

"Bingo." He rubbed his hands together. "I need to make some calls. Then, look over the camp schedule to fit in training sessions."

"Training?"

"Prepping for the games. Building up teamwork. You know, camp stuff."

I nodded. "And I suppose I'm part of this since I committed us in the first place?"

He leaned forward. His eyes landed on me with intensity. "You better believe it."

Part of me felt the threat—I'd caused this—but the rest of me grew eager with excitement. I'd never been part of a camp war before. Could be fun? I might need to make another clothing order.

"What can I do to help?" I asked.

He sat back. "Oh, I don't know. Maybe just..." He shrugged. "I'll text my friends about joining us." He slid out a cell phone. It wasn't some relic like Marcy joked.

"You could have done that from home."

He continued typing. "What?"

"You didn't need to come to the office to text your friends."

He looked up. "I know. But the camp schedule is here."

"You don't have that downloaded to your phone? Or in cloud storage? Do you know what cloud storage—"

"Yes, I know what cloud storage is." He stood and pocketed the phone. "I've got...other work to do." He walked past me into his office. He closed the door.

A moment later the door opened and he came out. "Are you staying here all weekend?"

"Where else would I be?" I laughed.

"You're allowed to leave."

Tread carefully. He didn't know my full reason for being here. I'd for sure end up on his grumpy side if he did.

"I know." I folded my hands in front of me on the desk. "I also have work to do." Which I'd done already.

He stepped right in front of the desk, bringing me into his aura of Lucas scents: a coffee base layered with a woodsy musk. Perhaps an aftershave or cologne and not simply the woods. Though if anyone could absorb the true essence of trees and leaves, it was him. "If you need to run into town for anything, let me know. Heck, you've driven my truck, so you can take the keys if you want."

This was an interesting development. "Why are you being nice to me?"

His usual scowl twitched. "I'm hard on you sometimes. I'm sorry."

"But I'm responsible for getting us into several messes with the camp."

He shrugged. "It was also kind of a wake-up call. If we don't stand up for ourselves, what does that say about us?"

It probably said we were a children's camp for gentle exploration, but I liked this intentional, adventurous vibe Lucas was riding. "We're not quitters."

He pointed at me. "That's right." He looked at his finger, then lowered it. "I should stop doing that so much. The pointing. Anyway. How about we get some food at the Mess?"

"It's open today?"

He pulled out a keyring from his cargo pants side pocket. "It is if you're the camp director."

Chapter 17

Lucas

HUDSON SWUNG HER LEGS from her position on the kitchen counter in the Mess. We'd cracked open a can of sticky sweet peaches and cut off portions from a leftover sub sandwich I found in the camp kitchen fridge.

I could have been grilling steaks at my apartment instead of eating camp food, but the thought of Hudson alone here for the weekend didn't sit well with me. Not after what I'd read online about her situation.

As long as I kept things professional, I'd be here as support. A friend. So far, she hadn't told me to leave, so I took it as a good sign. She could have taken her food and returned to her empty cabin for some peace and quiet.

The kind of peace and quiet I usually liked, but instead found myself here, in the camp kitchen, with Hudson chattering away.

"I'd like to explore the grounds more," she was saying.

The word explore hit a switch in me. "Yeah?"

"I'd like to see what's the opposite direction from the other camp. Is that the direction we went for the leaf walk?"

"Yeah. There are trails that extend about a half mile to our property line. More trails wind up toward the main road. We should do that."

"You'd go with me on a hike?"

I'd go with her to a mall right now if she asked. Thankfully, she didn't. "It's part of my job to inspect the trails for fallen tree limbs and other hazards."

She hopped off the counter, newly energized. "Well, I'd love to help with inspections."

"I'll grab the bug spray."

Strictly professional. We were simply two camp staff going on rounds together in the woods.

We headed out and I locked up the Mess. The day was perfect. Warm but overcast, with clouds warning of potential rain. The air didn't smell like rain, so it would likely miss us.

As we progressed through the woods, Hudson asked me about the trees, random wildflowers, and general hiking stuff. Kind of like how the campers did, with curiosity and an eagerness to learn.

"Do you know about medicinal plants?" she asked.

I nodded. "It's crucial in wilderness survival to know which plants can hurt and which can heal." She seemed interested, so I talked about that for a bit as we walked. She slowed a few times to snap pictures. "Oh, and did you know lavender is a natural mosquito repellent?"

She perked up. "Really?"

"Yup. So is lemon grass, lemon balm, peppermint, and even catnip. I've heard you can whip up a homemade concoction with herbs and essential oils."

She stopped abruptly on the trail. "*You* know about essential oils?"

I shrugged. "Not really. A naturalist I met on a hike uses them. That's all out of my wheelhouse, but sounds like something you might be into."

She gave me a contemplative look before walking. Contemplating whether I was full of it, probably. But hey, maybe it could be future video material.

Which gave me an idea. "Let me show you something."

She put her hands on her hips. "It better not be another slasher cabin."

I grinned. "Nope. No tricks this time."

I checked that she followed and took a fork in the path marked by a wooden post. We walked a short distance until I stopped.

I watched Hudson for her reaction.

She stood side by side with me, her mouth slightly parted. She inhaled softly, her eyes wide and consuming. "It's beautiful."

We stood before a clearing filled with wildflowers. A small sanctuary of untamed nature.

"It's so colorful." She took a tentative step forward. "I don't want to crush any. Is it okay if I walk farther in?"

"You're fine. There's a faint trail that goes through if you keep your eye on it."

She stepped with care on the narrow path. She crouched to examine a patch of yellow blooms.

"Alice, one of the camp owners, this is her favorite spot. She planted a number of these flowers. They're all native plants, so they grow and spread on their own. I thought you might want to take pictures here."

She didn't reach for her phone. Instead, she continued to absorb the scene around us. I knelt beside her. I wanted to experience the beauty as she saw it. I appreciated flowers for their practical purposes, but could admit to simply enjoying their beauty. Unexpected delights made the harsher elements worth braving.

Hudson all but glowed. "Thank you for bringing me here."

She stood again and continued through the clearing with careful steps. Finally, she snapped photos from different angles. She circled back to the trail where I waited.

"No selfie?" I asked. "Or I could take a picture of you."

"Oh, um. Sure." She fumbled with the phone. "How about both of us?"

"I'm not really into selfies."

She smirked. "Imagine that. Come on. Squeeze next to me and I'll hold the camera."

I positioned myself beside her. With the flowers behind us, she held the phone up and out. She clicked, then checked the image. "Look. You seem at ease. Content. Dare I say happy?"

A low sound came from my throat.

"Do you grumble when you're happy?"

"Alright, I'm leaving."

She didn't comment again until we reached a point in the trail that edged the water. No sand here, only rocks and rough terrain leading out to the lake.

"I don't think I appreciated lakes like this when I was a kid," she said.

I stopped next to her. "Yeah, it hits different. When I was younger, I only cared about diving in. Or tubing behind a boat."

"That sounds fun." She shaded her eyes with her hands, though she had on sunglasses. "Those houses across the lake are gorgeous. I'd love to live in one of those."

"That's a far commute from California."

She lowered to sit on a large rock overlooking the lake. "I'm not going back." She shook her head. "I mean, I'll go back because I have things there, but I don't...I don't want to live there anymore."

Her words came almost as a whisper. Almost like she was saying them out loud for the first time.

I found my own dry rock to sit on. "That's a big decision." I wasn't sure what else to say. Her famous ex lived out there, so I guess she wanted to steer clear of him. Couldn't blame her for that. "Where do you think you'll go?"

She stared at the water. "Maybe I'll travel. There are so many places to choose from. What about you? Where would you go if you weren't here?"

"Easy. Colorado."

"Oh, I've heard it's beautiful. Lots of skiing, if you're into that."

I shrugged. "Not my thing."

"What's the draw for you?"

Only the highest-tier, premier outdoor adventure company, aka my dream job. I hesitated, but something told me Hudson wouldn't laugh at my dream. "It's kinda my big goal. To live and work out there leading expeditions into the wilderness. Survivalist trips. Moderate to advanced hiking. That sort of thing."

Sure enough, she didn't laugh. "That sounds incredible. It sounds perfect for you."

"Yeah?"

"You must feel cramped in that old camp office." She looked over the gentle waves marking the lake. "You want to be out there, leading. *Living.*"

She could have plucked those words out of my own brain. "Exactly." How was it someone so different from me understood so completely?

"Sounds like my nightmare." She snickered. "The survivalist part, at least. I'm sure the mountains are pretty."

Right. Just because she understood my dream didn't mean my interests were anywhere near what she'd want herself. Proof we *were* completely different.

"Anyway, I'm sure I'll figure out something." She let out a nervous laugh. "That's what this summer is supposed to be. A time to figure things out."

Funny, I looked at my own time at camp as a stepping stone to bigger boulders, so to speak. Instead of fishing lakes, I'd hike near mountain streams. Do solo quests with the land as my companion.

She gathered her knees and wrapped her arms around them. "Do you mind if we sit here for little while? To just...be?"

I couldn't think of anything I'd like more. But I didn't say that. Those were the kind of words I thought but rarely made audible. "Yeah."

So we sat. I didn't count the time or look at my watch. I wished I could say I didn't peek at Hudson every few seconds, but I'd be lying.

She closed her eyes and breathed in a gentle in and out. Moments like this, where obligations didn't demand attention, were few and too far between. I decided to give her privacy and left my spot to walk along the shore.

When I turned back after ten minutes, darkening clouds shaded the sky ahead. I picked up my pace. By the time I reached Hudson, a distant rumble sounded.

She gasped. "Was that thunder? Is it going to rain?"

"My weather app said a forty percent chance." Yesterday. I hadn't checked today for updates. "I bet most of it will miss us."

"Should we head back?"

Her worried expression and that cute gasp were pretty dang endearing. "We'll be fine." I gestured with my head to return to the trail.

I cleared several fallen branches near the property line. Only the teen campers tended to walk this far for their supervised trail time, but we still aimed to keep the paths free of obstacles.

The sky growled again, louder.

"That doesn't sound promising." Hudson rubbed her arms. "Did you feel a chill? I swear I felt a chill."

I smelled it now. Rain and pending storms. A burst of light streaked across the sky. Hudson gasped again. "Lightning."

"Okay, we'll head out." I tapped the weather app on my phone to check the radar, but the connection stalled out.

We returned toward camp on the same trail, walking in peaceful silence until the sky opened up. Rain began as a steady trickle and quickly progressed to heavy sheets.

Hudson shrieked and covered her head with her hands.

"This way." I lightly touched the back of her arm to steer her toward another bend in the trail. "Keep your eye on the path so you don't trip."

Another burst of lightning flashed, followed by a boom of thunder. I glanced her way. Hudson followed at my heels, focused on the path as I'd advised.

Finally, I stopped and fished for my key ring.

Hudson gaped at our detour destination. "You've got to be kidding me."

I opened the door to a familiar, dilapidated cabin I swore I wouldn't bring her back to.

Hudson leaned against the closed door. "I can't believe I'm grateful to be in the murder hut."

Rain streaked across her face and soaked her clothes. Her pink hair matted against her face. And because she was Hudson, the effect came off as if she'd stepped out of a perfume ad, with drenched hair and clothes as part of the look.

My boots made tracks across the wood floor. I opened the closet and pulled out a blanket. Stray pieces of grass and a leaf stuck to one side, but it was dry. "Here. Wrap up in this."

Hudson took the blanket. "I'm not even going to ask if this is evidence in a past crime."

I laughed to myself. "I'm sorry I didn't have a better gauge on the weather. I assumed the rain would pass us."

And truthfully, I liked being out on the trail with Hudson so much, I might not have turned back even if I knew we'd get soaked.

Only a small puddle of water existed in the front corner of the cabin where the old siding parted. "The roof is decent. We should be good here until the rain lets up."

Hudson settled onto the floor. She looked in disgust across the room. "That mattress."

"Red paint. Not blood. We used it for a Halloween thing last year with camp staff."

She appeared a smidge less tense. "Sure, I knew that."

I took a seat on the floor across from her with enough distance to remain professional. "You didn't really think something bad happened out here, did you?"

She shrugged one shoulder. "Who's to say it didn't?"

Thunder sounded again, causing Hudson to flinch. She scooted across the floor until she faced the same direction as me with her right arm pressed against my left. "Don't make fun of me for being scared of thunder and lightning."

I turned my head a fraction to see her better. Her closeness set my heart to a new pace. "I won't."

Her breathing came light and shallow. "Especially thunder and lightning while we're sitting ducks in a creepy cabin in the woods."

"If it makes you feel better, any bad guys out there have to deal with the rain to get to us."

She swatted me. "You don't watch scary movies, do you?"

"Never liked them."

"Killers *like* rain. They *thrive* in it."

I wanted to laugh, but she looked freaked. The whole reason we were trapped out here together was because I didn't want her to be alone today. Her world had upended, and she'd been bombarded with hateful comments online. And that video. She'd been Krom's pawn where he threw all his blame.

She didn't know I knew any of that. We could discuss details later. Right now, she was practically screaming, in her own way, that she didn't feel safe.

Well, this was my camp, and I wouldn't let her feel unsafe. "There's an ax in the closet." I swung my arm around her, my heart pounding the whole time. "I'll protect you."

I couldn't believe I'd gotten the words out—they were that painfully cheesy. An offense my cousins would shred me for if they ever heard about it.

But Hudson didn't crack a joke. She nestled in closer to me, letting me hold her, as the thunder rolled on.

Chapter 18

Hudson

WE'D SURVIVED. LUCAS AND I survived in the murder hut during that awful thunderstorm.

I felt like a huge baby acting scared about a dumb storm. All my emotions crashed together, resulting in spewed nonsense about horror movies coming to life.

Lucas hadn't teased me. He possibly pitied me for being such a scaredy cat.

But also? His steady, strong arm grounded me. His warmth like a seal of protection. He'd given me exactly what I needed in that moment.

Also, he had that ax in the closet. Just in case.

After the rain eased up, we made a careful dash through muddy trails to camp and parted ways for the day. I was embarrassed by my outbursts. Lucas likely sensed it and gave me space.

He didn't even know the full truth about my reason for being here. I needed to come clean with him at some point, but right now, I held that truth close. The less he knew, the better.

I showered, then settled in reading one of Maggie's fantasy novels from her stash inside the roller desk.

That night, as I plugged my phone into the charger, I skimmed through the day's photos. The wildflower field had been pure magic. Beautiful. Romantic.

I want to show you something. Lucas had thought of me when he'd suggested going to the clearing with those beautiful flowers. He'd expected I'd want to photograph them, which I very much did. But the beauty took me off guard. I wanted to experience them, to touch them, and smell them. Not just digitize them.

My photo review landed on the selfie of me and Lucas. I could imagine us other places together, posing in front of lakes and flowers like Lucas enjoyed. Or at a concert or a busy restaurant, the stuff I liked. Us with a group of friends.

I set the phone aside and drifted off to the best sleep I'd had since starting my camp adventure.

The next weekly session of camp began Sunday afternoon with a new batch of campers ranging in age from eight to twelve. No word from the outside world meant another week of Miss Hudson the camp counselor.

I got cracking with the camp social media after receiving official approval (this approval came from Twila, but it counted since she ran the office). I wouldn't go too wild, but improvement was a guarantee when the start was rock bottom.

Literally, the last post made seven weeks prior on the camp's Instagram was of a rock. No caption and nary a hashtag. Just a rock on an account hovering on life support.

"Let's get you all lined up facing the lake, and then I'm going to move behind you," I instructed Bianca's cabin of adorkable campers. We'd already handled a skinned knee and a bee freak-out and it wasn't even ten a.m. "Grab the hand of the camper beside you."

The girls linked hands. Perfect. Picture perfect.

"But Miss Hudson," a freckled ten-year-old turned toward me with a wide grin. "If you're back there for the picture, you'll only see our butts!"

The girls collapsed into laughter at this amazing display of comedy.

"I'm showing your *backs* silhouetted against the lake," I explained. "Also, we can't legally show your faces on social media."

The most fashionable girl of the group gasped and struck a pose. "We're gonna be on social media?"

"Your silhouettes," I reminded. "Because this is cheaper than stock photo."

These photos plus the pics I'd snapped on the walk with Lucas would all go toward building content for the Camp Junebug accounts. I'd followed every other camp account in the tri-state area (other than the Trail Blazers, because *no*), and proceeded on a like and comment spree. Networking, baby. We could all support each other like I did in my skincare community. Well, before the drama. I'd even started a DM conversation with a scout leader in Cheboygan who had a hot tip on some excess canoes. Free boats? I deserved a raise.

In fact, I deserved some accolades for a show of restraint with my influencer accounts. I'd only experienced a single weak moment yesterday during my time online in the office. Yes, searching my own name as a hashtag was a dumb idea. Yes, it led to light doomscrolling and spiraling. But I pulled myself out.

Not before commenting to a troll in my defense under my private lurker skincare account, but a girl can only handle so much.

Maggie approached as I stood along on the shore while campers collected interesting stones for a project. "Did Lucas tell you?

Tonight, we're training for the camp games. We'll rotate out so we have staff coverage for Campfire."

I'd only seen Lucas in passing here and there since Saturday. It was now Tuesday afternoon. "About that—I'm sorry I challenged the other camp and involved all of you."

She crossed her arms. "We're all in, so don't feel bad. Pocket Pete and the kitchen crew have been salivating for a chance to decimate the Trail Blazers." She straightened, glancing around for any campers within earshot. She spoke louder. "By decimate, I mean participate in a friendly tournament with sportsmanlike attitudes."

"It's fine, no one's listening."

She lowered her voice. "They're always listening."

As if on cue, the tiniest fifth grader peeked around Maggie's torso with a hand outstretched. "Is this a rock, Miss Maggie?"

"See?" Maggie mouthed to me before turning to examine the object in the girl's hand. "That looks like melted plastic who's had a rough day."

The girl giggled.

Maggie held out her hand. "I'll take it and trash it." She scrutinized it further once the girl scampered off. "This has the Trail Blazers' logo colors swirled in there. Those punks are polluting our waters. Probably burned the plastic and an animal carried it off." Each word grew more severe and clipped.

Maybe pure revenge would fuel us to victory. "Do you know what games we'll be playing?"

"Playing?" She huffed a loud breath. "This is war. In fact, I'm sure they'll start with exactly that: Tug of War."

Flashbacks to my childhood gym days danced in my head. I'd been that kid who despite being active, didn't manage to be active in the right way for gym class. Excess energy: yes. Dancing to my own beat: absolutely. Paying attention when maroon-colored bouncy balls sailed my way? Sadly, no. One point for the bouncy ball, zero for Hudson's nose.

Maggie continued chattering about the war games. "You have no idea how much we want to beat those snobs."

Her apparent thirst for competition came across not a small bit worrying. Truth: I worried. "I hate to be a downer, but those Trail Blazers looked pretty fit. Is there any way we could practice on a ropes course similar to theirs? I've never done anything like it."

"Hey, Boss," Maggie said, looking past me rather than responding to my question. "What's our rope inventory? Any chance we can rig up something in the trees mimicking a course?"

Lucas headed toward us with a neatly trimmed beard and a gray T-shirt begging to be snuggled up to. That was to say, he wore a perfectly clean shirt. A nice, clean T-shirt appropriate for a camp director on a hot, hot day.

Was it hot out here, or what?

Dang, did Lucas look good when he wanted to. And something told me he wanted to. He looked at me, almost as if waiting on me to speak to him.

"Hudson?" He said my name and my left knee creaked.

"Um, yes?"

Lucas looked at me directly. "I asked if you'd checked in with Rena about the camper with suspected hives."

Oops, he *had* been waiting for me to speak to him. "Oh, right. Did the herbal salve work?"

He blinked. "Herbal salve?"

"Her skin showed irritation, so I applied a salve. Maggie thinks it's a heat rash, not hives. It's all natural and great for sensitive skin."

"You." He pointed a stern finger my way. "Are not to *apply* anything to a child. Ever. That is Nurse Rena territory."

"The salve is hypo-allergenic. It—"

"No."

Ah, so grumpy, pointing Lucas had replaced comforting, rain shelter Lucas.

"I'm sorry." And here I'd thought I'd healed a child.

Lucas appeared to be internally assessing. "No, I'm sorry. Just...don't put stuff on campers."

He looked at Maggie, then at me.

Maggie whistled loud, using only her mouth—impressive. "You! There! Halt and do not touch the turtle!" She barreled toward a cluster of campers gathered around a girl holding up a tiny turtle *Lion King*-style.

I shook my head. Camp life.

With Maggie's attention now taken, Lucas leaned in. "I'm sorry. About the pointing. I'm trying to cut back."

"You're right about not using untested salves on campers. I should only product test on adults."

He snapped his head toward me. "Product test? What do you mean?"

Oops. I'd been experimenting with essential oil recipes using ingredients Twila found at a health food store the next town over. Oils and natural ingredients were fascinating to learn about. Key word being learn, and I was a far cry from an herbalist. "Never mind."

That evening, the adults and a handful of the college and teen counselors gathered to talk strategy for the upcoming Summer Trail Games. Lucas managed to get a few friends from his outdoors meet-up group to join us as fake staff for the games. We now had Shawn, Preston, and Meg as part of the group. Three sturdy, fit adults to balance out our competition ranks.

After a round of introductions and initial discussion, Lucas clapped his hands for our attention. "Let's set up a relay race and play out some possible team combinations."

Lucas exuded confidence as he spoke. He had an understated charm. With his friends here, he smiled more. I liked seeing him smile.

He caught my eye as he spoke. Was it me, or did his gaze linger?

I kind of hoped it lingered. Okay, not kind of. I hoped. I hoped for the linger. I couldn't stop thinking about our time together in nature. Both gentle and extreme. I liked the multiple versions of Lucas I'd witnessed in the wild: the thoughtful exploring of wildflowers version and the threatening phantom murderers with an ax version.

My focus landed on Meg, one of Lucas' friends from his outdoors group. She wore cute athletic gear highlighting toned arms and muscular legs. She had a carefree look about her. She in all likelihood knew how to canoe without going in circles.

Which was what happened to me earlier today in a boat with three ten-year-olds. Bianca had to row over and save us.

Lucas and Meg had way more in common than he and I did. Not to say Meg took any interest in him, but if not, what was wrong with her? Lucas was a catch. Grumpiness aside, he had a lot going for him.

"Hudson?" Maggie's voice cut into my thoughts.

"Yeah?" Everyone grew quiet. And looked at me.

"We're counting off."

"Oh okay. One."

"No, you're three. Pocket Pete next to you is two and I'm a one."

Sounded like she could have counted for me then. "Sorry. Three."

I scanned the group as they completed counting off into randomized teams. They were all sporty types. They knew the games we'd be playing because they'd done them or similar.

How much could I actually contribute to this team?

So, I did what I did best. In between running relay races and jumping over weird obstacles, I created content. I photographed and filmed little snippets for social media. Not only would it be good content to show off the camp, but we'd show those Trail Blazers we were coming for them.

But after capturing the scene in video and stills, I found myself wanting to just run around and have fun. Filming felt like a distraction. So I did.

Catching my breath, I welcomed our water break.

Lucas opened a cooler and held out a water bottle for me. "Doing okay? You're working hard out there."

He seemed proud. I supposed any concerted effort toward camp participation counted after I'd pranced into camp in heels and a kaftan.

"Meg's nice." I sipped the water.

"Yeah, Meg's great. How's that door hinge working for you? I fixed it today—the bathroom door in your cabin."

"You fixed it? Wow, thanks." In my last apartment, it took weeks to get my maintenance requests looked at. "So, this Meg, is she good at canoeing?"

"We're not doing water sports for the camp games. We set it as a ground rule."

I looked over at Meg who had a hand on Shawn's arm as she laughed. Flirting? Friendly? Either way, she wasn't over here gunning for Lucas' attention.

I shook my head at myself. Jealous. I was freaking jealous of the mere potential of Meg being into Lucas.

"Come on," he said and nudged me toward his friends. "I think you'll like them."

Lucas being social? What a sight to behold.

I fell into conversation surprisingly easily using my method to ask new people questions about themselves. I watched Lucas interact with his friends. A friendly, smiling, downright talkative guy replaced any hint of grouch. Talkative for Lucas, at least. Leaps and bounds beyond one word answers or simple grunts.

As the meet-up group absorbed into our rag-tag camp team, it was as if Lucas became more comfortable with the rest of us too.

With me. A development I very much enjoyed.

Chapter 19

Lucas

"LET'S GO AGAIN ON three. One, two three!"

Team Blue put our full weight into the pull. I gripped the thick rope and tugged harder to move Team Red into the sand pit between us.

"You call this Tug of War?" Maggie yelled across the divide. "You're all weak!"

"It's your lucky day," Twila shot back, part of Team Blue and decked out in spandex with an old-school sweatband at her brow. "I took my calcium pills. I'm *fortified*. Aarraggh!" She grunted and yanked harder.

"Not sure that's very intimidating," my buddy Shawn, pulled from my outdoors meet-up group, said in front of me.

But the extra effort worked. Team Red crossed into the pit.

Hudson, at the front of Team Red, hit the sand on her knees. This had to be rougher than her usual Pilates class.

"Let's break." Maggie clapped twice, like she did with the campers. And still, we followed her directions.

It was Wednesday, our second practice, and we now knew the game day against the Trail Blazers would be in two weeks. Every practice counted. It had taken all I had not to delete the email from Brycen without reading it, but we couldn't drop out of the competition. Not after we'd agreed and especially not after I'd been caught sneaking on his grounds.

I confirmed receipt and asked for a list of planned team activities, offering a few suggestions, so we had some say in the whole thing.

A response followed, and we had our list.

Our practice ended as nightfall set in, and we dispersed. The teen counselors remained on full watch over the campers. We'd invited the campers to watch us, but apparently, they determined we were boring.

I walked my friends out to the camp lot. Said our goodbyes until the weekend, our next practice. I turned to find Hudson waiting on the office steps. She had her phone out, so maybe not waiting on me.

"Have you checked our accounts today?" she asked, seamlessly as if we'd been in a discussion already.

"Bank accounts?"

She let her head fall pointedly to one side. "The social accounts. For the camp. Look." She faced her phone screen at me.

I walked closer. The profile showed Camp Junebug with a picture of the camp logo, a description and website link. Beneath that, a bunch of pictures that looked like what I'd seen on other camps' websites. "You better have permission to use those photos. You can't pull stuff off the internet and post them like they're yours. Especially for a business."

"Are you mansplaining image copyright to me? To someone who earns actual money from their online content?"

I bristled. I hated that term. *Mansplaining*. Like explaining anything as a man was bad. But also, I'd just explained image copyright to someone who worked daily with digital images. "Then where did you get the money for those photos?"

"I took the photos. Look closer. This is our camp."

Sure enough, on closer inspection, I noticed our rain shelter in the distance of a photo featuring a water bottle with the camp's name. Another with kids silhouetted against the lake. Our lake. And the wildflowers. "These are good. You took these pictures with a phone?"

She nodded. "I know the kids' faces and identifying information can't be shown. I did some editing on this one here to blur the background. The caption for each post covers a point from the mission statement. That's the theme this week—to educate on the mission of the camp. Every post directs to the link in the profile which goes to the camp website. And I created daily Stories content and followed a bunch of local businesses. We're already up one hundred followers!"

Okay, she obviously knew far more than I did about how to do this stuff. "Sorry for ragging on you about the photos. This looks great. But don't make it too great or we won't be able to keep up."

"Why are you so afraid of succeeding?"

"Me, or the camp?"

She didn't respond and the empty beat made the question hit deeper. I wanted to succeed. That wasn't the problem. I *couldn't* succeed. Not here. Period.

But that sounded like a crummy thing to say about a kid's camp, so I didn't. "I don't want to make a bunch of work for the next person."

"Is someone taking over after you?"

If only it were so easy to have someone lined up. "I'm just trying to get through the summer." I dug my keys out of my pocket. "It's late. I'm going to hit the road." She was doing that lingering thing like she had in the office the other day. "Want me to walk you to your cottage?"

She grinned. "Don't you mean cabin?"

I gave her a playful smile back. "Sure. Same thing, really."

She started walking and I fell into step beside her. "You did good today at practice. Did you have fun?"

"You know...I *did*." She said it like she had the realization right now. "Do camps for adults exist? I feel like they should. This is all so much more fun than running around in gym class."

"Or a stuffy workout studio."

"That's what I'm used to." She shrugged. "Do we have a shot at winning? Really, truthfully?"

I liked that she said *we*. She'd been all-in with camp almost from the start, now that I'd thought about it. Made friends easily, the kids loved her, and she'd worked hard in our practice both nights. Now that we had some momentum, I even looked forward to game day. "I think we have a shot."

She veered right to the path toward her cabin. "What do we win?"

"Bragging rights. Dominance."

"Ego stuff."

"Yup." We made it in sight of the cabin and I lowered my voice. Bedtime for the campers and all. "Uh, so, see you tomorrow."

She sighed and stretched her arms in front of her. "Trouble is, I'm not tired."

My stomach woke up. Not sure what it had been doing, but it was up to something new. "What does that mean?"

"What's there to do at night around camp?"

With Hudson? A whole host of thoughts came at me fast. Some I'd never 'fess up to. If I had any sense, I'd turn and run. The less time spent at camp, the less I cared. The less I saw Hudson, the more easily I held onto the idea I was her boss and nothing else.

Trouble was, I liked being here. And I liked...Hudson.

"A campfire in the main pit might be distracting." I nodded toward the campers' cabins down the path which had sight lines to the fire pit. "There's always the lake. I've got a boat."

The light from the cabin's porch lit a sparkle in her eye, like a firefly's soft glow. "The lake sounds fun. But I'm not getting in a canoe. Not at night." She shuddered.

"We've got a boathouse with a motorboat. It belongs to the camp owners. Alan said to asked to take her out whenever I want and keep her running smooth. Have to keep it slow this time of night because of the lake curfew. We've got some lake time left. If we're quick."

"The lake has a curfew?" Her tone told me she did not believe me, but she followed me toward the lake regardless.

"To keep noise down and people safe. I thought you grew up in Michigan? Didn't you know anybody with a boat?"

"Sure, but I don't remember lakes having curfews. Plus, it's not like I lived on a fishing lake. Water parks and the rec center pool were more my family's thing."

"I assume no camping as a kid."

"Not even once. Just *The Parent Trap*."

"Man, that's a shame. You missed out—no offense. Camping was everything to me."

"I'd assume as much if you're in a job like this. Wanting a job with even less of this." She pointed to the Mess Hall in the distance as we neared the lake. "What do you eat when you're questing in the woods? Have you ever eaten off the land? Like that one show where they drop people off in the Canadian wilderness?"

"Do you get all your ideas of the outdoors from TV and movies?"

"You're forgetting the internet. Everything is on the internet."

We reached the boathouse. I gestured for Hudson to wait on shore while I tested the deck and checked out the boat. With the all clear, I helped her into the boat and eased us out onto the lake. Even at a slow pace, the familiar excitement I craved rolled over my skin. The cool air ignited my sense of adventure. Of forging my own path. Even on a little fishing lake like this.

The sky opened up, dotted with stars. A clear summer night. Couldn't get much better.

I glanced at my traveling companion. Nope, not any better than this.

Chapter 20

Hudson

I COULDN'T BELIEVE I'D convinced Lucas to take me out on his private boat. It was a far cry from a yacht, but it certainly wasn't shabby. Two seats at the front and a little bench seat in the back. Now here we were, drifting beneath a beautiful night sky to the gentle soundtrack of crickets and calm waters.

I wasn't sure what I'd been aiming for exactly when I'd told him I wasn't tired. I'd just been up for *something*. Whatever would keep me away from that lumpy bunk bed and nearer to...him.

Lucas cut the engine after putting distance between us and the shore. We coasted beyond camp property, passing private homes bordering the lake. "Did you grow up on a lake?" I asked him.

"Nope. I lived in neighborhood outside of Detroit—no lake."

"Oh, right, by Marcy." I'd been to Marcy's family's house in a dense suburban Detroit neighborhood. Her apartment wasn't too far from where her family lived.

"That love of camping I had as a kid never left my system. When I worked construction, I did any sort of outdoor activity in my free time. Camping trips with friends, rock climbing, those extreme obstacle courses in the mud—maybe you've seen those online?"

"I have. Where you're racing as team, crawling on all fours in some mud-soaked pit?" An image came to mind. A dirty image. Lucas coated in mud. His T-shirt slick against his skin, outlining every muscle.

I wouldn't hate to see that. I might pay real money to see that.

"Some of it involved crawling," he went on. "And climbing. The mud makes it so much tougher. I did team and individual competitions."

This was chatty Lucas. Like he acted with his friends. "Did you ever run? Like marathons?" He was bulkier than most runners, but still had a leanness to his physique.

"Never a marathon, but shorter races. I'll run for exercise, but it isn't my thing, competitively. That's why I like the meet-up group. We try out lots of activities, but it's usually not competition."

I trailed a hand in the water, enjoying the cool sensation against my skin. "Did you do sports in high school? I could see you tearing up a football field."

"Yeah. Wrestling, baseball."

"And college?"

He waited a beat before answering. "Didn't go to college."

"Ah, sorry. Silly of me to assume." His posture, which had been relaxed only a moment ago, turned rigid. I hit a sore spot.

His plan with Brycen had been to work at the camp for two years. Maybe he needed those two years specifically for the job he truly wanted. He mentioned Colorado—the dream. When the camp split, the plan went down in flames, and he was stuck. He'd stayed to run the camp because he had to, only he wasn't doing any, or much, of the adventure trekking he'd been hired for.

"You have a dream job," I stated.

"Huh?" He glanced at me across the short distance between our seats.

"The job you're aiming for after putting in your time here. Your big plan, and the reason you don't want the camp to succeed because then you'd care too much and never leave. Is that what's in Colorado?"

He made a low sound in his throat. We were back to grunting. Maybe I shouldn't press him on things he wasn't interested in talking about. Clearly, I'd struck something important or he wouldn't have clammed up. And if Lucas was miserable at camp, regardless of how much he pretended he wasn't, perhaps he needed a nudge.

I was a pretty good with a nudge.

I could assume Lucas had deep, soul-searching conversations with someone else. His meet-up group buddies. Or maybe his cousins. But my instincts about people were pretty good—billionaire bro aside—and my gut told me he wasn't. This guy was clammed up and pent up and needed a swift kick in the you-know-where to get his life moving forward.

"How about you?" he asked, before I could launch into a new line of questions.

"How about me what?"

"You're working at a children's summer camp when you don't have experience with kids or camps. You're a graduate from a good university and living in a cabin with a bunk bed and eating cafeteria sloppy joes. What's *your* two-year plan?"

Harsh. This was harsh and uncalled for. "You know what? Go jump in the lake."

His eyes turned sharp. "Too cold. And it's dark."

"Fine. *I'll* jump in the lake." I stood and the boat swayed.

He stood with me. "Hudson. Don't fling yourself in the water. Can you swim?"

"Sure can." I kicked off my shoes.

"This isn't a good idea."

Before he could protest further, I slipped off my T-shirt to my sports bra. My shorts were staying on because honestly, I was not ready for a full undies reveal. I grabbed Lucas' hand and pulled him to the boat's edge.

"Hudson—"

I yanked him forward as far as I could, then let go, and jumped.

The cold hit like a shock. It really had been a good long while since I'd jumped into a lake and not a heated pool. The water felt good. Incredibly good. Cold and revitalizing.

A splash hit the water beside me. I grinned. Lucas followed me in. This was exactly what we both needed. I treaded water and drifted closer to the boat.

Suddenly, a force tugged at my foot. I went under. A split second of panic hit, before arms cinched my waist and pulled me to the surface again. I sputtered in Lucas' face now inches from mine. "What—why did you do that?!"

He was close, so close, and still holding on to me. "Because you deserved it. Want me to dunk you again?"

Bare arms held me to him. He'd ditched his shirt. Water droplets clung to his beard, dripping off slowly one by one. So close, so close. "Yes," I said in a near whisper.

"Yes, what? A dunk?" His voice came low and deep, almost a growl. Not an angry or annoyed growl. This was something else.

My gaze fixated on him. Trails of water marked his smooth skin under the glow of stars and moonlight. "Not a dunk."

He swung one arm to the edge of the boat where a ladder dipped into the water. With the other arm, he pulled me even closer until our legs entwined. Then he tipped his head and met his lips with mine.

I may have blacked out. Somehow, Lucas and I ended up back in the boat, on the bench seat, kissing. My mind flashed to when we'd been in the water, also kissing. Moments ago—seconds, minutes?

I wasn't sure what was hotter: being cold in the lake kissing or freezing out of the water, kissing.

His hands were present, but not groping. His lips firm, deliberate, and intentional. Once he knew I was in, he didn't hold back.

I slid a hand along his chest to his shoulder. Strong, lean muscle met my touch. I managed to pull apart from him. My heart, my breath, my head. So many sensations hit at once.

He looked me over with mild alarm. "Are you okay? Is this okay? You seemed into it and then—"

"I'm just cold." And disoriented. I'd never experienced actual dizziness from a kiss. I could sense the fading impression of his lips against mine. I wanted that feeling again. I eased him toward me and kissed him. Gentle, but assuring. *This is okay. I want this.*

This was the most sure I'd felt about anything in weeks.

We separated again, looking at each other as if for the first time. He laughed. I laughed.

"You have avoidance issues," he said.

I blinked water from my lashes. "What? You kiss me like that and you tell me I have issues?"

"You'd rather dunk yourself in cold lake water than talk about your life plans," he murmured close to my cheek. "You'd rather kiss your temporary camp boss than deal with reality."

Okay, I definitely didn't like this conversation trajectory. "Yeah, so what?" A comeback for the ages. He released his grasp, but I didn't move far. "I like kissing you." Shoot, was I supposed to admit that? Out loud?

He grinned. "I like kissing you too."

"Why do you think I'm treating this like a distraction? Just because I wasn't planning on kissing you doesn't mean it's a bad thing. I didn't plan to become a skincare influencer. It happened because I was good at it so I kept going and that's where I landed."

Something about my own words struck me in a new way. This wasn't a new revelation, but the concept, the shape of the words, felt new. I wanted to save a career I'd never purposefully intended. When my YouTube caught attention from thousands of followers, I took it as a sign of success. The next step was to monetize the account. Then look for brands to rep. Grow the brand. Add in a business Instagram account focused on beauty content, branded to fit in with the trends, and I had a thing. A real thing.

As I built my Beauty Butterfly brand, each step brought me closer to earning respect from my family. If millions of strangers could recognize my talent, surely my own parents and siblings could.

That drive had somehow morphed into L.A. celebrity obsessions and dating a larger-than-life figurehead like Kristoff. Now, that life seemed like old content. Like a social media profile I abandoned and no longer used.

That's not what I want.

The thought grew louder, clearer. *That's not what I want. I don't want that life.*

I'd already told Lucas I didn't want to live in Los Angeles. I wasn't sure I even wanted another brand ambassadorship. After all, I never liked playing by other people's rules.

But if that was true, I had a problem. It left me with one very big unanswered question, and dozens and hundreds of smaller questions to follow.

I blinked to the present. Lucas watched me. He had lovely brown eyes and jealousy-inducing lashes. It was a crime how long those lashes reached for a guy who'd presumably never once used a serum. "I'm a mess, huh?"

He grazed a hand across my cheek, sending a cool shiver down my spine. "Maybe a little. But so am I. You're right, if I really cared about the camp, I'd be recruiting a full-time director to replace me to ensure its success. Not simply riding out my time."

Now we were getting somewhere. And doing so sexily.

I could handle life planning if it involved slow kisses and cheek caresses from this mountain man. Never mind no mountains. I'd follow this guy into the woods.

"Stand up a sec," he said.

I stood and he opened the bench seat we'd been sitting on. He pulled out a towel and wrapped it around me.

"Come with me to the front."

That was only two steps. I followed him and sat in the passenger seat. He turned the ignition and returned us to the boat house. Without speaking, he parked the boat. We gathered our things and climbed onto the dock.

"Walk you back to your cabin?" he asked.

A nice closed loop on the same question he'd asked earlier tonight. "Yes."

We made it to the split in the path toward the cabins. "Here is good," I said. "In case any of the counselors are out, it's probably best we part here."

"I don't think there's a rule. About staff, you know…"

"Sneaking out to the lake at night to make out?"

"With their boss."

"Maybe we shouldn't make that public knowledge. You know, for the sake of the children."

"Angelica would be so disappointed."

I bit my lip. So the little girl from our runway show had made an impression on him. The kid had good instincts.

Standing together in the dark, he adjusted my towel around my shoulders. "Let's promise we'll both work on those two-year plans. Maybe even make a five-year one. Whatever that means."

"Okay." I didn't have much left in me at the moment. A full day with campers followed by an evening running relays with flags and tugging a massive rope, and now this. Lucas and his wet skin, his probing questions, his deliberate kisses.

It was the best day I'd had in years.

"Goodnight, Lucas," I said.

He kissed me on the cheek. "Sweet dreams, Hudson."

Chapter 21

Lucas

SECRETLY DATING ONE OF my camp staff had not been in this summer's plans. Maybe dating went too far, but this connection between me and Hudson sure felt like something.

The next two days involved the usual camp activities like any other week. Only I had the bonus of stolen moments with Hudson in the camp office when Twila stepped out. In the rain shelter while the campers canoed on the lake. Passing glances. Longer ones where we touched. A light kiss, a graze of the wrist.

I couldn't get enough of her. I felt like a high school kid obsessively crushing all over again. I was this short of writing an actual note and passing it to her in the Mess.

We'd made the mistake of sitting next to each other in the Mess which nearly gave us away. The kids were too curious. Too many questions. The teen girls, even more eagle-eyed.

After the campers cleared out Friday afternoon, the staff split off according to their planned schedules. No happy hour tonight as Maggie left camp for a much needed full weekend away. She'd return Tuesday, while Jasmine took lead on the coming week's new batch of campers.

Twila shouted her goodbye, followed by Rena. The front office door closed. A few minutes later the door opened again and Hudson appeared in my office doorway.

She'd already changed out of her camp clothes into an outfit closer to what she'd worn her first day. Trendy and camp-inappropriate shoes. She wanted to go out.

Which was perfect, because I'd intentionally worn a nicer shirt and pants along with my good leather boots. Trimmed up my beard and used the beard combs and a balm I'd been gifted for Christmas last year. I'd told myself this morning it was because parents might stop by the office on pick-up day.

That was a lie.

I was taking Hudson to dinner. To a restaurant that didn't serve nachos in a boat. I'd planned to ask her right now, and here Hudson came already dressed for the occasion.

I met her beneath the door's frame.

"Hey, Mr. Director." She lifted her chin and kissed the corner of my mouth.

Who knew that spot was so sensitive? I slid my hand to her waist and bent to kiss her fully. "This still okay?" We hadn't had much, if any, time alone since our night out on the water. Only moments.

"Yes. I'm not a TikTok algorithm."

"I could have told you that. Because I don't know what one is."

"Ever changing," she quipped. She took a breath before smiling up at me. "So. We have a weekend."

"Tonight, Saturday, and Sunday morning." I wasn't sure why I stated the obvious. Maybe nerves. This was all new. What did a weekend alone with Hudson mean now that we'd kissed? We had so much to learn about each other.

She ran her hands across my chest. I loved it. "I was thinking—"

The front office door banged open. "Knock-knock. Hell-ooo?"

Hudson's eyes widened. "Marcy?"

She whipped around and marched toward the door. My cousin stood live and in person with a duffle bag slung over her shoulder. She wore a dorky visor and a Hawaiian print shirt over her T-shirt and shorts. "Hey, girl. Look who's here!"

"Wow—Marcy and—"

Behind her, two more women appeared. A blond and a brunette carrying bags and big stuffed purses.

"Surprise!" the blond one drew Hudson into her arms. Marcy and the other joined for a group hug. "Sleepaway camp sleepover!"

Hudson peeked her head up and craned it my direction. She mouthed words at me. *I didn't know, I swear.*

But I had. Marcy told me on the phone she wanted to visit. She'd even suggested *this weekend*. I'd entirely forgotten. With Hudson having nowhere to go, given she was hiding out and all, Marcy didn't have any reason to suspect Hudson would have plans. The perfect opportunity to launch a surprise.

I shrugged in response, tossing her a helpless look. So, no date. No weekend alone with Hudson. What a bummer. On the upside, Hudson needed to see her friends. And I could finally get around to organizing my hiking gear.

Yeah, my life was that pitiful.

Marcy set down her bag and directed her enthusiasm my way. "Hey, cuz." She hugged me, then examined me in far too similar a way as our mothers did. "You're looking sharp, Lucas. I know you don't dress like this every day. You have a date or something?"

My cheeks lit hot. Why did Marcy have to go for the jugular every time?

She pressed her lips together, but it didn't squelch the high-pitched sound she was making in her mouth. "Lucas. You have somebody?" She gripped my arm, shifting her voice quieter, which still sounded many decibels higher than a whisper. "Tell me. You've got a townie stashed somewhere?"

I shook my head. "Stop. Now."

She threw her hands up in surrender. "Okay, I'll back off. But you know I'll get details before I leave."

I was afraid of that. Very afraid.

She turned to her friends. "Lucas, these are the girls: Jillian and Noah. These are my college roommates I'm forever talking about. In the flesh. I can't believe you've never met them. Y'all haven't met Lucas before, right?"

"Nope, just heard stories," the brunette, Noah, said. "Lots of stories."

I cringed. "My cousins embellish. Heavily." I caught Hudson's eye. She shot me another apologetic look, but she also wore a big smile. Her friends were here, and she practically glowed with excitement. I didn't want her to feel torn about it.

I clapped once, gripping my hands together. "Well. Sounds like we need a couple air mattresses for the cabin. I assume you'll all want to bunk with Hudson. We've got clean sheets for Maggie's bed while she's out. Unless you all want to stay in one of the campers' cabins?"

Hudson appeared to refocus. "My cabin's good. It's a cozy fit," she said to the others. "But it should be fun for a night."

"Or two," Marcy said. "If Lucas doesn't kick us out."

As if I'd dare. "No issues here."

She did a little dance to her own internal music. "Good. Because you'll love our next surprise."

Dread hit me like ice. "There's another surprise?"

Marcy winked at me. "If you knew everything, there's no fun in that." She yanked the front door open wider. "Hey," she called out the screen door. "We're in here!"

Not a minute later, three guys barreled in, loaded with coolers, pillows, and bags. Matteo, Robby, and Patrick—my two cousins and their BFF. Our childhood crew.

"Surprise!" Matteo, Marcy's oldest brother said. "This is officially a party weekend."

Chapter 22

Hudson

"This is the most fun sleepover we've ever had," Jillian announced. "We're sleeping over at a real-life summer camp."

Marcy flung a sock at Jillian. "You never went to camp as a kid?"

She unleashed a comforter from one of those plastic bags that vacuum-sucked out all the air. "I did science camp, but we stayed in dorms on a college campus."

"I camped in a tent once," Noah offered. "It stormed all night and raccoons dug through our garbage. Never did that again."

My friends' chatter and busy movement filled the front room of the tiny cabin. I had no idea they would show up today. I couldn't be mad even for a second. I nearly shed happy tears in the office, but I was tired of crying. I wanted to have some fun.

Lucas caught me for a moment before I'd left the office, under the guise of helping him find the extra sheets and towels in the closet in the nurse's room.

"I planned to ask you to dinner," he said.

"I would have accepted your invitation to dinner."

He smiled. "This is unexpected, but should be fun."

He looked a little doubtful, but I was still excited, despite the whiplash effect. "Do we tell them?"

He let out the slightest breath. "I don't know."

"Yeah, I don't either."

He kissed me. A noise sounded in the hall and we split apart.

We didn't decide anything. So, this would be fun.

At the cabin, we went with one air mattress since someone could sleep on the couch. Two beds with the bunk beds. Snacks and drinks appeared, bags were overturned and blankets tossed onto the floor as seating. It was like our old dorm days all over again.

"I was thinking about what you said the other day," Marcy said as she chewed on licorice. "About the *Golden Girls*. That's not a bad idea." Marcy filled the others in on our conversation. "Jillian, I told Hudson the living together part was out because you'll be moving in soon with your man."

Jillian covered her cheeks with her hands. "It's way too soon to predict that. I know he used to be my boyfriend, but this two-point-oh business is very new."

Marcy made a rolling motion with her hands. "Look, it's only a matter of time, and we don't need to enter into a lease agreement if you're immediately going to break it."

Jillian looked offended for two seconds, but we all knew Marcy came with love and care in mind, so she quickly moved on. "So how are we like the *Golden Girls*?"

All eyes landed on me. "It seems like we're all at a place where we're changing or maybe not changing enough. I want to us to help each other through those changes. Intentionally. Like, set goals, make plans, and check in with each other."

The others nodded. Jillian could barely contain herself. "You know I love a good plan. I found these cute notebooks. Here. Everybody take one."

She passed out little spiral bound notebooks each with a different inspirational phrase on the cover. "How did you know we'd need notebooks?" I asked.

"I didn't. I can't resist buying them. I also have stickers."

We tore into her bag of sticker joy, which was enough of a distraction for me. Until I realized I needed to actually form a plan and not merely talk about one.

"Back to the fun name," Noah said. "Since we're all in the Midwest, how about a name that ties into that. Like Marvelous Midwest...or Midwest Marvelles."

Marcy made a face. "That sounds like a 1960s singing group. Which is fine and cute, but none of us sing."

"What about mavens?" I visualized the name. "Midwest Mavens."

Jillian carefully placed a sticker on her notebook cover so it lined up perfectly with the edge. "I like it. It has flair to it."

"So, we call ourselves the Midwest Mavens and what, put stickers in a book?" Noah asked.

"We set goals and hold each other accountable," I said. "And give each other a boost if we need it. Or a shoulder to cry on. We commit to meeting more regularly and we have to at least talk once about our plans and goals. However small or big."

"I like it," Marcy said. "I like it a lot. Because I'm telling you, my family is making me doubt every decision I've ever made. I can't stand my job but what I want feels out of reach. I'm either trying to keep the peace or trying not to tear my hair out. And I finally got a haircut I really like, so the thought of ruining that is added stress."

I set my stickers aside. "Marcy, I had no idea. You're like the glue that holds everyone together."

"And I'm getting real tired of hearing it," she grumbled.

Yikes. "Sorry." I got the impression people said that to her with the expectation she would continue to hold them together. Which was unfair. "You planned this whole weekend, didn't you?"

She nodded.

"Two surprises—for me and for Lucas." I hadn't decided if or when I'd spill about the changes between us, but that was clearly for another time. "You found me this job, exactly when I needed it. And made sure I could get to your place safely, and bought me the burner phone..." She'd done so much while she had so much else on her mind and her to-do list. "Thank you."

We all hugged. It made me feel a little less messy knowing she struggled too. Not that I wanted Marcy to struggle. Just that beneath her put-together exterior, her own doubts and insecurities existed.

"We'll help each other," Jillian agreed. "But before that, I need to eat."

The guys had already been assigned food duty (by Marcy of course), so by the time we headed to the owner's cabin, take-out had been ordered with delivery on its way.

"If I know you like I think, I'm guessing you were eager to go out tonight," Marcy said to me as we hoofed it past the office to the owner's cabin. "We decided it would be safer to stay here. With the whole lay low theme."

She was probably right, though I desperately needed a dip back into civilization. "Thanks. That's really considerate."

"Any news?" she asked.

"Nope. I got a check-in text from the attorney yesterday. She had nothing to report. Do your brothers know? And Patrick?"

Marcy's cheeks tinged pink. Possibly from the walk since we headed up at an incline. "Patrick's like family. I know I've told you that, but it's true. He and my brothers only know essentials.

I told them no social media this weekend to avoid any accidental location reveals."

"That's smart." My life, how it had changed. Normally, I'd film everything and share clips to friends or fans.

"Once my brothers heard Krom dissed you with that video, I had to verbally threaten them to back off from retaliation plans. I caught Robby looking up Krom's house on Google maps. I told him to stop being scary."

We reached Lucas' cabin, aka the owner's suite, gently tucked into a wooded area. Massive overarching trees had been trimmed to frame the house, and a high fence behind it marked this end of the property line. The place was larger than where I stayed with Maggie, but more of a weekend retreat than a full-time residence.

The covered front porch held two rocking chairs. The door burst open and Marcy's youngest (and to be honest, hottest) brother Robby held a megaphone in one hand and a sparkling soda in the other.

"You ladies ready to rock?" he called out through the megaphone.

I snorted. Marcy threw her sandal at him. He ducked easily and pumped a fist in the air. "That's a yes!"

Music kicked in behind him from the house.

We climbed the steps and entered a cozy, woodsy space. A table by the front door held a massive amount of snacks and drinks. We still had the delivery order on the way.

To our left, in an open kitchen, Lucas waved his smart phone in front of Marcy's older brother Matteo. "For the last time, I don't use a flip phone!"

He'd ditched the dressier shirt and pants for jeans and a band T-shirt. A totally different look than I'd seen on him so far. *Weekend Lucas.*

A jab hit my side. "Stare much?" Noah grinned at me.

Caught. She saw me staring and she saw who I stared at. "How'd you know?"

"I didn't. You just confirmed."

Dang, my friends were sharp. "Don't say anything."

She winked at me. I could trust Noah not to blurt out I had a thing for Lucas, but I could also count on her to dance around the topic so frequently it forced me to confess. Good times ahead.

Lucas caught my gaze from across the room. His weekend look hit me right in the sweet spot. It took determined strength to not dash across the room and fling my arms around him.

I smiled back at him, then quickly glanced to my friends if anyone noticed. Lucas grinned. Almost as if he energized by our secret.

We hit the snacks head-on, followed by delivery from a Greek food take-out with gyros, salad, pitas, and baba ghanoush. We spread out across the dining area and combined living room, which stretched the full length of the cabin, with windows at either end and a couch facing a floor-to-ceiling stone fireplace. The other half was comprised of a simple but functional kitchen and a hall leading to a bathroom and bedroom.

After eating, Robby grabbed an acoustic guitar from a hook on the wall. He began a gentle strum, then jammed harder, seeming to lose all sense of time and place.

"He's the youngest," Matteo said. "He's special."

"I'll start a fire," Lucas offered. "Unless you all want to go to the fire pit at camp. We have the place to ourselves."

"Run of the camp?" Robby stood. "Lead the way."

Patrick held up a hand. "We should get a group consensus. Who wants to go to the fire pit?"

"Future politician," Marcy said to me as she raised her hand. "He's always *practicing*."

He folded his arms. "I heard that."

The group gathered jackets, coolers, the guitar, and moved outside. Lucas and I were the last ones out.

As I began to cross through the doorway, he hooked a finger onto my sleeve and pulled me inside again. He swept me closer for a kiss. "I need a little hit."

I kissed him back and ran my hand along his jawline. He smelled like woodsy perfection. "Maybe we can find a chance to sneak away."

"They'll follow us. My cousins are ruthless."

"Noah already suspects something."

"Marcy will find out."

"Who are we missing?" Marcy called out loudly from outside. "Hudson and Lucas—what are you two doing?"

I went in for a last-second kiss. His lips lingered and I stupidly sank into his embrace as a door creaked open. We pulled apart. As I suspected, we had an audience.

Chapter 23

Lucas

WITH ALL THE SURPRISE excitement of my crew showing up, I'd forgotten we planned another practice for the camp games competition that weekend. Maggie and some of the counselors were gone, but Pocket Pete and the kitchen staff came out Saturday afternoon along with the meet-up group folks. We were one big happy mash of camp family and friends.

Hudson said she wished for a camp for adults, and that's exactly what we did. I couldn't imagine anything better than camp with my best friends, my new friends, and Hudson.

I gathered everybody to the central activity area by the fire pit.

"You know what this means, Lucas." Matteo clapped a hand to my shoulder. "Three words."

Oh, I knew. "Capture. The. Flag."

My cousins and Patrick went wild cheering. The rest of the group looked around questioningly.

"What's the big deal with Capture the Flag?" Hudson asked.

"It's only the greatest game of all time," Marcy answered. Immediately, she started in with a rundown of why we loved the game and provided a high-level overview of how to play.

"We'll get into more detail as we split into teams," she said.

We counted off and divided into teams. Hudson and I made it on the same team. She grinned at me. I grinned back.

Patrick jacked me in the ribs. "Can't believe you tried to hide it from us."

I waved him off. "I don't know what you're talking about."

Marcy, in the midst of her game explanation, broke away without missing a beat. "We could tell the second we saw you two together you were fools for each other."

Hudson rolled her eyes. Her blushing made her even more adorable.

Now everybody looked at me. "It's not like we had some master plan. It just sort of happened. Then you all showed up."

Funny, not much had changed since my younger days. Any time I thought I'd scored time with a girl, somehow my cousins found out and ruined my plans. Only now, this wasn't so bad. I ran this place. I could kick them out if I wanted.

We returned to game prep. Flag zones and guards were established and flags placed. We peeled off to our respective hiding spots.

The afternoon flew by. I'd say I felt like a kid again, but my full adult self experienced the game with all the knowledge I'd picked up through the years. Nostalgia hit hard. I didn't need elaborate hiking adventures if I could just do *this* every so often.

The score was currently tied and I had a clear shot at the flag. I ran for it. Out of nowhere, a tackle hit me from the side. We rolled to the ground.

Noah. "Caught!"

I scrambled to my feet and reached a hand out to help her up. "You okay? That was a hard fall."

She sprung up without assistance. Green paint streaked across her face. And, were those fangs drawn below her mouth? With red painted blood trails?

"Jail for you." She pointed to the holding area where I'd need to stay put until a teammate tagged me out. She growled and fled into the woods.

Wow. That was, uh, quite a friend group Marcy put together. Marcy, my hyper-involved cousin, Hudson the diva, Jillian the brain scientist, and whatever *that* was with Noah.

Preston from meet-up group tagged me out from jail. We dashed in the direction of the other team's flag, working out a plan. That plan involved going the long way around through thick woods and brush. A thin, faint trail cut through it. Not one we took campers through, but I knew the route.

Preston tapped me on the back. "Hit the deck."

We ducked behind cover. I spied a figure in the distance walking slow. I angled around a tree for a better view. Huh. Couldn't tell who it was. I mouthed, "Who is that?

Preston crouched forward, squinting. Turned to me and shrugged.

I looked again. A man. Dressed in muted colors. Not camo, but clothing that blended into the woods. Ball cap with no logo. White guy maybe thirty-five. And he wasn't a part of our game.

I pointed at Preston again. "Trespasser," I said in a low voice.

Preston's eyes grew wide. "What do we do?"

I returned to watching the stranger. We were near the property border. If he'd come from the other camp, he'd climbed the fence. If he was a lost hiker, he'd still have climbed that fence. Either that, or he'd walked in through our front entrance and wound his way through the woods. The gate up front closed off the driveway at night and on weekends, but this wasn't Fort Knox.

The fourteen of us playing had covered a lot of ground running around during the game. This guy would have caught someone's attention by now if he'd come in from any other direction.

Preston followed my lead to stay hidden and move toward the voices of our friends while keeping watch over the guy. I spied

Pocket Pete on our team. Moving with as little sound as possible, I caught up to him and filled him in.

Pete flexed his hands. "You want me to confront him?"

"If he stops at the clearing and looks like he's staying out of sight, then we go in."

Marcy squealed in the distance. Women's laughter carried over. I recognized Hudson's voice. I could make out their figures through the scattered trees which thinned to a clearing a few hundred feet ahead.

Sure enough, the guy advanced. He slowed and paused at the clearing. Focusing ahead of him, he squatted behind cover. And waited.

So much for the lost hiker theory. This guy didn't want to be found or spotted.

More laughter traveled over from the women. They had no clue they were being watched.

The creeper moved a hand into his vest pocket.

Something primal in me lit. I launched forward and ran.

Preston and Pete joined, a mere step behind. We crashed through brush and leaves—no secret we were coming for this guy.

Alerted to our ambush, the man leapt to his feet. He was fast. He cut through the woods toward the boundary fence. Back toward the Trail Blazers' camp.

"The property line!" I called to the others.

From my left, Matteo bolted toward me. "Prepare to get tagged, fool!"

"Get that guy!" I pointed ahead of me to the runner.

But Matteo had too much momentum. He plowed into me, sending me to the ground. As I fell, Preston tripped and cried out in pain.

Pete kept running. "I'm going for it."

"Got you, sucker," Matteo yelled at my face. He stopped at the sight of me. "What?"

My breath came hard and quick. "There's a trespasser. He was watching Marcy and Hudson."

Matteo swore and pulled me up. "Sorry, brother. Which way?"

We ran toward the fence. By the time we reached it, Pete was pacing and breathing heavily. "Sorry, man. I couldn't...catch him."

I growled in frustration and kicked a tree stump.

Matteo took me by both shoulders. "You saw him watching them?"

I nodded, my heart screaming, not from the run, but from an acute need to defend. "All three of us did. I didn't recognize him." Brycen hired a slew of new staff since the split. The nerve of him sending a scout to do his dirty work spying on us.

Preston hobbled over, favoring his right ankle. "He looked military."

Brycen might have recruited former military to train kids boot camp-style. I wouldn't put it past him. His camp methods were a far cry from little girls peering at caterpillars on nature walks.

"We can't let that man live," Matteo said.

"This isn't an action movie," I told him. I looked over my shoulder toward the direction of excited yells and a flag score. "But you better believe I won't let this go."

The plan was to keep the trespasser incident to ourselves for now as to not incite worry or panic.

We reached the nearest flag where several players gathered. Matteo threw his arms wide. "Y'all, we just chased off a stalker!"

"A stalker?" Marcy yelled.

I shoved Matteo. "We had a plan, man."

He scoffed. "Did you hear me agree?"

I hadn't. Only Pete and Preston agreed. Figured.

"Call the others in," I told my cousin.

Matteo hollered for a game break. The rest of the teams emerged from the woods and gathered. Hudson jogged over, looking at Marcy first, then me. I moved to her side and rested a hand at her shoulder. I wanted to wrap her in a bear hug but chose restraint to not freak her out. "Did you see anybody? Someone outside the group walking around?"

"Someone, like a trespasser?"

I nodded. She shook her head and her brow furrowed.

Matteo broke into recap. His version of events unfolded with more drama than necessary, and he hadn't even seen the guy.

"Pete and I didn't recognize him," I said. "The Trail Blazers have new hires we don't know."

Robby sneered. "Who sneak in, looking at our women?"

"We are not *your women*," Marcy shot back. "I'm older than you and I will take you down if I have to."

Robby's face didn't break into his usual smirk when she challenged him. "Nobody messes with my sister. Or her friends. Or my family."

"We sneaked into the Trail Blazers' camp," Hudson said, glancing at me. "And we were caught. Maybe it's retaliation?"

Pete whipped toward me. His jaw tightened. "What were you doing sneaking around the other camp?"

I knew this would come back to bite me. "It was a mistake—"

"And why didn't you ask me?" he asked with a sly grin. "I've been itching to go over there and wreck something. You know what that punk Brycen said to me?"

"Brycen is that guy who sold you out, cousin?" Robby ground a fist in his palm. "Do we need to go over there and have words?"

Yes, yes, we did. But that was for me to do. Alone. Not with this amped up crew.

Marcy shot a look to her brothers. "Will you guys settle down? You're acting like untrained house pets."

The brothers muttered as Marcy continued to chastise them.

Hudson's face paled. "Thank goodness the kids aren't here."

The kids. If camp had been in session while some creep lurked in the woods, my problems would be much bigger. We didn't know for sure he'd come from the other camp, but it provided the most logical explanation.

Across from me, Patrick paced, seeming to need an outlet for his sudden onset of stress. "We need to deal with this. *Now.*"

Jillian raised her hand. "It's the middle of day. The sun is out. Could he have been a lost hiker?"

"Then why'd he run?" Pete asked.

Patrick's fists clenched. "And why was this man watching Marcy. And...and her friend."

Marcy flashed a look at Patrick I couldn't read. She moved to Hudson and spoke low.

I looked between them. "You two better come clean if you know something."

Hudson couldn't hide her emotions—her guilt flared like a sunburn. "I'm sure it's nothing. I got worried about something for a second."

Thoughts came rapid fire. Hudson running from her glamorous life after her public breakup. Staying off the internet unless it was camp related. She came here to hide. Maybe more existed to this hiding.

If there was more, then she was using us. Using this camp. Was she using me too? And to what end?

As much as I regretted taking the director role, I'd signed on. That meant doing my job to keep the campers safe.

I turned a harsh stare at Hudson. "I know you're using the camp to hide." Murmurs coursed through the group. I kept my focus. "I know about your ex and how you needed a place to escape. And how not many people know where you are. For your *safety*."

She flashed a look to Marcy. "What did you tell him?"

"As little as possible." Marcy sighed and cast me a hopeful look. "Hudson shouldn't be in any real danger. The staying off the internet stuff is a precaution, right?" She caught Hudson's eye again.

"A precaution for what?" Robby blurted. "You think that Krom clown is going to come find you at this summer camp? And what, beg your forgiveness for acting like a loser?"

"Krom who?" Pocket Pete scanned the group. "Not that billionaire bro Kristoff—"

"Yeah, Hudson dated him!" Robby burst out. "You're too good for him, Hudson. Don't take his ratty butt back."

The group chatter grew louder. I only knew fragments of Hudson's obviously much larger story. My unease grew deeper, darker. I did not like where my mind wandered on this topic. "If this camp is under threat of danger, I needed answers. Now."

Hudson's face twisted. She avoided my gaze. It seemed a real struggle for her to gather her words.

I clapped once. "Okay. Let's break for the day. We need time to figure this out."

Pocket Pete crossed his arms. "I'm not leaving. A threat to the camp is a threat to me. And I want to hear about this Kristoff guy. How is he connected?"

Robby let out an exasperated sigh. "I just told you, man. He's Hudson's ex."

"He already moved on to some new bimbo," Noah offered. "Not that he only dates bimbos," she said quickly. "Or maybe his new girlfriend isn't a bimbo at all because that's a pretty rotten thing to call a woman. I'll stop talking now."

My head pounded. We were getting nowhere. "Look. I run this camp, and if we have a threat, I need to take this seriously. I'm going to call the sheriff—"

"No!"

The Nos came instantly and from every direction. I looked at Matteo and Robby.

"Cops, man." Robby shook his head.

"What, are you running from the law?" Robby ran his mouth about cops, but usually for no real reason other than to act like a tough guy.

He tugged at the bottom hem of his jersey. "No, but I'd prefer not to call attention to myself."

Figured.

"Hear me out." Matteo rubbed his hands together. "We set up a perimeter—"

"Stop." I put my hand over his mouth, something I knew he hated. Yeah, I was pulling out old tactics from childhood. I used my most intimidating tone. "Do I need to repeat that *I* run this camp? It's my responsibility to report any threats." I looked across the faces of my friends. My own family stirring up the worst of the drama. "We've got campers coming in tomorrow. *Children.*" I looked at Hudson. "Is there a reason there might be someone on camp grounds looking for you?" I measured my tone. "Please, Hudson. I have to know."

She swallowed and looked past me to some distant point. "I...I need to make a call. To my agent."

I didn't even attempt to hide an eye roll. "Really? Your talent agent? Now?"

Her brow furrowed with obvious confusion. "No. My agent contact. At the FBI."

Chapter 24

Hudson

AGENT MULDER DID NOT sound happy. And he highly disliked that I called him Agent Mulder.

I *had* done the responsible thing by calling him. I should have gotten points for that.

Worry crept into every paranoid thought. I'd been careful. No one should have known my location other than my friends and the camp staff, so contacting the agent was only a precaution. Just checking in to make sure he knew this threat of danger that was more than likely only a Trail Blazer spying on us ahead of the camp games.

And my other decidedly unhappy camper? Lucas. His eyes lit with molten lava at the admission I had a federal agent contact. Equally not happy I'd saved said agent's number to a burner phone.

I guess that wasn't typical of children's camp counselors.

I hadn't intended to keep the full story from Lucas. Not forever, at least. Besides, he could have looked me up at any time. He could have connected my need for an escape plan. Marcy told him only the basics, assuming I'd fill Lucas in when ready.

Only I hadn't.

Marcy and Lucas went with me to the camp office as I related the latest information to the agent. Suspected stalker and all. I had permission from him to use speaker phone after disclosing who was with me.

The agent's gravelly sigh punctuated the end of my wrap-up. "A children's camp?" The burner phone offered a surprisingly crisp connection. "That's certainly an interesting choice."

My heart raced. "Kelly Q. Pierce told me I wasn't in direct danger." My shoulders tensed—was she on the line listening? I hated to shove her under the bus, but well, her name came out of my mouth. "I've barely been online. I swear. Not on my real phone or on my main accounts."

A beat of silence passed. "Are you on accounts that are not your *main* accounts?"

His attempt at controlling his tone reminded me of my dad after I'd run up his credit card at sixteen. Dad had handed the card over for my birthday weekend and told me outright to have fun. How did I know his idea of fun didn't translate to a Sephora shopping spree and my first day spa experience with my friends? Look, I'd known the credit card had a limit, I just hadn't known that limit applied to my birthday.

I still felt bad about it.

Focus. "I've been checking on my accounts—not logged in—from a desktop computer at the camp office. I've been managing the camp's Instagram but—"

My words fell off. My breath came shallow.

Heat crawled up my neck. I took out my real phone and turned it on.

Marcy and Lucas, who'd been talking low to each other in the corner of the room, looked at me. Watching, waiting.

"Hudson." My name dropped from the agent like a lead boot. "Please enlighten me so I can do my job."

I opened Instagram. My moment of weakness the other night. After searching my name, I found an all-Krom fandom account with a post blasting me. A static image pulled mid-frame from one of my videos, caught while speaking so I looked half awake and messy.

I'd made one comment. One comment in self-defense. From an anonymous skincare junkie using a private account.

Horror struck as my worst fear surfaced. I hadn't posted from the private account. I'd posted from Camp Junebug.

A reply showed beneath my comment. *Why is a kid's camp dishing dirt about Kristoff Krom?"*

"No. No, no, no." I sank to the floor behind Twila's desk, staring at the phone.

"That's not what I want to hear," the agent warned.

"What?" Marcy appeared at my side, her voice gentle, urging.

I couldn't look at Lucas.

I faced my phone to Marcy and spoke to the agent on the burner. "I was logged into the Camp Junebug account and made a comment in my defense." Right there on the screen, my rant against the troll. Not from a skincare fan's account, but with the camp account I'd been building up the past week. "I thought I was logged into my private account."

Marcy read the screen. "You clapped back to a troll and you used the camp account. So delete it. What's the issue?"

"The account has the location in the bio. The camp's location isn't a secret. And look at the user's name who called out my comment."

KromBroFan

Agent Mulder cleared his throat. "You posted in defense of yourself on an account with location information readily available. We have no knowledge this person believes it's you posting from the account. Or that Krom saw this post or that he or his followers would connect you to a children's camp. It was a sloppy move, but it doesn't mean the threat is related."

Lucas moved closer to the phone I held. "Sir, this the camp director. A new session begins tomorrow. I need to know if it's safe for the children to attend."

My mind flashed with the faces of the campers on their nature walks. Bianca and her craft mastery. Maggie's ability to sense a homesick kid before the first tears shed. I put them all at risk by being here.

This was my fault. "I'm so sorry. I thought..." of myself. I'd been thinking only of myself.

I couldn't resist defending my brand. Defending *me*. And I'd been careless about it.

"How about I alert the local field office as a precaution," Agent Mulder said. "Sir, go ahead and file your police report. A trespasser at a children's camp is reason enough to heighten security without the added Hollywood hoopla." He noisily cleared his throat. "With children involved, do what you need to do."

I chanced a look at Lucas. Determined, fierce eyes looked past me. Jaw set. He walked to his office and shut the door.

Agent Mulder left me with a few parting words, mainly about staying offline and not doing anything stupid, then defined stupid as anything that might alert anyone on earth to my whereabouts, and clicked off.

Marcy's arms encircled me. "You've been through a lot."

I didn't deserve sympathy. "I made this worse. So much worse than it needed to be."

"If you want to come home with me, you're welcome to."

My back met the wall, its cool touch mildly calming. I could leave. Ditch this low-tech existence and at least be somewhere with streaming TV and access to better take-out options.

But I didn't want to leave. I'd come close to grasping a sense of peace I hadn't experienced in so long. I needed more time. I needed more walks by the water, more time to think.

"Would leaving be worse? Running off after I put the camp in danger. Plus, the camp games—I committed to the team." Comparatively unimportant. If the threat came from the other camp, would we even want to play competitive games with them?

"Maybe Lucas can hire my brothers to work security," Marcy said with a snort. "They seemed real eager to defend you."

"Like Patrick jumping to defend *you*?"

She waved me off. "He's always tagging along doing whatever my brothers do. They jump at any chance to act macho."

Knowing they had my back, simply by virtue of knowing Marcy, brought more comfort than I cared to admit. Lucas included. I'd seen the fear in his eyes. Then again, maybe that fear was only for the kids he'd signed on to oversee. Kids I'd put in harm's way.

I'd been so naïve. So focused on myself.

We sat there like that for a few minutes. Neither of us spoke. My mind settled, though the undercurrent of worry clung to each breath.

Marcy held her hands out to help me to standing. "Whatever's going on in that head of yours, don't get too down on yourself. You've done everything else your people asked."

Lucas' office door swung open. He stomped across the room and stopped in front of us to look out the window. He sighed.

"What's the scoop, boss?" Marcy asked.

He physically bristled. "The *scoop*," he said and turned toward us. "Is the sheriff's office took down a description and said they'd run a patrol car by the camp. That's it." He sighed again. "Beyond that, we're on our own."

Chapter 25

Lucas

Across the fire pit, Hudson sat bundled in a sweatshirt and jeans surrounded by her friends. My meet-up buddies and the kitchen staff, with exception of Pete, had taken off, leaving nine of us at camp. The atmosphere was notably less party weekend now that we'd encountered the possible threat. But the group had another night together, so we decided to make the best of it. Fire pit, S'mores, coolers of snacks.

Only I couldn't get the day's events out of my head. Hudson had looked terrified during that phone call. Krom shredded her in that video, barely holding back a smirk while he did it. Krom had a legion of dedicated followers who believed he could do no wrong. Who knew what those fans would do if incited.

Stupid me, I hadn't put together the severity of her situation. The feds? A burner phone? Hiding out at camp wasn't some one-eighty turn after a bad breakup. This was laying low *under federal supervision*.

And no one told me.

While I'd waited for the sheriff's office on hold, I'd dug deeper searching Hudson's name on a social media site. Horrible posts surfaced claiming she conspired against Krom. That she'd been planning with an impressive list of political figures and questionable celebrities to set him up. Krom was framed, they insisted, by a girlboss loser who leached onto Krom's hard-earned fame. Now she "had to pay."

That last comment chilled me to the bone. I'd rather the threat have been from the other camp. A Brycen crony looking for intel on our tug-of-war tactics.

I prayed that was the case and not something worse.

Across from me, Hudson's skin glowed from the fire. The pink in her hair had faded more, giving her a less polished look that was even more beautiful to me.

I could hardly be mad at her knowing what she'd been through. I wanted to shelter her in my arms. Tell her I'd keep her safe. Hudson's pale face and frightened eyes haunted my thoughts. If real danger lurked, I had to protect her. She lived on camp property. She was my staff. My cousin's friend. My...something more.

Our last few days together, our kisses, our touches. Okay, she meant more to me than simply being my staff and my cousin's friend.

She caught my eye. Usually she'd throw me a smile, but now she looked at me with that neutral expression. She thought I was mad at her. I'd definitely growled once or twice in the office during that call with the agent. I didn't know how to tell her none of that mattered right now. All that did was making sure she stayed safe. If someone was targeting Hudson, they'd have to come through me.

The guys had been quiet around the fire for a while now. Too quiet, hunched over their phones with occasional whining about bad cell service in the woods. If I knew my cousins and Patrick, they had shenanigans up their sleeves.

"Maybe stop texting and enjoy this beautiful night," Marcy nearly yelled at them across the flickering flames.

They looked up. Guilty, each one of them.

"Who are you texting?" I asked.

Robby's phone buzzed in his hand. I snatched it from him.

"Hey!" He lunged at me, but I moved fast and sprang out of reach.

The text came from Matteo, who sat right next to him.

We go at midnight. Hop the fence and form a perimeter

Shenanigans—I knew it. "You're not going to the other camp." No secrets, I'd call out their plan in front of everybody.

"I'm taking them," Pete said, who true to his word, stayed for defense purposes. "I know the land."

I pointed at him. "No."

"Ah, a return to form," Marcy mumbled.

"I heard that." I cracked my knuckles. "No conspiring to sneak to the other camp. If Brycen sent that guy, we can't stoop to their level. I'll handle it myself."

Arguments flew back and forth. Hudson and her friends huddled, speaking quietly. The quiet ones you had to watch for.

"That goes for you lot, too." I nodded at the women. "I know you used to thieve from dumpsters."

Noah busted out laughing. "It was garbage. And we were like, nineteen."

Everyone talked at once, pleading their case for why we needed to confront the Trail Blazers. So much for a quiet campfire.

This was getting ridiculous.

But they had a point. A strange man had lurked on our camp property. We weren't getting down to business sitting here stuffing our faces. The sheriff's deputy doing a drive by the camp wasn't enough.

I stood and clapped three times. "Here's what we're going to do. No sneaking. No hopping the fence. We're going to the Trail Blazers' camp and we're going in through the front gate. All of us. Right now."

We met a locked front gate at the Trail Blazers' camp.

As it should have been, since it was night and a weekend. Same as our camp.

But the closed gate killed our roll up and intimidate plan, leaving us idling in my truck. Behind me, a car carried the women and Patrick. Pete followed in his own Jeep.

"This is a bad idea," I admitted to Robby and Matteo stuffed next to me in the front seat. I would have preferred Hudson squished beside me instead of two full-grown dudes who'd been running around for hours, followed by devouring a bag of Doritos each.

Robby jabbed me with his elbow. "Don't chicken out now. What will Hudson think?" He made clucking sounds.

"That won't work on me."

A car door opened and shut behind us. I stared through the dark as Patrick headed toward the gate as if a mission beacon called to him. He'd been watching Marcy like a freaking hawk all night. Now he had it in his mind to defend her honor or some nonsense.

Hudson's frightened expression replayed in my mind. Her eyes said it all. Fear, guilt, worry. I knew she felt bad not coming clean about her full situation. The threats I'd seen about her online floated back. *Now she has to pay.*

Not on my watch.

I shut off the truck and shoved my door open. I could play protector too.

The women parked and gathered at the gate.

"Don't bother telling us we should stay in the car because we deserve to be here as much as any of you," Marcy announced, lasering her stare at each of us in her family, and lastly, landing her scrutiny on Patrick.

Patrick slipped his hands into his shorts pockets. "Literally, no one is suggesting that."

Marcy huffed.

"Strength in numbers," I said. "There are nine of us. Perfect to intimidate and demand answers."

"Yeah!" Robby pumped a fist in the air.

"Let's do this." Filled with renewed determination, we bypassed the gate, which only blocked vehicles from entering, and marched down the gravel drive. Our flashlight beams served as a light source until the outline of the lodge appeared ahead. Soft light glowed from the first-floor windows.

Gravel crunched in the distance and a figure formed. I swung my flashlight beam up. A familiar face.

"Porter," I said. His last name, which he preferred to go by. We reached him beneath the halo of an outdoor light at the path leading to the lodge. "We're here for Brycen."

Porter, a lean guy in his early twenties, loved rock climbing and distance running. Questions practically shot from his face, but he simply said: "He's not here."

Robby pulled himself to his full not-quite five-foot-eight height. He puffed his chest and stepped closer. "Stop covering for him. We know he's here."

"Uh, actually he's not. Sorry." Porter shrugged. "Y'all want to come inside? We're about to start game night. We've got Settlers of Catan—"

"Why'd you send a scout to spy on us?" Patrick demanded. "And who are you *really* looking for?"

Porter lifted his hands in mock surrender. "Look, I don't know what this is. If it's some prank, I'm not in on it." He looked at me. "I know you and Brycen have a beef, but that's not me. I don't care. We have plenty of pizza if you guys want some."

Matteo whipped around to the group. "No one crosses the line."

Marcy swatted him. "Give up the macho act. This guy has no idea why we're here and he's not acting guilty."

As they bickered, I studied Porter's face. He'd always been a chill guy, and not in the way Brycen played chill where it seemed like an act. Porter avoided confrontation and complications. During the split, Porter simply drifted toward the most magnetic personality. I would never claim my personality as magnetic, so clearly I lost that battle.

Regardless, I didn't peg Porter for a conspiring sort of guy. I believed him that he didn't care about my issues with Brycen.

Well, so much for our plan. We weren't any closer to figuring this out.

Footsteps sounded. "What's all this?"

The man of the hour appeared. "Brycen."

Robby scoffed at Porter. "You said he wasn't here."

"I got back ten minutes ago," Brycen answered for Porter. He stopped in front of the group, looking us over with a mild smirk. "I don't have staff openings for all of you. Maybe we can filter out the best during the competition and go from there. Set up a few interviews?"

We were amped up on snacks, and in some cases, spiked sports drinks, so the reactions came fast and furious. My cousins slung meaningless threats. Marcy scoffed loudly, and Noah complained she'd never work for a granola lord. I'd laugh if I wasn't so mad.

"We don't want jobs," I ground out. "Someone from your camp trespassed onto our property. When we caught him lurking behind cover and watching our friends, he took off and hopped the fence."

Brycen rolled his eyes. "You're asking if we sent someone to spy on you? Now you're inventing reasons to be mad at us. You're delusional."

I inched forward. "The dude ran to *your* camp. Three of us saw him. If you're not lying right now and you didn't send him, then he was trespassing on your side too."

Brycen's smirk vanished. "What did he look like?"

"White guy, maybe early thirties. About six foot, built, wearing gear that blended with the woods. Plain ball cap. I'd bank on him being military."

Brycen glanced to Porter. "That's not any of us."

"Doesn't sound familiar," Porter agreed.

"We've got limited staff here this weekend," Brycen said. "It's our long break weekend. I was off-site all day until tonight. My staff would have contacted me if they'd seen someone. They would have reported the incident to the police."

A hint of worry threaded his tone. For all my issues with Brycen—his forced cool attitude, his turbo-charged vision of summer camp, he seemed to be telling the truth. An intruder on his grounds, particularly a military type, was not welcome news.

Brycen took out his phone. "Will you call me if you find out anything? I'm at my same number. And I'll ask the sheriff to run patrols by both camps."

"Already did that," I said. Brycen offered an olive branch. For the sake of the kids, I'd take it. Well, maybe just a leaf. "We've got a few authorities alerted and are taking additional precautions." I wouldn't out Hudson's FBI contact, but at least we covered some ground.

Brycen nodded. "Hey, thanks for letting us know." He gave a simple nod to the group and headed to the lodge with Porter.

Hudson appeared at my side. "You okay?"

I took a breath. I wasn't ready to forgive and forget everything Brycen had done during the camp split, but right now we had a common threat. "Yeah. Let's get out of here."

The next morning, we sent off our friends and family. Promises were made to keep in touch more often, and threats made that I better call if things heated up.

"Seriously," Patrick told me outside Matteo's car as the other guys packed in. "Tell me if you need anything. I can call in some favors for more support."

I laughed before I could help it. "You've got connections here? What, are you some kind of fixer?"

He narrowed his eyes. "You know I'm looking to run for local office. I know people."

"Sure, but not local here." What was I doing? He was focused on solutions and here I was ragging on him. Old habits died hard. "Sorry. Yeah, if you want to pull your strings, I won't complain."

A snort sounded behind me. "You not complaining. That's rich."

"Love you too, Marcy." I held up my phone. "I promise I'll call."

Her shoulders softened. "I'll hold you to it."

Hudson hugged each of her friends. They'd gone directly to her cabin after our mission to the other camp last night, so I hadn't had a chance to talk to her. Alone. To tell her I wasn't mad. That I'd protect her. So many things I wanted to say, but every second seemed to fill with distractions.

After final goodbyes, the cars departed, leaving Hudson and me standing in the camp parking lot.

Here it was, my opportunity to share the thoughts stewing in my brain since yesterday. Everything that filled my mind in between chucking stuff at snoring dudes during the night.

Only no words came. *Say something, anything.*

Hudson looked across the empty drive leading from camp, her mind a million miles from here. She was doing that thing where she wrapped her arms around herself. Like she had to hold herself together.

If only I could wrap myself around her and provide that protection. For today, for this week. Whatever it took so she'd feel safe again.

But how could I protect Hudson when I didn't know if she'd want me to? Brycen had called my accusations delusional; it was probably my own delusion to assume I could fix her problems when I could barely run this camp.

She turned to me. "Finally, everyone's gone." Her smile came slow and downright sexy. She hooked a finger into my shirt collar and pulled. "Come here."

I obeyed. I was useless to resist. She tilted her delicate face upward and pressed her lips to mine. She slid her arms around my neck, slowly, inch by inch as she deepened the kiss.

She knew I wasn't mad. How did she know? Did I care?

I took her cues and pulled her closer. Her scent was distinctly her. Sweet, fresh, possibly expensive. Her lips tasted like everything I'd hoped for but didn't know was within reach. She made no sense for me. Right now, I could think of no one else. Of nothing I wanted more than this moment, fossilized and forever captured.

Gently, I covered her back with my hands, wrapping slowly around her. A hug and an embrace. A circle of protection. All that I could offer.

I spoke with my kiss to prove I intended to be there for her. I would protect her. I would ensure her safety.

When we came up for air, I looked into her eyes. "I'm sorry."

"Okay." She blinked. "What for?"

For so much. For being hard on her. For not looking into her situation sooner or connecting the right dots. I felt responsible, even though she'd left out details and bore responsibility there too. Everything felt out of place and I liked neat rows. Scratch that, rows reminded me of spreadsheets which I hated. "I'm sorry for what happened to you."

"Oh." She danced her fingers along my arm. Mindless maybe, but my body reacted in a pleasing shiver. "Did you read any of the stuff online?"

I nodded. "A little."

"And?"

"I can see why you needed to be somewhere away from it all. Why you kept details to yourself. And why the agent advised you to stay off the internet."

She nodded. "I'm sorry too."

It was enough. I took her hand. "Come on, let's head back to camp."

We walked side by side. "You know, I've been starting to get used to this place."

I laughed. "You took to camp almost immediately. In your own way."

"Me? No." She laughed too, a musical sound I wanted more of. "I didn't know what to expect when I first walked in. But the kids are funny, even though there's always a drama queen or two in each cabin. And Maggie's lack of fashion sense is tough to witness on the daily, but her heart is so in the right place all the time. It's made me consider my friendships the past few years. People who on the surface seem supportive, but they're focused on making famous connections more than deepening actual friendships. And I became just like them."

I knew less than nothing about her world and the friends she'd had. "Seems like you're getting on track with the friendships that matter."

"Yeah. This weekend was great. Despite the parts that weren't." She slowed when we reached the office. "I like seeing you with your family and friends. It's a different side of you."

I scrubbed my free hand across my beard. "As soon as they got here, it was like old times." I'd been shouldering so much on my own. "I have people to lean on. This weekend reminded me of that."

"Same." Her smile brightened. "I would say it was like old times seeing the Mavens again, but it feels different. New. We're different."

"The Mavens?"

"It's this thing we're doing. We gave ourselves a group name and set personal goals. Life goals. There are notebooks and stickers." A blush colored her cheeks. "Anyway, it's got to be tough running a camp. No wonder you're stressed."

Stress. Not a word I'd used much in my life to be honest. I'd always had simple interests. Jobs requiring sweat and hard work but not really *stress*. Being responsible for people's lives, for children? This job made me feel stress.

And even more now that beefing up security measures became a top priority. I needed to get to the office and make some calls. "I should get to work."

"The counselors will be here soon. And campers." She sighed heavily. "The whole cycle starts again."

"Soon, but not yet." I pulled her in for another kiss, memorizing every detail.

Chapter 26

Hudson

THE VIBE FOR CAMP arrival day hit decidedly different than past weeks.

"Uh, what are all these teenagers doing here?" Lucas joined me in the parking lot for the latest arrivals, standing a safe and professional distance from me.

"It's teen week." He should have known that, right?

He looked at me with a blank expression.

"The fifteen and sixteen-year-olds—the oldest age bracket the camp allows," I went on. "Some will go on to be counselors next year. We even offer mini training sessions this week with the chance to earn a junior counselor badge."

"We don't do badges."

"We don't do *patches*. Seriously, you run this camp?"

Lucas scowled. I guess my grin wasn't enough to signal I was teasing.

He ran a hand across his beard. "Should have known that, you're right. I didn't pay attention to the age range on the schedule."

He said something else, but I'd already moved on to replay our last kiss for my brainwaves only. Lucas was so not my type and somehow completely hitting my buttons. Figuratively, obviously, since I had on a slouchy camp T-shirt and shorts with an elastic waistband. No actual buttons to be found.

"Is that okay?" Lucas looked at me.

"Oh, sure. Yes." I had no idea what I agreed to.

"Good." Lucas shifted toward me. He caught himself and straightened. "Good, good." He sauntered away.

I suppose I'd find out later what I committed to. It wasn't as if I could leave. Or more like, I'd committed to stay and committed to keeping the camp and staff safe.

We'd already had a meeting with the counselors to inform them of the trespasser and to radio Lucas immediately if they noticed anything off. Anything at all.

Jasmine and the other counselors were managing the bulk of the camper check-ins in Maggie's absence. Here I was, uselessly standing around.

"Welcome to Camp Junebug," I announced to the nearest cluster of girls.

The return looks varied from skeptical to mildly hostile. Teen angst or was I overboard with dork energy? I hadn't felt this out of place socially since...well, the night I met Kristoff.

I'd gotten the dream invitation to a super posh party with a mix of celebrities and L.A. mainstays. The kind of people that opened real doors, not just digital ones.

I'd been practically scaling walls to get this sort of invitation.

But the friend who'd invited me hadn't bothered to show up. Arriving in my borrowed dress with a rented designer handbag, I sensed the social level shift immediately. The people at this party were not home renovation sisters on basic cable or reality show contestants. No actors with a string of failed pilot episodes.

These were the people who ran Hollywood and the businesses around it. Powerful people who wore their wealth in their posture, who weren't flashy because they didn't have to be.

I was utterly out of place and hopelessly try-hard.

And then Kristoff found me. He had the most charisma of anyone I'd ever met. I vaguely knew who he was at the time, and was surprised when he approached me and pulled me into a conversation with his wealthy friends. He listened to me like I had something to say. I hadn't expected that. My strategy at parties was to introduce myself and then ask people lots of open-ended questions to get them talking about their favorite topic, themselves. But Kristoff, he'd wanted to know about *me*.

He'd made me feel special. In that frighteningly wealthy home with no one else to support me, he'd chosen *me*.

I snapped to reality as more teens arrived at check-in. Now that I had a chance to observe better, I noticed I was getting some looks.

The pink hair maybe? The color had paled further, and my roots showed. Usually I'd care more and would have scheduled a salon trip by now. With salons out, even a henna box dye could do the trick. But I sort of didn't care. Maybe the pink needed to fully fade and I'd find a new color to try.

Hold up. A girl had her phone out. We were in the parking lot, technically not deeper into camp where the phone would be confiscated or not work at all. She looked at me, then at the phone. Looked at me again.

Nope. This was not good.

"They've got their phones," I said to Jasmine.

"We allow phones for the older teens. They're restricted use. They have to secure them in their bunks for most of the day, but we let them have access."

I should have expected this. These girls were more likely to have seen my beauty channel than the younger girls. With a simple click and a location tag, my lay-low plan would bust for sure.

"Hey," a girl with a messy bun walked over. "Are you that butterfly skincare girl from YouTube?"

My vision narrowed. The secret was out.

All of this was my fault. I'd assumed staying at camp was some valiant move to keep my word by not running off. But I couldn't control any of these teen girls if I tried. They had phones and were trained and primed by the outside world to snap and post pics of anything and everything with infinite platforms available to instantly share.

"I..." I couldn't deny it. The girl was looking right at my face. She showed me her phone. My face was there too, on her small screen, with my YouTube account clearly marked below it. "Yes. Yes, that's me."

"Cool." She shrugged and slid the phone into her shorts pocket. She turned to her friend and their discussion switched to recapping their boring ride to camp.

Okay, so maybe I was overreacting. I'd become so full of myself I'd assumed these teenagers cared enough to share about me online.

"So, why are you here if you're a YouTube star?" another girl asked. She had her phone out too, looking from her screen to me. "You're like, famous."

Dangit.

Teen counselor Bianca appeared and slung an arm around me. "I can answer that. But let me get everybody together first."

Panic shot through me, but Bianca merely offered a wink.

Bianca stepped in front of me and motioned for the campers to gather. "Heads up girls!" She clapped three times. "Before we move into camp, I want to introduce our newest counselor. This is Hudson. She's a staffer here for the summer and she's also an influencer online. She went off-grid for the true organic experience. She's not using social media or any of her online accounts. To help her out, we don't share that she's here. Like, no social posts or pictures online. It's been a really cool experience for all of us so far."

Words failed. I shot Bianca a grateful look. She knew. She knew so much and I had no idea. I hadn't asked this of her or even hinted at it.

The girl in front of us looked in awe at Bianca. Forget me. To this girl, Bianca was a year older, trendy without trying hard, and a leader. A natural beauty. And she loved this camp.

I owed Bianca for life.

"So, we all need to agree," Bianca went on. "We're keeping Hudson out of our socials. Raise your hand and solemnly swear."

For life.

Maggie's absence was noticeable in every aspect when camp was in session. She'd be back tomorrow, and I'd tell her just how much she added to this camp. Lucas told me he'd alerted Maggie about the current security situation but urged her not to rush back.

I spotted Lucas around here and there but only in short glimpses. I knew he took the security risk seriously, so I aimed to stay out of his way.

Every moment since arrival was filled by talking to and managing the teen campers. They weren't satisfied with simple answers like the younger girls. Despite the solemn oath to not share about me online, it didn't dissuade them from constantly asking me about my life.

"How can I be a YouTube star?"

"How did you get so many followers on Instagram?"

"Can you tell me how to be famous?"

"What do you do to get free stuff?"

"What's going on with the rich guy ex-boyfriend?"

The last question stole my breath. I could talk about videos and social media marketing all day, but the personal stuff... How did I respond?

Thankfully, Bianca was within earshot. "Off limits."

"I..." I nodded. That was a good response. "Yes, that's an off-limits topic."

The questioning camper moved on.

But later at our first Campfire, the tone turned serious. These girls wanted to go *deep*. They moved on quickly from Jasmine's attempt at a scary ghost story to demand a round of truth or dare.

Bianca took the lead, laying out ground rules that no one should feel pressured to share what they weren't comfortable with and no dares could involve the lake (for safety) or public humiliation. Silly dares, yes. Dangerous or tragically embarrassing, no. This was clearly not her first round of camp truth or dare.

Truths shared involved confessions of crushes (back home, where no one would know their names—a safe truth), to admissions of struggles with schoolwork or even depression. I sat in awe of the support the girls provided for each other. While some of the campers returned year after year and were close with girls here, many had only known each other for a few hours.

They reminded me of my Mavens. These girls were meeting earlier than we had in college, but some here would make friends for life. This was a big deal.

The circle focused their attention on me. "Miss Hudson: Truth or dare."

I could opt out—I was an adult. But something told me not to. "Truth."

The campers looked at each other. No one came out of the gates bursting with a question. They'd pestered me half the day, so maybe there wasn't anything left to wonder about. Finally, one of the bolder girls asked: "Is it true you tried to ruin Kristoff Krom?"

Bianca shot up from her log bench. "Off limits."

I held up a hand. "It's okay."

"You don't have to answer," Bianca told me.

The girl lifted her chin. "Truth or dare *requires* an answer."

Bianca shot her a frosty glare. "I'll block your junior leadership badge."

"I'll answer," I said. "I did not intentionally ruin his business deals or rat him out to authorities. I know that's an expected answer. Of course I'd defend myself. But I want you all to know, I truly did not sabotage him. The truth is, I was too focused on myself to notice what he was doing. I really wanted that Sheek deal. Looking back, I can see I glossed right over a bunch of red flags with Kristoff because being in his circle of influence got me closer to what I wanted."

I paused to scan their faces. I expected bored expressions or eye rolls, but I had their attention.

"He would often leave in the middle of dinner at a restaurant to take a private phone call," I continued. "Busy people do that. I thought nothing of it. Once his driver made a sharp turn and the car sped up. The place we were going was only a few miles away but it took us an hour. Kristoff told me it was L.A. traffic. Now I think the driver was trying to outrun somebody following him."

Soft gasps sounded around the fire.

I glanced to Bianca. "I'm not going to stop you now," she said.

"For me, fame wasn't the end goal. But it sort of was." I rubbed my forehead in an attempt to gather my thoughts. "I wanted the skincare spokesperson deal so I could get paid and stop having to do all these side hustle jobs. The truth about influencers is a lot of it isn't as lucrative as it seems. For some, it totally is. For me, even with ad revenue and free samples and paid posts, I had to work odd jobs to stay afloat. The whole time I told myself I was better off making my own way than working some conventional job with a steady paycheck. I had thousands and thousands of followers but...I was miserable. And dating a billionaire tech genius didn't make me happy either."

I swallowed. As I spoke, my thoughts grew more clear. "I honestly haven't been happy in a long time. Not until...until I came here. When all of my usual distractions weren't taking up every inch of space in my life. I had to face that I have no idea what I want to do with my life. And that it's okay to feel that way. It's okay to want a reset."

Murmurs cascaded around the fire. I sat straighter. This was inappropriate. I was using campfire time like therapy. I wasn't a camper, I was an adult. "I'm sorry, that was too much for a truth."

"No," the girl who'd asked me the question spoke first, followed by more objections. "It's so good to hear the other side of fame. So many famous people don't talk about how it really is."

"I stayed with a boyfriend who wasn't good for me too," a blond with a pixie cut admitted. "I wouldn't listen to my friends. Finally, he broke up with me in a video chat that he recorded and put online. Like your ex did to you."

"What a jerk," I blurted. "I'm so sorry that happened."

The camper next to her gave her a hug.

My throat tightened. "Sometimes the person you believe is everything you want is the opposite. It can be really surprising who sees you for who you are."

Feet shuffling sounded behind me. My skin chilled. It was total darkness beyond the fire. A figure in a plaid shirt emerged.

"Lucas?" I called out.

A grumble sounded and he stepped nearer, now visible from the campfire's flames. "I'm keeping watch. I'm not...listening." A flash in his eyes told on him. I would gamble he'd heard me, at least whatever I'd most recently said.

The campers had been introduced to Lucas at the night's first Mess, and he'd informed them he'd be staying on site all week. He shuffled back, seeming to recognize we needed space.

Bianca tossed a knowing glance my way. She clasped her hands. "Thanks, Hudson, for sharing. Now who's next—truth or dare?"

Chapter 27

Lucas

I HOLED UP IN the camp office with an aggressive To-Do list. First, I looked at camp director job listings. Not for me, but to learn how to post one.

Camp Junebug deserved a director who was all-in. I'd give the job what I had day by day, but these past few weeks proved I needed to move on.

Hudson proved I needed to move on.

It can be surprising who sees you for who you are.

We had nothing in common. Nothing and somehow everything. This fashion diva who'd shown up to my corner of the wilderness managed to shake my world. She did foolish things and brave things. She faced and ran from her fears. But below the surface, she wanted what I did. To discover purpose. To do meaningful things. To find...love.

I found purpose and meaning outdoors. Not managing budgets and parent complaints. This job was a means to an end, but if I wasn't actively looking to move on, then I was hiding, just like her.

Almost as if I'd been hiding for a long time.

My truth, like the campers' truth or dare (which I wasn't intentionally listening to until it got to Hudson), was that fear held me back. Fear that my dream job didn't want me.

It couldn't reject me if I never applied.

Because I hadn't. I took one look at the requirements for the Colorado wilderness adventure job and talked myself out of it. This plan to get experience under my belt? A distraction. I could twist it any way I liked, but the bottom line practically screamed at me: *you're scared to live your dream, so you settle for what's safer.*

For a guy claiming he dreamed of leading survivalist expeditions, guiding ten-year-olds through the woods while checking off leaves on bingo cards sure played it safe.

It wasn't all bad here. The kids were funny (when they weren't crying), Maggie was a dependable team player, and the kitchen crew added a dose of reality when I needed it.

But this sure wasn't rock climbing in the mountains. Or fishing for the night's dinner.

Maybe my playing it safe was like Hudson with her videos. That immediate gratification of followers and making famous friends held her back from reaching bigger. Well, she'd reached for bigger, but she'd said outright it hadn't been what she really wanted.

What did she want? Did she want me? Was I more than a temporary distraction?

Everything about our interactions were based on happenstance. She needed a place to lay low. I was so desperate for camp staff we'd take anyone. She was coming off a breakup and I happened to be living and breathing near her.

I stood and paced my office. I was so different than Hudson's usual taste, maybe being with me seemed exciting or dangerous.

I liked to feel dangerous. I hadn't felt that way in a long time. Kind of hard to when daily camp life revolved around skinned knees and songs about bugs.

But once Hudson was out of here, or when I was out of here, what would be left of us?

I'd built this idea of becoming a wilderness guide for action-adventure seekers, but what if I couldn't hack it? Construction jobs offered more security. I could always go back to work that wasn't so complicated.

But that was an excuse. None of this was complicated. I was simply scared.

I sat again and pulled up the camp Instagram account on my office computer. Thanks to Hudson's recent efforts, Twila informed me that camp enrollment had filled for the summer. The proof was in the comments below every post:

Do you have camp sessions open? My 9-year-old is begging to go to camp.

Any open weeks left?

Are your rates the same as the website? That's a good deal!

Interest was up, I had an offer of free canoes if I was willing to drive to Cheboygan, and Twila was strangely not nosing into my business.

My phone lit with a text. Huh. Brycen.

Are we still on for the Summer Trail Games? I know it's been a rough week. We wanted to know if Wednesday would work instead of Saturday.

My thoughts raged. That threw our whole camp schedule off. And what about my meet-up group? They worked on weekdays.

I wasn't good with texts. I did the thing I swore I wouldn't. I called him.

"Hey," Brycen answered. "Assuming you got my message."

"Yeah. We've got campers here this week. How would that work?"

"We do too. Bring the kids over. We'll do an all-camp competition. Split into age groups. Campers and staff."

"Is this some angle to sell our kids on your flashy camp?"

A soft laugh came from the other end. "It's not a recruitment effort, no. Something in our schedule shifted and we thought it would be fun to host the games during the week where the campers could be involved. That's it. Your campers are welcome here. No strings."

That was the thing. This was all too welcoming. Our campers would experience the slick Trail Blazers' way of life and then complain the rest of the week at Camp Junebug.

Even if we beat them at the games, we couldn't compete camp against camp. It would be like the Terminator going against well, a literal junebug. *Squish*.

When I didn't respond, Brycen continued. "Look. I know I play a heavy hand teasing you guys, but I'm thinking I went too far. You actually believed we sent a tactical scout to *spy* on you. Even after we caught you on our side, we wouldn't send someone over in retaliation."

Now I said nothing. My trust had been lost with Brycen, and I wouldn't put anything past him.

"I'm sorry, Lucas," he said. "I never meant for things to turn out like this. I wanted you with the Trail Blazers. You were my first pick. You were my partner."

Partner was questionable. Even when we were friends, Brycen ran things the way he wanted. Brycen had taken what he wanted and ran with it. He took our staff and our land. I was bitter over it.

"It wasn't what your dad wanted for the camp," I finally said. "Your parents built this camp from scratch with the belief that camp was for everyone. Your dad wanted those values to continue." He knew this already, of course he did. "I only wanted to carry out his wishes."

Brycen had his own vision and he wouldn't be satisfied until he put his vision into action. Even if it meant going against his family's values. Even if it meant no longer talking to his parents. I didn't agree with his vision of an elite camp that excluded less wealthy or unathletic kids, so I couldn't partner with it.

But I couldn't argue that he had a purpose and acted on it.

"My dad started treatment for memory care," Brycen said. "For his Alzheimer's. My biggest regret is that I didn't clear the air with him sooner. I begged him to hear me out. Lucas, it's gotten bad."

I hadn't talked to the old man in a few weeks. He couldn't have turned for the worse that quickly. But I didn't know much about the condition. Maybe it was true he'd worsened.

Back when Alan would pop into camp regularly with Brycen in charge, he'd sometimes repeat things he'd already said. A few times he'd comment sharply, seeming irritated or even confused by basic things. Mostly, he'd seemed in his right mind. Perhaps I saw him on good days. I didn't know what his daily life was like.

When Brycen's father pulled me aside one day, distraught that his only son wanted to gut the camp of its core values, I believed him. I believed him over my friend.

What if that wasn't the full story?

"Thanks for the apology," I said. Brycen seemed sincere, but I had a lot to work through before I'd forget how much he'd hurt his family and Camp Junebug. "I'll ask my staff about Wednesday."

"Sounds good. Take care, Lucas."

Chapter 28

Hudson

MAGGIE RETURNED TO CAMP pink skinned with more freckles across her nose. Despite her rested and refreshed appearance, she immediately focused on business. "I see Lucas installed more secure locks in the bunkhouses. Did he review lock and key protocol with the counselors?"

I'd been fielding questions from her all morning.

Meanwhile, Lucas confirmed regular patrols by the sheriff and let us know the Trail Blazers had counselors doing rounds across camp grounds reaching to the property lines. We'd spoken a handful of times, always brief, since the weekend. I could tell he was stressed.

A camper named Vera, a quiet one with incredible artistic skills, approached Maggie and me as we rotated groups from volleyball to craft stations. The older girls could do more advanced crafting and some of them were seriously talented. I'd been "helping" them all morning in between Maggie drilling me for updates.

Vera held up her phone. "Miss Hudson, I was online—on our morning break, with permission," she said quickly to Maggie, whose six-foot presence was new and imposing to campers who hadn't been here before. "And saw this."

She faced her phone at me. It was a message forum thread and the topic was...*me*. I gulped.

Before I could formulate a response, Maggie took the phone and started reading. She looked between me and Vera, and to the phone again. She snorted. "What a load of hooey. Imagine that—one of our camp counselors dating a celebrity billionaire."

An uncomfortable silence followed.

Maggie blinked rapidly. "It's not *true*. Those people sound like wackos. They're talking about some girl boss influencer stealing bitcoin. You have *yarn in your hair*."

I'd attempted a crochet headband of sorts. B plus for effort? C minus for execution. Failing grade for any fashion sense.

"The stealing part isn't true, right, Miss Hudson?" Vera flashed at look at me, mouthing *I'm sorry*. She meant involving Maggie, but it was on me that Maggie didn't know those details.

The silence became too much. "You dated *Kristoff Krom*?" There was no mistaking Maggie's reaction. She did not like this information. "You never—" She huffed and returned to the screen. "Well, the rest of this is total nonsense. How do you steal bitcoin? Wait—I don't want to know. None of this sounds like you, Hudson." She handed the phone to Vera. "People lie on the internet all the time. You can't always believe what you read."

True. But I'd hurt Maggie by keeping my real life a secret. What was new? It seemed a common theme. Maybe I could build a career out of it.

Maggie shook her head and directed herself toward the volley-ball players.

"Maggie, wait—"

She didn't turn back.

"Sorry," Vera said to me.

"You did nothing wrong. Can I see that again?" I gestured to her phone.

As I read the forum post, she recapped. "This guy is saying he knows Kristoff and there's an account he doesn't have access to. That you have access to it. And..."

I landed on the comment she referred to. This person wanted to find me. Somebody who believed I'd stolen something from Kristoff was intent on *enacting justice*. I shuddered. Even though these posts were pure fiction, if this person really believed I had something belonging to Kristoff, if they really knew Kristoff personally, which I doubted, then this was freaking scary.

The comment existed on a subforum with few replies or upvotes on a massive website. "How did you even find this?"

"We want to look out for you, Miss Hudson. We've been thinking of ways to support you."

If my heart was butter, it had transformed into an oily, melted mess. "That's incredibly sweet, but I'm afraid I overshared the other night. It's not your responsibility to take care of me. I really appreciate it, but please don't go looking for posts like this."

I handed the phone back. Vera's shoulders sank. "Sorry. We were trying to help."

My oily heart oozed again. "Don't feel bad or apologize. I'm the one who shared too much of my personal life. Maggie would never have stood for that." I pressed my lips together. "You didn't hear me say that. Maggie is incredible. She's just tall and comes off a little intimidating with all her rules."

Vera smiled now. "No worries."

She trotted off to the rain shelter with the craft stations even though I swore she was up for volleyball next.

Later at dinner, the campers at my table buzzed with conversation until a lull hit. I was about to bust out an icebreaker question when Bianca slid beside me on the lunch table bench.

She made eye contact with a few girls before turning to me. "We've identified a threat."

I waited for the punchline. Her face was serious. Oh—oh no. "Radio Lucas." I twisted and scanned the Mess. He wasn't here. "What did you see? Is it—"

"Not here at camp—online." Bianca lowered her voice. "Vera told me she showed you that post." She held up a hand. "Don't get mad at her. She did the right thing. We checked out this guy's digital footprint. We think he's legit."

My mind swirled with responses, from reprimands to denials. "What do you mean, legit? And I'm not mad, but you shouldn't be involving yourself with this. Or be on your phones when you're supposed to be doing...organic stuff."

A girl across from me at the table giggled, but it was short lived. "Miss Hudson, we really are worried. This isn't a joke or made up."

"Here's the thing," Bianca said, revealing what was one hundred percent a contraband item: her cell phone. She knew the rule better than anybody: there were no phones allowed at the Mess or outside the bunkhouse.

But what she said next hit hard.

"They know where you are."

This was not good. Very not good.

We split from the Mess for an emergency bunkhouse huddle. I let Bianca lead the way. I needed to hear them out to determine if this threat was legitimately legit or an invented time-waster the girls risked getting in trouble for. They were allowed phones to use sparingly, and I hated to be *that counselor*, but they were violating the very rules Camp Junebug held so strong.

The campers arranged themselves in the center of the bunkhouse to present digital evidence of the threats against me.

"I don't have anything belonging to Kristoff," I told them before they began. "I understand these scum suckers think I do, but I don't. I barely packed anything. If I didn't have these camp clothes, I'd be wearing the same handful of outfits over and over. And as far as bitcoin goes, I never invested in it. Kristoff didn't add me to his accounts. We weren't even dating that long."

Bianca sighed dramatically. "You're missing the point. Even if it's not true, these people believe it is. Therefore, you're in danger."

No, *I put you all in danger*. I needed to tell Lucas. I needed to alert Agent Mulder. But what would I say? A cabin of fifteen-year-olds uncovered a stalker trail the FBI couldn't find?

"I already told them about the skeezy guy in the woods this weekend," Bianca said.

Great, just great. Teen counselors for the win. "*As you know*," I said pointedly to Bianca. "The camp has taken safety precautions, and we don't have any evidence that he had anything to do with me. Most likely not." I hoped. I really, really hoped. "Anyway, the local sheriff has been patrolling and I have an FBI contact who notified the local office." There. Now they all knew.

Undeterred, they launched into a detailed recap of the user's digital trail on the website, following a link the user posted in another thread that led to their personal blog, which obsessed over cryptocurrency. Also, weirdly, Crocs footwear.

I was a terrible camp counselor. If these girls' parents knew their camp money was funding an undercover investigation intersecting with an infamous billionaire's open fraud case, they'd blow many and all gaskets. There wasn't a badge for this sort of camp craft.

"Okay, I don't see evidence that this user knows where I am."

Three phones shot up with girls talking at once.

My head throbbed.

"Here." One of them stood. "On this other website there's a public chat thread that says where your hometown is and that you went to college at University of Michigan. They found pictures of you on Facebook."

That information was public. The pictures were old. "That doesn't tie me to the camp. We're miles away from where I grew up and where I went to college."

Another girl spoke up. "This one here says they found out from a source you flew to the Midwest and you're researching subleasing your apartment in Los Angeles."

Okay, *that* was creepy. But the simplest explanation was an educated guess. Someone on the run likely wouldn't return to a known address. Though officially, I was laying low, not on the run.

"No, this is the one," the third girl showed me her phone. "It's Instagram. A lady posted that she got free Sheek lipstick in a restaurant bathroom from the pink-haired make-up YouTuber. Look at her location."

My breath froze. Free lipstick in a restaurant bathroom. That was during happy hour in town my first week. The location of the user was a town nearby the camp.

Stupid me needing to give out my freebies. I'd been caged in social butterfly captivity and couldn't resist. "Hold on, I was wearing a hat." Yes, I'd definitely worn a hat when we went out. "Wait—I took it off at the mirror."

This gave the girls new fuel to burn. "I told you!"

"They know she's here!"

The women from the bathroom hadn't said they'd recognized me at the time, but maybe they'd connected it later. Not good.

"Now look at the comments," Bianca said over my shoulder.

Isn't she the one Kristoff Krom broke up with?

Where are you, Michigan? Why would she be slumming it out there?

Hey, watch your mouth! Michigan is the Great Lakes State!

Michigan pride aside, this was like a dart making it onto the dartboard. Not a bullseye, but not a total miss. Only it didn't prove

Kristoff or his buddies had any awareness I was here. These were unconnected posts across multiple platforms.

"Credit due for your investigative skills, girls, but I'm afraid these don't add up to solid evidence." And thankfully for me, it was unlikely any of this resulted in a real threat.

The girls all talked at once. If only they'd been this excited over our leaf walk earlier today. I clapped my hands. "Okay. Settle down. Thank you for taking time to look into this. Focus on what camp has to offer. I promise I'll be careful and we'll watch out for anything odd. Promise me you'll report anything suspicious to your counselor and radio Maggie or Lucas."

"I understand camp protocol," Bianca stated. Which was not an agreement to what I'd asked.

The campers reluctantly agreed.

"The feds are all fine and good, but we'll need reinforcements," Bianca said with a straight face. "We have our own plans."

Vera popped up behind the girls sitting closest to me. She held a lined, spiral notebook. Diagrams and sketches covered the page.

Did I dare ask? "Um, what is that?"

"It's our master plan."

Oh, boy.

This entire discussion brought sharpened awareness to a thought I could no longer ignore. I needed to talk to Lucas about exiting camp. Even if the threat seemed unlikely, my presence put the campers at risk. Regardless of reality, online obsessives who believed wild theories they could enact justice *were* a threat. The girls proved enough pieces existed online that an obsessive focused on their version of justice could potentially piece them together.

I couldn't let that happen.

I left the bunkhouse after radioing for Jasmine to assist Bianca with after dinner activities. Bianca herself needed supervision or the girls would continue their makeshift Machiavellian strategies.

I marched to the main office hoping to find Lucas. The office was locked. I radioed Lucas, but he didn't respond.

My heartbeat kicked up a notch. Where was he? Was he in trouble? In danger?

"Hudson."

I yelped and nearly jumped out of my skin. I swatted Lucas. "You scared me."

"Sorry. You were standing there staring into space."

I threw my arms around him. "Why didn't you respond to the radio?"

"I just got back from town. Maggie was on point for any emergencies. Is everything okay?"

How to sum up okay? "The girls are curious," I started. No, too vague. "Don't be mad, but—" I watched his face harden as the words left my mouth. This approach never worked when I tried with my parents either. Why would it with Lucas as my boss? They always got mad at the request to not get mad. "There's chatter online from some weirdo who claims I have something of Kristoff's. Bianca's girls are all worked up about it. It's my fault. I shared too much with them the other day. I assumed it would put an end to their questions for good, but it's like a whole barrel of worms cracked open." I made a face.

"A barrel holds a lot of worms."

"I know—don't remind me." Hello, missing the point? "I don't want the kids reporting their online sleuthing skills to their parents. It will unravel all the work you've done to keep this camp focused on crafts and nature." I sighed. "Maybe it's a lost cause. Maybe we're all doomed to doomscroll."

"Hey." Lucas laid a hand on my arm. His body heat was scorching against my skin. Did he run hot? "Don't get upset, okay? We're doing everything we can."

"But is it enough? If I wasn't here at camp, they wouldn't have to worry about this at all."

"But you *are* here. We're not going to let anyone find you."

"That's out of your control. It's out of *my* control." I swallowed. "Lucas, I should leave."

"Into town? Do you need something? I could take you. We could—"

"No. I mean, leave camp."

He returned a look that stuttered my heart. Hurt. We both knew what it meant if I left early. Not only would he lose his new hire, but we'd both lose on this new thing between us. We'd barely gotten started and now I was running off. But hiding here had been a selfish move. I should have known not to involve so many people in my situation, especially kids.

"Did you tell the girls to back off on the theories?" he asked.

I nodded.

"Good. Then you've done your job. I hired a buddy who's off work to walk the grounds tomorrow while we're at the Trail Blazers' camp. You know, for the games."

Right, they were rescheduled for tomorrow. "Good idea."

"The campers will be with us all day at the other camp. Our two camps can pool resources. I...talked to Brycen again."

"Oh?" He seemed tentative to share.

"Yeah."

He said nothing further. So that was that. "I should still—"

"Don't go." His voice came low, deep. Shadows crossed his face from sunlight escaping through tree branches overhead. He maintained a calmness, a steadiness I couldn't deny eased my worries.

He made me feel wanted in a real and natural way, unlike the artificial world surrounding Kristoff. I'd fallen for Kristoff's charms and the dazzle of celebrity, but I was falling for Lucas for every opposite reason. His lack of charisma was charming in itself; I had to work for a smile, a laugh, but when he did, he meant it. Lucas admitted he didn't always understand things I said, but he didn't ask me to change either.

Moreso, I didn't find myself molding my life around Lucas. Kristoff may have been my access to the Sheek deal, but I'd also stopped calling my friends and spent all my time with him. I'd poured myself entirely into my image, only to have it ruined by something I couldn't control.

None of that happened with Lucas.

"I don't want to go," I told him. "But I have to."

He grazed his hand across my cheek. Into my hair. His breath ghosted across my lips. "One more day. Please. Stay through the camp games. Then we can talk."

One more day. It made sense. I wouldn't have anywhere to go for the night anyway. Marcy was several hours' drive from here. And I wouldn't ask that of her unless it was an absolute emergency.

"Okay," I found myself saying.

Our lips found each other's. I escaped into the kiss. Relaxed into his embrace. He wanted me here. He wanted me.

He pulled back first and our comforting little bubble burst. His touch came warm and unbelievably tempting, but I could tell he hesitated. A guarded look crossed his face that told me he'd gotten my message. This was all temporary. Even if I didn't leave tomorrow, eventually I would.

"Did you get my gift?" he asked, a total shift in gears.

"Huh? What gift?" My stomach did a little dance. I loved gifts. They didn't have to be expensive, just thoughtful.

"Remember I told you to check the camp office?"

"Umm..."

"The other day. I told you I had a surprise for you. I told you to check on Tuesday."

Ah, the thing I agreed to but forgot about.

He unlocked the office and I followed. A cardboard shipping box sat on the table between Twila's desk and his office.

Okay, no fancy wrapping, but it was the thought that counted.

Inside the box I uncovered...bug spray. Two slim cans. "How...thoughtful," I said carefully.

Lucas grinned from ear to ear. "Did you see the label? *Non-toxic*. No harsh chemicals will touch your skin."

That little buttery heart of mine softened a bit more.

Chapter 29

Lucas

THE SUMMER TRAIL GAMES kicked off after morning Mess. Brycen offered to bring our campers over using their camp's pontoon party boat, but I declined. Adding a water hazard to an already busy day? No. Being dependent on them to return to our camp? Hard pass.

I headed over to the Trail Blazers with the kitchen crew and Shawn, the only one from meet-up group who didn't have day job responsibilities today. So much for our increased muscle.

The remaining staff and the campers would take the camp bus the long way around the lake.

The Trail Blazers pulled out all the stops for our welcome. A balloon arch, tables with sports drinks, fresh fruit, and protein bars. Music blasted from an impressive sound system. Show-offs.

"Sure seems like they're sugar coating this whole welcome to our camp thing," Twila grumbled, suddenly beside me.

She'd been quiet this week. Which had me suspicious. It was nice to hear a catty comment so I knew she was okay.

Then I caught sight of her. Twila wore full tactical gear. Military style boots, aviator shades, cargo pants made from a synthetic lightweight material. A fitted shirt with a vest over top and an F.B.I.

patch on the front. Pockets across every surface. She unzipped one and pulled out Chapstick in a hot pink tube.

"What's with the gear?" I asked.

"Army surplus. Isn't it great?" She turned. On the back of her vest, in a cutesy cursive font, read *FBI: Figurines By Ida*.

I would probably regret this. "Who's Ida?"

"*FBI* is my Etsy shop. For selling figurines."

Further regret. "But your name's not Ida..."

"Like I'd use my real name on the *internet*." She rolled her eyes. "Come on, Lucas. That's day one stuff."

The rumble of our camp bus sounded. Campers poured out making excited noises at the sight of free food.

Hudson approached. "This is certainly interesting."

My skin reacted to her closeness. It'd been a strange few days, low on anything physical with her. I missed it. I missed her. "Yeah, they sure have a handle on snacks and PA equipment."

Her mouth quirked. "I meant *that*. Look."

I turned to where she gestured. Our campers, all teenage girls, approached the Trail Blazers, a mix of genders, all teenagers. It was like two warring factions on a battlefield, only the first strike came not from a sword, but a teen boy lifting his chin to say, "'Sup."

Giggles erupted. Hair was tossed over shoulders. Dudes cleared throats and flexed.

I stared. "This could be a disaster."

"You've made the girls *so* happy." Hudson's smile reached through her words, but her eyes held sadness.

She said one more day. We had today.

"Thankfully, not all of the campers are obsessed with crushes and dating," she went on. "We've got a few campers more excited about the games than the...merchandise."

I laughed an uneasy laugh. The starry-eyed look some of these girls had? No. Just no. Let them stay young and curious about nature and crafts a little longer.

We had our work cut out for us. In more ways than I'd expected.

Hudson whipped off her cap and shook her hair out. I did a double take. "Your hair." I pointed. "It's not pink." A soft purple-ish red colored the strands. Not bright like the pink. She of course looked incredible.

She smiled. "I asked Twila to bring me a henna box dye. Bianca's cabin suggested an impromptu makeover night. How could I pass on that?"

"Was that hard? To use some cheap product from the drug-store?"

"Aw, you're so *concerned*. No, it's fine. It's a brand I've used before. I actually do most of my color work myself." She paused. "The salon costs a lot."

This coming from someone who dated a billionaire. Maybe we weren't so far apart in our lives after all.

"Either way, you look great."

The music cut off and Brycen grabbed a microphone. He hopped over to the lodge porch. "Hello, everyone. Welcome to the Summer Trail Games!"

Counselors and campers from both sides gathered closer, chatting and making noise.

"Some of you may remember when we were all one camp," Brycen stated. The crowd noise died down. "It's been a tough summer so far, and we've felt the loss."

"What is this crap," Maggie muttered beside me. "Watch—he'll drop an insult and make a move to steal our staff. Or our campers."

I was suspicious too, but Brycen had been sincere in every interaction since we'd confronted them about the trespasser. Now he openly referred to the split as a loss. This was new.

"We want these games to be a celebration of what summer camp has to offer," Brycen announced. "Two camps. Two visions. One day of joy."

The crowd clapped, mostly the Trail Blazers. If we were going to move on from our grudge, I should model better behavior. I joined in clapping and nudged Twila beside me.

"A big thanks to Camp Junebug Director Lucas for agreeing to our day of games," Brycen searched the crowd and made eye contact. "Dude, thank you."

This was embarrassing. Maggie and Twila both muttered beside me. Was this what I sounded like to everyone else—a muttering grump?

I didn't have time to think further. Brycen bounded from the deck into the crowd. "Now, let the games begin!"

Having the campers with us eased some of the competitive tension, but these girls were down to win any chance they got.

It was neck and neck with a Trail Blazers team versus Camp Junebug for the relay race obstacle course. In the end, the Trail Blazers took the win.

The balloon toss win went to the Junebug camp staff.

After a break for snacks, we moved to Tug of War. With mixed teams of campers and staff, I could tell right away we were out muscled.

Pocket Pete slapped a hand at my shoulder. "We've got grit. I can bench one-eighty."

"Is that good?" I was never much for indoor gyms and weights.

"Yeah, man. Look at me. You call me *Pocket*."

We assumed our positions. And went to war.

"Yarrggh!" Twila called out like a battle cry.

We moved the Trail Blazers closer to the middle sand pit. Did we have a shot here? Our girls had some strength.

"One, two, three, pull!" Maggie yelled.

We tugged again. Cries of pain and struggle emitted from the other team.

Maggie yelled for a pull again. We were gaining ground, but the other team countered hard. Ground lost.

We struggled back and forth, gaining and losing inches. I put forth every bit of strength in me. All I had left. Maybe running a camp wasn't my strength, but no one could count me out when it came to throwing myself fully into this competition.

My strength drained as the rope war continued.

Hudson, in front of me, called over her shoulder. "We're losing our grip. I don't know how much longer we can last."

"We're doing this!" Maggie barked. "One, two, three, pull!"

We heaved with all our might. Was it happening? Were we winning?

Voices cried out from the other team. A sharp force yanked us forward. A Junebug camper screamed.

A whistle cut through the air. "Trail Blazers win!"

Cheers erupted from the other team. Our side collapsed. Rubbed our sore hands. The defeat hit hard.

Brycen appeared in front of me with a hand outstretched. "Good game."

It was the sportsmanlike thing to do. His team filed behind him, each repeating "good game" to our campers and staff.

My anger, the grudge against Brycen, dug its heels in. *Don't forgive. Don't give in.*

"Hey, man," Brycen said, returning to me after commending our team for a hard-fought game. "We should talk."

Alan and Alice came to mind, and how hurt they'd been when Brycen wouldn't listen to them. How Alice cried that her only son was cruel enough to involve lawyers to divide the camp. I remembered what Brycen said about his dad. His memory issues were worsening. He might not have another chance to reconcile.

That's what this was, wasn't it? An attempt to reconcile?

My phone vibrated in my pocket. Seven missed calls. A bunch of texts. "Hold on," I told Brycen.

I flipped to the messages. My buddy working security at the camp.

I think someone broke into the cabins. A door is open that was closed earlier.

I went in, it's a counselor cabin. The bedroom is tossed. Jewelry and clothes all over the floor.

My heart raced. I scanned the area for Hudson. She stood in a huddle with a group from both camps, laughing and talking.

I saw a man run into the woods. Chased but lost him. I'm calling it in.

"What?" Brycen asked, in front of me. "Talk to me."

I spoke fast. "I've got a guy watching our camp. Sounds like trouble. Somebody broke into a locked staff cabin."

The last text came in only minutes ago.

I hit the call button and started talking as soon as my buddy answered. "Which way did he run?"

"Into the woods, east side of the lake."

"East side?" I looked at Brycen as I spoke. "That's the boundary line between camps."

Brycen whistled through his teeth and gestured to a group of Trail Blazers staff. Porter jogged over. "Possible threat. Trespasser at the boundary line between camps."

I ended the call. "I can handle it."

"This affects all of us," Brycen said. "We'll catch him. Porter, take two staff and cover the woods leading to the main road. If they're armed, do not engage. Steer them away from camp. Lucas—you and me, we take the direct path by the ropes course."

"What's going on?" Bianca demanded. "Is something wrong?"

"We're handling it." I looked past her to the campers. Vulnerable campers I was responsible for. "Do a head count. Keep track of every Junebugger."

Bianca whipped around. "Operation Downvote Activate! I repeat: Activate!"

What the...

A cluster of Junebug campers removed their caps and chucked them aside. I squinted. "Is their hair...*pink?*"

"It's a temporary spray, don't worry," Bianca said. "Nobody's parents will get mad." She slipped off her own cap, revealing hot pink chunks of hair. "Mine are clip-in extensions. The spray doesn't work well over dark hair." She bounced off.

As if that explained any of this.

"Did she say Operation Downvote?" Brycen asked. "Never mind. We need to go."

We could ask questions and not get straight answers later. I bolted for the woods. In a passing glance, I searched for one particular person without pink hair. Hudson stared after us, bewildered.

Brycen moved ahead of me, moving fast on the familiar terrain. "This way," he called out as he zipped past a tree toward a shaded path.

I slowed instinctively at the same time as Brycen did to quiet our steps. No way was this guy getting away this time.

We cut through the path reaching the obstacle course first, then the thicker trees and brush beyond. We combed the woods, circled around, and back again. Nothing.

I wiped sweat from my forehead. "Where is this guy?"

"Maybe he never jumped the fence." Brycen paced in a tight circle. "He could have reached the boundary and followed the fence line up to the main road on your side."

I checked my phone again. Texted back to my camp security. *We've got nothing.*

Sorry, man. Sheriff isn't available now either.

I sighed and showed Brycen the text.

"Let's head to camp and regroup."

Back at the Trail Blazers, the camp was eerily quiet. Desolate even. "Where is everybody?"

"Probably in the lodge," Brycen answered. "Smart."

Something yellow caught my eye. Round and sailing through the air. Sailing....at *me*.

I ducked but was too late. "Ah!" The object made impact and exploded against my arm. A shower of water sprayed my face and body.

Three pink-haired heads shot up from behind the deck railing at the lodge. "Mr. Lucas? Is that you?" a girl's voice called out.

I shook off the water and grumbled something unintelligible. Heck, it was unintelligible to *me*.

"Sorry!" That came from Bianca.

"Come on out," Brycen yelled. "No more water balloons."

Campers emerged from the cover of trees and other hidden areas. A teen boy with braces approached. "In case anybody came at us this way, we were prepared."

Prepared. With water balloons. Against a guy with a who-knew-what agenda. "Whose idea was that?" I couldn't help asking.

The boy scuffed his feet. "I think her name's Bianca. But we were all in. It was all of us. Together. Filling balloons and taking position."

I shot Brycen a look. He took in a calming breath, but he looked anything but Zen. "Thanks, Eli. Go on and get your friends ready for lunch."

Hudson jogged over. "Don't get mad." She winced at her own words. "I did not condone or encourage the water balloon attack strategy. Or the pink hair. Turns out they're very protective."

"You've got some loyal campers." Brycen looked between the two of us. "Loyal staff, too. Look, once this threat clears, we should talk, Lucas. About the future of our camps."

"Sure." Agreeing got Brycen off my back for the moment. I had too much else on my mind to consider anything other than the immediate danger to Hudson and the campers. "Hudson, can I talk to you?"

She nodded and veered off to a spot out of earshot from campers and staff. I followed, dreading what I had to tell her.

She spun to face me. "I'm leaving camp. I have to."

I began to object when she raised a hand. "I saw you and Brycen tearing into the woods and knew it was bad. One of the girls overheard you say a cabin was broken into." Her lip trembled. "I'm assuming it was mine. Someone *is* looking for me, aren't they?"

"We still don't know that. We only know someone was on-site. We don't even know if it's the same person coming back for what they couldn't do the last time. We just don't know."

She bit her lip. I was desperate to pull her into my arms, to tell her everything would be okay. But I needed answers.

Hudson stepped closer. "I keep telling them the posts they found online are too disconnected, too far-fetched. But what if it's true?"

I rubbed my palms against my shorts—still wet from splash damage. "We need to go back to our camp and assess. Make a plan. We'll leave the campers here with Maggie, the counselors, and the Trail Blazers staff."

Brycen walked over. "Sorry to interrupt, but we should go to your side of the camp and check out the damage. The kids can stay here."

I sort of hated how our minds were so in sync. But maybe that was my crusty grudge talking. It sure wasn't interested in letting go. "Yeah, that's what I was thinking. Hudson will come too. Bring anyone you'd like. We can fit three in my truck—"

"Lucas." Brycen grinned, shaking his head. "I've got my boat."

# Chapter 30

Hudson

WE CUT ACROSS THE lake in Brycen's speed boat, making quick time. I practically heard the urgency of a clock ticking down. But to what? And how much time did we have?

Brycen brought along one of his staff, a buff guy who bragged about his martial arts skills and proficiency with nunchucks. Which he carried with him. My life was now a full-on action-adventure movie.

Or maybe a parody of an action movie. Because our A-Team was about to go S.W.A.T. on a children's camp.

After docking the boat, we hopped out and followed Lucas toward the heart of camp. His friend working security met us by the main fire pit.

"Sorry, man," he told us. "I wish I'd caught the guy."

"You did exactly what I hired you for." Lucas clapped a hand against the guy's back.

We arrived at my cabin. Mr. Nunchucks insisted on going in first with Lucas and Brycen right behind.

"Watch for that mud," Lucas called over to me.

I was last in and couldn't help the gasp that escaped. Cushions angled off the couch. Anything not nailed down was out of place or tipped over. I stood, frozen, taking it in.

Lucas laid a gentle hand at my shoulder. "You should take a look at the bedroom. See if you notice anything missing."

The tiny room was even more a disaster than the living room. Sheets and blankets wadded on the floor, drawers open with clothes strewn across every available surface.

A small jewelry pouch gaped open and my accessories scattered across the floor. Earrings, bracelets, necklaces twisted together.

This was a violation. This was our space, mine and Maggie's. Our small, private space to recuperate.

My hideaway.

Someone had torn through our belongings on a mission, but for what?

"Do you have valuables?" Brycen asked.

I shook my head numbly. "Unless this guy was looking for a high-end face serum. My nicer jewelry and a handbag are locked in the camp office Nothing too extravagant." I crouched and picked up a locket gifted to me by my grandmother on my sixteenth birthday. It lay tangled with a beaded bracelet. I breathed in relief. It wasn't broken. I hadn't worn it in months, but I'd never meant for it to be tossed around carelessly.

Lucas paced outside the bedroom door. "The cabin doesn't have a TV. Maggie has a laptop, but look—it's charging at the table in the kitchen."

Brycen joined Lucas in the other room. I wandered out after them.

"If this was a smash and grab, they would have taken the laptop," Brycen said. "They would have broken into the office. Was the office hit?"

Lucas' security guy bypassed Nunchucks, who practiced stealthy poses by the front door. "The office is secure. No signs of breaking or entering."

"What about the owner's cabin?" Lucas asked.

His friend shook his head. "Didn't check there, sorry. Is that past the office?"

Lucas nodded.

My throat tightened and the room grew blurry. This intruder hadn't come here to steal obvious things like electronics. They were looking for something and came all the way into camp to seek it out.

A shout sounded from outside, followed by the bang of a distant door.

Lucas stilled. "What was that?"

Nunchuck Guy sprang onto the cabin's porch, readying himself for action.

The remaining guys moved to the door, quietly.

More banging and another yelp. A man's voice.

"Somebody's out there." Nunchuck Guy here saving the day, stating the obvious. "Let's move out." He pointed first to himself, then at the others, and gestured for them to follow.

Lucas rolled his eyes and stomped past him, loudly, down the cabin's steps and onto the dirt path.

We followed in a herd as a figure stumbled out of the nearest girls' cabin.

"Stop right there," Lucas bellowed.

His growl sent shivers across my skin. He'd gone full Papa Bear and stalked toward the man in the near distance.

The man appeared to try running but tripped immediately. He scrambled up. Was he wearing...business clothes? The clothes were covered in something. White splotches.

The man doubled over, coughing.

All of which gave our A-Team time to surround him.

Lucas yanked him up by the back of his shirt.

I ran toward them, my heart begging to escape my chest. Some sort of white powder was splattered across the man's face and body. His hair too. His dark, slick hair.

I gaped at the scene in front of me. "*Kristoff?*"

Before he could respond, a body moving at an impossible speed burst from the trees. Another man. A man who tackled Kristoff to the ground. "Don't move. You are under arrest!"

Then, behind us, voices called out. Young ones. "Hudson! We did it! We saved you!"

Chapter 31

Hudson

A CIRCUS. CAMP JUNEBUG had turned into a circus.

Three rings? Four? Who could count?

Too many things happened at once. Teen girls with sprayed pink hair cascaded toward us from the camp entrance, declaring victory. An air horn blasted followed by Twila shouting, "Operation Downvote Complete!"

In front of us, Kristoff, one of the world's most recent and famous billionaires, and also my very, very ex-boyfriend, struggled beneath the weight of a man who flashed an F.B.I. badge.

The feds.

Nunchucks Guy swung his nunchucks and landed a hit on Kristoff's side. Kristoff cried out in pain. Brycen told Nunchucks to back off, and when he swung the weapon again, Brycen tackled him.

I had my own physical lockdown in the form of Lucas. His strong arms wrapped around me as he slowly steered me farther from the Kristoff chaos.

"Are you okay?" Lucas spoke in a low voice against my cheek. "You're okay?"

A chill ripped through my body despite sweat sticking my shirt to my back. My throat as dry as skin with acute dermatitis. Lucas held me.

"I'm okay." My childhood dog Bacon probably felt like this when I loved on him a little too hard.

My eyes went blurry again. Lucas was holding onto me for dear life.

"Do you know who I am?" Kristoff ground out as his face pressed against, well, the ground.

The F.B.I. guy stood, hauling Kristoff up with him. He recited the Miranda rights and got out honest-to-goodness zip ties to secure the billionaire's hands.

"I'm totally recording this," Twila announced excitedly. "How's this for viral!"

Kristoff twisted in Fed Guy's grip. "What, you're going to arrest me for walking through camp grounds?"

The sound of his voice triggered a shock wave of emotions. I couldn't believe Kristoff was here. Standing in front of me. In my camp. In my home state. And he was a *total* mess. "What are you *doing* here?" I blurted.

He flashed me a deadly look. "Finishing what others failed to do."

"You know that's going to be held against you in the court of law," Bianca helpfully stated.

"All on tape," Twila added. "We used to call it tape," she told Bianca.

Kristoff muttered to himself before focusing on me. "If you'd answered my calls, my texts, none of this would be necessary."

What texts? "I blocked your number."

"Like she'd keep your dumb butt in her phone!" Twila continued filming. "That's like breakup 1o1 for the digital age. *Delete the ex from all devices.* Huh. I should write a book."

"Can you shut her up?" Kristoff said in a near growl. His gaze darted in panic, desperate for a way out. "Let me go and my lawyers will handle this. I'm not doing anything illegal."

Our federal hero, a plain man with pale skin and regular brown hair, gripped Kristoff tighter. "Trespassing, breaking and entering—"

"It's a cabin," Kristoff exclaimed. "In the woods!"

Fed Guy wasn't having it. "It's a children's camp, and you are neither a child nor camp staff. You've got bigger problems than this. Starting with violating the order to not leave the state of California during the open investigation." He put space between himself and Kristoff while continuing to hold him. "What's this white stuff?"

"Flour!" a camper yelled. "From one of our traps!"

A deep sound of dread emitted from Lucas. He loosened his embrace but didn't let me go. "What are you girls doing here? You're supposed to be at the other camp."

Twila scoffed. "And miss this hot action?"

"You." He pointed at her. "Are complicit. You drove them here in the bus."

She lifted her chin. "Call it complicit. I call it camp spirit. Am I right, girls?"

Cheers erupted from the campers. Bianca broke from the crowd, bringing two other pink-haireds with her.

She assessed Kristoff, not wavering in confidence. "He set off our flour trap. Pocket Pete hooked us up. We greased the floor with the camp's butter flavored liquid—gross—and look, he must have tipped over the bucket of burrs we planted by the grease."

Sure enough, little round plant burrs clustered against his dress shirt and pants. Those were a beast to pick off. His shoes, expensive Italian leather, coated in mud. That mud pit by my cabin's porch...it hadn't rained all week. It was almost as if the pit had been artificially created.

By protective campers.

"I told you girls not to involve yourselves." What if Kristoff had stumbled upon the girls mid-trap planning? What if he kidnapped someone and used them for leverage?

The horror was too much. I was responsible for this.

"The pink hair was a decoy maneuver," Bianca continued, unfazed. "In case Krom's bros were looking for your pink hair, they'd get confused because *twelve* of us have pink hair."

My mouth hung open. I figured they'd wanted to copy my look because it was cute. "And that's why you said we should do salon night last night. You tricked me into coloring my hair a new shade so you could set up the decoy."

Bianca shrugged. She looked so proud of herself.

Too many thoughts crowded my mind. I still didn't know what Kristoff was after.

I faced him, faced this, us, and whatever this mess was really about. "Look, I don't have anything of yours. If you're looking for something, I don't know what it is."

Kristoff's eyes flashed. He arranged his face to a neutral, disaffected expression, which I now understood signaled he was lying. "I won't speak of it here. But you know what you have. And you'll pay if you use it."

Lucas broke free and moved within an inch of Kristoff, standing nose to nose. "Talk to her like that again, and I'll put you back in that dirt. Where you belong."

Kristoff blinked and attempted a smirk to cover his panic. "So, you found a new boy toy, Hudson, huh? A real mountain man."

I marched over and hooked my arm through Lucas'. "He's *my* mountain man. And he's more man than you'll ever be."

"Yeah!" the girls cheered. Twila angled for a better view for her video. She *tsk*ed at Kristoff. "My girl Bianca tried to warn you, Krom. What you say is gonna be held against you. You and that nasty suit."

Kristoff's faux cool exterior cracked. One thing he couldn't stand was to be made fun of. Once while hanging out at his mansion, he spent two solid hours combing gossip sites for snipes against him, then sent directives to his staff to file libel cases against every blog and tabloid.

Again, the red flags. So plentiful.

"Alright, stand back," the agent told us. "My back-up support is headed into camp now. We'll take care of this guy."

"I need to know what this is all about," I told Kristoff. "Whatever you believe I have, I don't. I swear. We need to put an end to this. Now."

He flashed a look at the new group arriving toward us on the path—the local sheriff and a couple of deputies. A woman in a suit and a buff guy who looked like a cousin to Vin Diesel. Definitely more A-Team.

Kristoff glared at me. "The key. You have it."

Key...I for sure did not have a key. He'd never given me one. Not to his house or a car or a safe. Nothing. I shook my head. "I don't."

"On the chain." He gave me a pointed look.

Frantically, I called up my memories like a search engine. Input: *Key. Chain.* A key chain? Nothing.

He patted his chest. Bare. He usually wore a long silver chain with a slim silver pendant. It looked like the long skinny Tetris block. I'd even said as much to him once and felt like an idiot for doing it.

"Your necklace? Was that a key? Why would I have it?" Still confused.

The new group closed in, directing the campers to move back.

"You have the spare," he said as the new bodies filled in around us. "I put it in your jewelry bag. I didn't think I'd need it. Until I did."

My jewelry bag...I'd left it open once on the bathroom counter at his house. When I'd packed to come here, I'd tossed more jewelry and accessories into the bag. I didn't take anything out.

The locker in the office. Where'd I'd stashed my extra things. It had to be there.

Twila sauntered forward. "You mean...this." She pulled out the exact silver chain and pendant from beneath her shirt and vest, swinging the pendant back and forth like a pendulum.

"Twila!" I gasped.

"That's *mine*." Kristoff lunged at her.

No fewer than six adults intervened, including Lucas, Nunchucks Guy, and all the new law enforcement.

"Sounds to me like you *gave* it to Hudson," Twila spoke over the commotion. She looked over her shoulder at Bianca who now had Twila's phone, recording. She turned to me. "I was borrowing it, honey. It's such an interesting piece with these little numbers etched into the silver. It was sitting so lonely in that locker..."

"The bitcoin account password," Vera the camper announced in a daze. "That's what the guys online were saying. The account password is the key. The key is the pendant, and it's right there on that necklace!"

I pressed a hand to my throbbing forehead. Had these girls been doing *anything* else besides investigating Kristoff? "Your parents are going to murder us."

No, they'd throw this on Lucas. They'd freak when news of Krom's arrest went public. They'd demand Lucas step down—he'd have to. Lucas would lose out on the very thing he'd been working so hard toward.

No job reference. No dream job.

I should have left camp by now. No, I shouldn't have ever come here at all.

"I'm afraid we'll need that." The agent held his hand out to Twila but looked at me. "Assuming you'll cooperate?"

I was too stuck on pink hair and mud pits and ruining Lucas' career to fully grasp a cryptocurrency account password engraved on a necklace and the fact I'd carried this duplicate in my possession for weeks.

I nodded. "Just take it. Take him." I was done here. Done with Kristoff and done with this camp. Done with whatever additional drama unfolded from either.

But I'd do whatever I had to in order to spare Lucas.

"Nice vest," the federal agent said in a dry tone to Twila, noting the F.B.I. patch. "Don't get any big ideas about sharing that video. This is an open case."

"Oops." That came from Bianca.

A cloud of smoke billowed around Lucas—his mood was that strong. "This is why we don't have cell phones at camp."

"Can someone call that girl's parents?" the agent said. "And confiscate the phone."

Chapter 32

Lucas

LAW ENFORCEMENT CLEARED OUT after thoroughly searching the grounds for further threats. Finding none, the rest of the campers were able to return.

Even so, I decided, with Brycen and Maggie's input, to move everyone to the Trail Blazers camp for the night. The big lodge had space for the kids. More secure with more staff. Strength in numbers.

What mattered was the kids were safe. Hudson was safe.

Hudson. After Krom was taken away, she took off to her cabin. Maggie went after her. I would have, I wanted to, but I had a full afternoon ahead of notifying parents.

No, that was a lie. I wasn't sure she wanted me around. If I followed her and she pushed me away, I wasn't sure I could handle it.

So back to the camp office I went to face my worst duty yet.

Twila—who miraculously remained employed, only because I needed her—tackled calling parents with me to update them on the day's *festivities*.

Damage control, pure and simple. I used the suggested language from the federal agent, but I was honest in my answers to their questions. They deserved to know what happened, even if I couldn't share every detail.

Two parents were on their way to pick up their girls. The rest, after hearing their kids were safe and had been off-site during the incident, grilled me for details as if this was a true crime podcast.

The video Bianca posted from Twila's phone had been taken down before it had the chance to spread. Sounded like it never fully uploaded anyway, likely due to the bad connection out here at camp.

Once again, proving my point that not everyone needed to be online all the time. Little good it did.

Ready to shut down for the day—and forever—I clicked on my open email at the same time a new message blinked into existence.

The Colorado job.

My breath stalled as I tapped open the message.

Lucas Russo:

We've reviewed your resume and qualifications and would love to set up a video interview. We're eager to fill the vacancy and have availability this week. Let us know which times work for you.

I pumped a fist in the air. *Yes.* They wanted me. Maybe. Key thing was they'd responded. After reviewing my limited camp experience and short stint as a director, they were *interested.*

All the fear I'd built up about not being qualified, and I already had an interview request.

My eyes fell shut. I envisioned a skyline of the Rocky Mountains. Me, right there and living the dream.

One person above all came to mind who I wanted to tell first.

Dusk settled in. With Twila on her way home, I closed up shop at the office and headed out.

I stopped short after exiting my office. Hudson appeared in the office doorway. She set down a bag and purse. Her rolling suitcase wobbled unsteadily beside her.

A sense of dread hit. "You're leaving."

She tugged at her hair. "Yeah."

Please stay.

But the words wouldn't come. She'd said she give one more day and she had. And it had been a disaster.

I approached her carefully. "It's not your fault."

"It's *absolutely* my fault." She had on the drapey robe again, the thing she'd worn her first day. She wore it over a plain shirt and shorts. A sort of half in, half out of camp look. "I heard Maggie's friend at the Trail Blazers is coming back to replace me."

As if she could be replaced. By anybody. "Maggie did some reconciling of her own. We all met—Maggie, Brycen, and me, to make some tentative plans for the two camps."

She remained in the doorway. *Go to her. Hold her. Protect her.*

But I sensed she didn't want that from me.

I scuffed my boot against the floor. "I've got a plan...with Brycen. It feels weird saying that. He apologized for, well, a lot of things. The split, and how he didn't listen to us when we stressed the importance of our camp's values. The Trail Blazers had a big cancellation with one of their groups coming in. Some of his plans went sideways, and a few counselors quit. Things aren't as perfect as they'd seemed."

None of this really mattered right now, but I found myself filling the silence anyway. "We talked about merging resources. There's a lot to figure out. For now, I'm here."

"You're not fired." She said it like a statement, as if not quite believing it.

"No." I'd handled the trespassing the best I knew how and the parents confirmed that. "Only two families pulled their kids. And they weren't mad so much as shaken up."

She let out a big sigh. "That's good news. I thought I cost you your job. I've been sort of hiding out until the last minute. Until I had to go."

Hiding from me. And us.

And now she was leaving.

"My days here are numbered," I said. "It just depends how things shake out."

She flinched.

I hit a nerve. "I'm not blaming you. I was never cut out for this job. You helped me see I could reach for bigger things. That I hadn't even been trying to go for what I said I wanted. So, I went for it. I applied for the job in Colorado."

Her face brightened. "Yeah?"

"While I was on the phone with a parent asking me to describe whether, and I quote, *the cops were hot*, an email came in about my job application. They want an interview."

"That's amazing, Lucas." When she smiled, my chest strained. She wrapped her arms around herself in that way she did to hold herself together.

"It's a video interview. If they like me, I fly out to check out the program in person."

She nodded, staring past me before connecting her attention again. "Really, Lucas. It's great. I'm proud of you. It takes guts to put yourself out there."

Out there being nowhere near Hudson. Whether she returned to Los Angeles or came back to Michigan, I'd be thousands of miles from her either way. Maybe she'd go off traveling and we'd be even farther apart.

But this job was my dream. I had to give it a shot.

And that was why I couldn't ask her to stay. She wouldn't ask me to give up my dream, and I couldn't ask her to stay at this camp any longer than she had to. With the Krom threat contained, she had no reason to be here.

Not even for me.

She moved into my space, filling my senses with her pretty, pleasant presence. That soft scent she had. Her gentle curves.

She kissed me on the cheek. "Thank you for everything. I wish I could repay you. I don't even know how."

"Your last paycheck—where should I send it?"

I cursed at myself for asking such a practical question when my heart screamed to beg her to give us a fighting chance.

"Marcy's address works." She offered a shy smile. "I think she's here now. Um, I'm gonna go."

Don't go.

But she had to. I had to. We both were meant to go separate directions.

Watching her walk out of camp might have been the toughest thing I'd ever done. But as hard as my heart took it, I sure wasn't going to be the one to hold her back.

Chapter 33

Hudson

"I THEREFORE BRING THIS inaugural meeting of the Midwest Mavens to order. All in agreement?"

"Aye!" Marcy responded to Jillian on her laptop's screen.

"Is this formality necessary?" Noah asked from another window on the video call. "Seems overkill."

"Hudson wanted structure," Jillian said. "I've been on a lot of committees and this is how meetings in a professional sphere work. Noah, would you like to take minutes?"

"No. This is my free time, not my job."

Jillian huffed out a breath. "This is *important* to *Hudson*."

Beside me, Marcy jabbed me lightly in our shared space on her couch. "Hudson, how about you go first since you have the most to catch us up on."

I nodded. "Sure. Right."

It had only been a mere twenty-four hours since I'd left Camp Junebug and...everything behind. I'd slept a good chunk of the following day in Marcy's guest room on her shockingly comfortable futon. Who ever knew such a combo existed.

I hadn't done much beyond letting Marcy feed me baked treats and honey and ginger tea, but I'd checked in with Kelly Q. Pierce and Agent Mulder this afternoon. With Kristoff violating his order to not leave the state, plus the breaking and entering at a children's camp and the discovery of the hidden crypto account now under investigation, the attorney and agent sorted out how I fit into those details. By Kristoff's own admission, caught on video, he'd stashed the crypto account key in my belongings without my awareness or consent.

Not that Kristoff's most dedicated followers would care about that. My name may have been cleared in the fraud case, but my brand and reputation suffered major damage.

And despite all that, it didn't feel right to just give up Beauty Butterfly. To let the trolls win. But I knew I needed a change. I just wasn't sure yet what that meant.

"First," I began to my Mavens. "I need to head back to L.A. and pack my stuff. Look for a subleaser for my apartment. Then..." What? Go where?

"My apartment is open for as long as you need," Marcy said for the sake of the group.

She'd told me as much, but I'd been too frazzled from the previous days' events to think through it further. "I called my parents and they want to see me before I go to California. My mom said I could stay with them. I'm sure she has a helpful friend with a new idea for a boring job I can settle into. Maybe that's not such a bad idea. I could use some stability right now."

"Yeah, but you don't need to settle yet," Noah said. "This is the perfect opportunity to focus on what you want to do. You don't have a job right now, so you aren't required to give two weeks' notice or disappoint anyone by leaving a job you took out of obligation or desperation. Start with your skills and put together a resume. I'll help you. Look for opportunities matching your skill set. Go from there."

All sound advice. I had more than one offer of a place to stay that provided time to sort out details. Even if I cringed at the idea of moving in with my parents, I wasn't out here on my own. They cared about me, even if they didn't fully understand me.

Part of this idea with the Mavens was to establish tangible plans. I needed tangible. "I liked the marketing work I did for the camp. It felt meaningful. I used my social media knowledge but focused it on a worthwhile cause. I wouldn't mind a marketing position for a non-profit." It was a starting point at least. "You know, I hope the back-to-nature spirit at Camp Junebug remains. It would be a shame if the Trail Blazers swallowed them whole and they lost the organic aspect. If it meant so much to me, imagine how impactful it is for the campers. Even if Lucas leaves for Colorado, he cared enough about the camp to keep that small, simple camp experience going."

My friends did not fill the silence. Not even Marcy who always had something to say.

"How did you leave things with Lucas?" Jillian finally asked.

"Amicably," I stated. "I mean, if we're honest, we both knew whatever was between us was temporary. We were never going to be anything more."

A humming sound of doubt came from Marcy. On the screen, Noah scrunched her nose and Jillian made an unidentifiable face.

"What?" I asked. "Come on. He hates being online, loves the woods and silence, and I..." I almost said I was the opposite, but that didn't feel right. I'd enjoyed my time off-grid in ways I hadn't expected. The boat rides, the hikes, becoming a yarn craft master.

And Lucas. His protective sense felt natural, not manufactured. Not like he was supposed to protect me as a man, but because he valued me, and he wanted the best for those he valued. I saw it in his daily actions with the camp. As much as he grumbled over the job, he'd sacrificed his own dreams and goals to help others.

And he'd listened to me. He'd *seen* me.

Not many people beyond those on this video call had seen into my real self. Because I hadn't let them. I'd let my online brand speak for me, ever the social butterfly, flitting around those who had connections and pivoting to gain access to what I wanted.

I shook sense into myself. "Lucas has a dream to lead outdoor expeditions for that company in Colorado. It sounds incredible. He has a video interview. I wish him the best."

Marcy snorted. "He's never even been to Colorado."

I must have heard her wrong. "What are you talking about? It's his entire career goal."

"I know for a fact he's never been there. He believes it's some kind of utopia for outdoor adventuring. He's never lived more than a few hours from where he grew up. He visits his mother every month. I don't buy that he's going to take off and live some place he's never even visited."

"Nope, me neither," said Noah. "We witnessed you two together. Look, I'll say it because Marcy can't. Lucas is a babe. And he completely and totally fell for you. I don't know how you walk away from that."

How could I walk away? Because I had to. He might never have taken the chance on his dream if I stuck around, keeping his world small and safe. Whether he'd been to Colorado or not, he'd hung his hopes there.

He'd done the same. He'd let me go. We were on different paths in life and he knew it same as I did. No way would I ever be capable of surviving in the woods without my creature comforts, nor did I want to, and he detested just about everything I liked doing. What a disaster.

"I see Hudson's struggle," Jillian said since I hadn't spoken. "She needs to figure out what she needs and wants and not mold her life around a guy. No matter how great that guy is."

The three of them volleyed opinions back and forth. My mind wandered to Lucas and how short he'd sold himself. I'd meant it when I said I was proud of him for going for his dream. Especially now knowing he'd never uprooted to such extremes.

We'd done the right thing. The right, sad, lonely thing.

Noah was on to something. I wouldn't be satisfied if I took a random receptionist job and lived with my parents. I needed to think bigger. To reach higher and actually take action.

Later that night, alone in Marcy's spare room, I logged into my Beauty Butterfly Instagram account. So much of myself had gone into my posts. Before my account became my brand, before I'd met celebrities and influencers, it was just me and a camera posting what I wanted. Silly videos on YouTube when I had barely ten subscribers. I had fun with it. I posted because I liked connecting with people. That's what I wanted to get back to.

Nuking the account felt too extreme. I'd regret it later. But something had to change if I started posting again. I couldn't go back to business as usual. Nothing about my life fit *usual*.

I spent some time scrolling, eventually going down a rabbit hole reading about actual butterflies. Most butterflies only lived days to months in their adult form. Hardly any time at all. But still, they left their mark on the world. A beautiful mark.

After a bit more searching, I found a lovely butterfly photo on a site featuring free image distribution.

I posted the single image with a caption reading:

Thank you, but not goodbye.

I'd be back, changed, and then I'd spread my wings.

The butterfly image I'd chosen was an Atala, a naturally poisonous butterfly. Because beauty didn't have to mean fragile, and I when I came back, whatever the form, I'd be stronger than ever.

Chapter 34

Lucas

I CLICKED THE INTERNET browser window closed on the camp office computer. Whew. That was done with.

My office door opened and Twila walked in. "How'd the interview go, Boss?"

"How did you know?" I hadn't told her a thing.

She shot back a self-satisfied smile. "Give me credit. You can't keep secrets from me."

I folded my arms, refusing to let her dig under my skin. "I won't leave the camp high and dry. I have a plan."

"Oh, I'm sure you do. So how did it go?"

I sat forward. "Hard to say. I'm not great at interviews." Especially on video. Something about it made me choke up. "They said my experience lines up. That they'd be in touch soon. They're in a crunch after losing two staff—one to injury, the other to a family issue where somebody needed to relocate. If this goes well, it could move quickly."

Twila grinned. "I'm just *tickled* to see you excited. Kind of like when Hudson was here and you'd get that gleam in your eye."

I stared at her. Didn't she know discussing Hudson was off-limits?

Twila hummed to herself. "She was a delight. I miss the girl and it's only been a few days. And wow, that adventure with the feds! My book club set an emergency meeting to get the details."

The front office door opened and Maggie walked in, right on time. "Come on in."

Twila shifted aside to let Maggie into my office. "I'll leave this door open a crack."

I grunted. "Close it."

The door closed.

Maggie sat. "Hey, Lucas. How are you doing?"

How to sum that up? How about I didn't. "I wanted to be first to tell you I'm looking elsewhere for employment. It's not a done deal, but if it works out, I could be leaving very soon."

"Yeah, I knew that from Twila."

My fists clenched involuntarily. "Okay. Well, I don't think she knows this. I choose you for the camp director job. I trust you completely to run Camp Junebug."

"Oh." She straightened and smoothed her wild ponytail. "That's flattering. Truly."

Maggie always had been modest. "You deserve it."

"Thank you. I appreciate that. But I can't accept."

It took a second to realize what she'd said. "What? Why?"

"Because I love my job. I like being front and center with the kids. I like wrangling the teen counselors even if I complain about them. Now my bestie is here again working with me. Things are good."

I hadn't foreseen this. Her rejection of the director role added a huge crack to my concrete plan. "But you'd be great at it. The job pays more money. You can do anything you want with the camp."

She appeared thoughtful. "I appreciate your faith in me. I don't doubt I could run this camp. But I don't want to."

I stood and paced behind my desk. "Then who will? I can't leave if no one takes the job."

She smirked. "Ah, so handing off the director job is convenient for *you*. I get it."

"No, that's not—" Yeah, she nailed it. "I mean it when I say you could run this camp. I guess I assumed you'd want to."

I could hand her the keys and start over with my new job in Colorado. Never look back. Never have to see reminders in every corner of this camp that glowed a faint pink.

"I could have offered to take over during the split," Maggie said. "I knew you dreaded the director job. But you were committed to the vision and I knew I could support you. If you want to leave, I'll support your decision. You'll have to post the job listing yourself. Or talk to Brycen."

I leaned against a dusty bookcase. "I already talked to Brycen. We're sharing some camp staff for coverage. You know that."

"I mean talk long term. He regrets the split. I heard him say as much. To you. When we all met the other day."

Yeah, so he did. "I can't hand the camp over to Brycen. Not after everything."

She toyed with a woven friendship bracelet on her wrist. "Are you protecting the camp or is this some other quest you have to punish Brycen?"

I started to object but fell quiet. Dang it. Why couldn't she take the director job and I'd be on my way? Possibly on my way. "When Alan and Alice told me they trusted me with the camp, I took that to heart. They trusted me over their own son. How could I say no?"

"I just told you no."

"Yeah, but this is different."

She looked at me. I looked at her.

"Talk to Brycen." Maggie stood. "Hear him out. Maybe you can both get what you want."

Brycen met me at an agreed upon spot. A place away from our day-to-day existence that would put both of us at ease. A hiking trail about ten miles outside of camp.

After a few minutes walking a shady uphill path, Brycen slowed his pace. "That Kristoff Krom arrest sure was wild. I can't believe he turned up at the camp. And I can't believe I ever looked up to him. The man is unhinged."

I had a lot of opinions on Krom. None of them kind. "No argument there."

"You handled the disruption well. Credit to you. You're doing great running the camp."

I waved him off. "No. I'm terrible."

"What? No, you're not. Stop being modest." He walked several paces before speaking again. "I thought I had this camp thing all figured out. But the parents are so demanding. The schools we're working with for the sports camp keep listing more requirements. We've spent so much money getting facilities up to code—" He stopped. "What I meant to get at it is you're making the camp work in a way I couldn't grasp while I worked under my parents' thumb."

"We're not doing anything different."

"Whoever you hired for your online media is doing a fantastic job. The branding, the stories on Instagram. It got me nostalgic for my old camp days."

"Hudson," I said. "You're right. She's done tremendous work." She'd claimed she wasn't a web designer, but she'd spiffed up the website too.

"Definitely hang onto her."

Failed on that front. I'd sure managed to bungle a great partnership. If I'd been smart, I would have offered Hudson to stay on managing the social media as a freelancer. But I couldn't. She needed to move on without strings attached. Me, I was *strings*.

The conversation lulled, giving me an opening to tell Brycen what I needed. Still, I hesitated. If I told him I wanted to leave, he could seize back the camp for himself.

And...what? What was I so afraid of?

"I think...I was jealous," I admitted. "You had this incredible job, a legacy, with the camp. I quit my construction job to work for the camp because I was inspired by your drive toward success. I wanted that for myself. I figured it would happen once I wanted it enough."

We stepped aside to let other hikers pass. "But when that legacy wasn't enough for you," I continued, "I didn't understand. I couldn't make sense of your vision. You were reaching higher, building on the camp's values, but I didn't see it that way at the time. I saw higher cost and fancier facilities. A shift to sports training over outdoor exploration. When your folks told me they wanted me to preserve the camp the old-fashioned way, I took their side. I completely dismissed yours."

"I was arrogant. I should have listened more."

"If I'm being honest, I should have heard you out too. Your ideas were good. Ambitious, but good. I don't know if Camp Junebug would have survived much longer without some kind of kick in the pants."

We walked with only the sounds of leaves rustling and distant voices from other hikers. "I don't want to wreck that vision," Brycen said. "This summer has shown me what works and what doesn't. Seeing my dad's health decline, the simple values stand out more clearly. I went to see my parents after we met the other night. I apologized. I told them I wanted to combine the camps again and offer two varied experiences. The rustic camp and the more sports-focused camp. Even with Dad's struggles, he seemed to understand what I was asking."

"That's great. I'm glad to hear it."

"I'd love for you to lead both."

I stared at him. "You want me to run *both* camps?"

"You'd be great at it."

A slow chuckle fell from my mouth. Then another. I outright laughed.

"What? I'm serious."

I took my hat off, shook it out, and put it back on. "I hate being a camp director."

"You do? But you're good."

"I offered Maggie the Camp Junebug director job for the same reason. She'd be incredible. She turned me down."

"Huh. Do you think *she'd* want to run both camps?"

Now we both laughed.

"I swear, I'm not trying to dump this on you," Brycen said. "I thought maybe you were bitter about losing out on running both camps when we split."

"I was bitter because this—" I pointed between us. "Broke. We used to be friends. Then we became enemies."

Brycen looked at the sky. "Yeah. That's on me and my big vision. It didn't leave room for much else. Again, I'm sorry."

I believed him. He'd been apologizing since the trespassing incident. Time to ditch this grudge. Forgive and move on. "Thanks. I'm sorry too, for taking your folks' side without looking at the bigger picture. And for what it's worth, you're doing a good job as director. So what if you've had a few setbacks. Staff will always turn over. Campers will cancel. Stuff will break and need fixing. That's expected. You're running a good camp."

We reached the summit of our small hill. Nowhere near a height like the Rocky Mountains, but a nice view overlooking trees, the park, and a glimpse of a nearby neighborhood.

"I'm planning to leave," I told him. "That Colorado expedition company has an opening. I already had a video interview."

Brycen grinned. "Wow, man. That's great. That's what you wanted all along, isn't it? You only agreed to work at our little camp to get where you wanted in the long run. I forgot about that."

"I don't have the job yet. If they're serious about me, I fly out to Colorado for the next step."

"If I can be of any help, a recommendation letter, anything, I will. I owe you that. And you deserve it."

"Thanks, man."

He stretched his arms wide, taking in the fresh air and view. "I have nothing but confidence in you."

Good thing. Because as within reach as my dreams had become, my confidence felt as unsteady as ever.

I posted the camp director job. Regardless of whether I got the Colorado gig, someone else needed to run Camp Junebug. My first big decision since refusing to run after Hudson.

The usual comforting silence of my apartment rang loud and intrusive.

Something was missing.

Yeah, the wind in my hair, a fishing pole in my hand. Living off the land. If the new job fell into place, I'd get exactly what I wanted.

In the meantime, I felt restless. I picked up my phone and found myself going to YouTube, to the last video I'd viewed.

Hudson's smile flashed at me. Her hair the old pink in this one. I watched her, mesmerized by her ease in front of the camera. If only she'd been around to give me some pointers for my interview.

If only she was here, in my arms, so I could hold her.

I watched seven full videos. I now knew about face contouring with different shades of makeup and skin care cycling. I had no idea what I'd do with that information, but I had it.

I didn't have Hudson.

That night I couldn't sleep. I tried imagining myself in the Rockies leading adults on challenging quests. Adults who didn't request constant potty breaks. Only every time, my thoughts derailed to noisy little girls and a certain fashion-minded lady with lotions and spritzes to aid every type of ouchie.

Memories surfaced of diving into the lake after her. Of her soft skin pressed against mine. Of watching her sit in contemplative silence. She may not have been into the idea of survivalist trips but she loved nature in her own way.

It was useless. I'd never get over her.

The next morning, I got the call. They wanted me to come out for a second interview.

Colorado. The dream. Everything was coming together.

I waited to feel excitement. Instead, panic set in.

I needed to do...everything. Book a flight. Hotel. Rental car?

If I got the job, then what? Where would I live? What about my stuff? How would I get it there?

I grabbed my laptop. "Cool it, dude. Just book the flight."

After searching three travel sites for hotel and flight options, I couldn't decide on anything, so I opened a new tab and pulled up a map of the surrounding towns by the expedition HQ. Took a peek at rental listings. Yikes. Expensive. I returned to the flights. Also, expensive.

That's fear talking.

I didn't know a soul in Colorado. I'd be starting from scratch. Completely.

My cousins and friends, all thousands of miles away.

Make new friends.

But Hudson...

I clicked out of the browser. My thoughts ran sideways. So I did what I usually did when I had a problem I couldn't reason out. I called Marcy.

Chapter 35

Hudson

I SPENT MY FIRST week back in California thoroughly cleaning my apartment and working on my plan.

Subleasing options: in motion

Resume: updated and approved (by Noah, Jillian, *and* Marcy)

Jobs: searched and bookmarked

Relationship status: single and not-at-all ready to mingle

I intended to return to Michigan to stay with Marcy. I gave myself a deadline for job hunting. If none of the options that interested me panned out by the date I set, I'd take a less exciting offer for a steady paycheck.

Those jobs may or may not end up being in Michigan. The world was open to me. I could go anywhere. I knew I didn't want to stay in Los Angeles, so I had that figured out at least.

My plan progressed quickly. I found a subleaser for my apartment. With several options to choose from, I picked the person who needed a place soonest. They even accepted my offer to buy my couch and bed, as neither would fit in my car. My other odds and ends furniture I scheduled for a pick-up from a charity outlet who would donate the furniture to recently relocated refugees.

I checked their website for open positions to flex my job-hunting muscles. No dice.

Since I needed my car, I planned to drive it across the country to Michigan. Now with a set move date, I let Marcy know she could book her flight to L.A. She came up with the brilliant idea to fly out one way and drive back with me. She'd take up valuable space in the car but her company? Priceless.

While I hadn't decided the true fate of my Beauty Butterfly accounts, I'd been cleared to post so long as I continued to avoid mentioning anything related to Kristoff or the ongoing case. I'd been provided a new sample statement, which I ignored. Okay, I read it. I wouldn't post it.

I'd been away long enough that returning to my usual scrolling habits felt strange. Online life had continued without me while I'd played camp counselor in the backwoods. I scrolled mindlessly, still unsure of what I'd post as my comeback. Whatever my comeback looked like.

Bored with Instagram, I switched over to my camera roll. Only three pictures existed of my time with Lucas where he appeared in the frame. Two taken during the weekend with the Mavens and Marcy's brothers, and the selfie of us by the wildflower field.

That one was my favorite.

Lucas smiled in every photo. He didn't look miserable or grumpy. I'd glimpsed first-hand his ease with his cousins and friends. A snapshot of Lucas without the pressure of running the camp.

Marcy promised she'd tell me if he got the Colorado job. I could call him myself—I had his number, which I hadn't brought myself to delete. Not calling felt like a boundary that needed to remain in place. At least for now.

A mere few days later, I crammed my remaining belongings into my car. I handed over the keys to my subleaser, and closed the door on another chapter of my life.

Weirdly, I was headed to the airport. I'd fetch Marcy and we'd start our next chapter, a two-thousand-mile trek across the country. Coincidentally, with a direct path through Colorado.

If the stars aligned, well, I was open to just about anything.

I texted Marcy after I parked at LAX.

Me: *Let me know when you land. I'm in short-term parking.*

A few minutes later she responded.

Marcy: *Okay! Head to Delta. You can't leave a girl to wander the parking lot for you. I'll meet you outside.*

I noted the location and made my way to the arrivals by her airline.

The day was a scorcher. Welcome to L.A. in the summer. I already missed Michigan. Including the gross humidity, which I'd adjusted my skincare routine to accommodate.

People swarmed past, the faces a blur. No sign of Marcy. Maybe I was in the wrong spot.

I turned and ran headlong into a body.

"Uf! I'm sorry I—" My words vanished. I couldn't believe my eyes.

"Hudson."

"Lucas." His name came as a disbelieving whisper. "What...how..."

"Change of plans." He shouldered a backpack. "I packed light. I promise."

This didn't make sense. "You're here."

"I couldn't stand being anywhere else. Without you."

A heady sensation hit all at once. "But I'm leaving."

"I know. I want to go where you go. I hear it's back to Michigan, at least for now."

I could hardly believe Lucas stood here in front of me. Seeing him outside of his woodland element in full California sun must have been like seeing me land in camp in my resort wear.

My thoughts raced. "But...Colorado. What happened? With the job?" Oh, right. It must have been bad news if he was here.

"I told them I wasn't ready," he said.

"Lucas—"

"Hear me out. When I looked at booking my tickets for the in-person interview, it struck me how much my life would change. New job, new friends, new state, new expenses. But it wasn't those things that scared me. It was the thought of never seeing you again. Of making a commitment I couldn't easily reverse when I wasn't sure I even wanted it anymore."

How could he not want the job? "I don't understand."

"I didn't take the job because I didn't want to move my entire life for an unknown. Not without exploring first. Did you know I've never even been to Colorado?"

"I heard something about that. From Marcy. It was Marcy who told me."

He shook his head, laughing. "Even if I went for a day ahead of the interview, it wasn't enough time to consider everything I've got in my head. They were understanding, by the way. In fact, they said to keep them top of mind if my plans changed. So there's always another chance."

He reached for my hands. His grasp came cool and firm. "I'm changed because of you, Hudson. I had a plan, but I was scared to act on it. Now I'm not afraid of the future. I want you in it, whatever that looks like. Even if it's not Colorado. Even if it's not Michigan. I'll go anywhere. Getting a chance at that job showed me I have options."

I clenched his hands, my emotions a mess. No, not a mess. A *joy* of confusion.

"All of that to say, a dream job doesn't matter if I can't see you again," he said. "That's why I'm here. I want to go on a journey with you, Hudson, wherever that may lead."

He'd detoured his dream for me. No, he named me as *part* of the dream. How was it possible? "I left so you could pursue your passions without any strings."

He slid a finger beneath the thin spaghetti strap at my shoulder. "Turns out, I like your strings."

Lucas—bringing the flirt! I couldn't help grinning at the attention. "I don't want you abandoning your longtime goal for me. I can't survive in the woods, Lucas. I can't even pilot a canoe."

"Canoes don't need pilots and you don't need to survive in the woods. I promise, if we ever do an overnight hike, we'll book a yurt."

"A yurt?"

"It's like a tent with more structure, insulated, and in a cute round shape."

"Ooh, that sounds intriguing." A car honked nearby and I blinked to reality. "Hold up. Marcy...so she's not coming. You two *conspired* against me!"

"Conspired *for you*. By now, you should know she's crafty."

And not the kind of crafty with yarn. "So, how does this work? You're riding with me? Across two thousand miles?"

He hesitated. "If you'll have me."

I was speechless.

"It's a big ask, I know," he went on. "No pressure with me standing here having flown on a one-way ticket." He winced through a nervous laugh. "Plan B is I can book a flight home. Marcy's on stand-by to fly out if you want to stick to your original plan. Or you fly back and I drive your car to Michigan. We have options."

"No," I said quickly and with confidence. I reached for his chest, to his well-worn T-shirt. "Stay."

His steady gaze never left mine. "But you're leaving."

A welcome flush went through me. "Want to come?"

He pulled me the rest of the way to him, grazing his hands along my shoulders. I slid a hand into his hair and joined my lips to his.

His kiss was familiar and new at once. Exciting and filled with possibility.

I pulled back. "We haven't known each other long."

"Crazy how it feels like longer." He brushed a strand of hair from my face and all noise around us dulled. "I can't promise I know what the future holds, but I know I want to experience it with you."

I reached for him again. He kissed me with a fierceness, as if he poured his intentions and hopes into each breath against my lips.

This was wild. This idea of us venturing across the country together. Wild and exhilarating. I felt the most excited I'd been maybe ever.

This excitement was no mere hit of dopamine. I didn't care about posting an update to prove my worth. This energy came from hope. From possibility. This next chapter offered plenty of adventure with an open road to make my mark on the world.

And my mountain man would be right beside me.

Epilogue

Hudson

Six Weeks Later

"So you spent your first date on a cross country road trip?" The older woman's eyes bugged out, looking between me and Lucas.

"Our first official date," I corrected. Technically, the road trip itself served as one big mega date. Talk about total immersion. "We'd known each other for a few weeks by then. We lived at the same camp together."

The woman scrunched her nose in confusion. "Like at a camp-ground?"

"A children's camp," I said. "He was my boss."

I could tell what she was thinking. Who in their right mind invited their grumpy former boss on a trip with the only directive to head east and not hurry?

"It's *very* romantic." Marcy swooped in carrying a tray of blissful distraction. "Here. Have a watermelon popsicle." She handed the woman—her mom's former coworker—a red frozen treat. Marcy glanced at me. I shot back a look. She returned her attention to the elder party guest. "Hey, Helen. Let me introduce you to our neighbor. She just came back from Vegas and has the best stories."

Marcy escorted Helen across her parents' backyard where multiple generations of the Russo family and their friends gathered to talk, eat, and celebrate the end of summer.

A deep voice spoke low in my ear. "Does Helen think we don't have good stories? We went to Vegas."

I twined my fingers through Lucas' big, warm hand. "We *drove* through Vegas. We only stopped for selfies at the Welcome to Las Vegas sign. And of course, the ramen."

"Best bowl of ramen I've ever had." He landed a gentle kiss at my forehead as if to seal the memories running through our minds.

We'd discovered the restaurant on a travel app and declared it our first off-the-beaten path side quest. Our desire for delicious noodles took us well off the Vegas strip, to an area of the city seen more by residents than tourists. The food had been fantastic, but the company even better.

Vegas and ramen had been our first real stop, other than for gas, after leaving California. Our first sit-down meal together outside of the confines of camp. Other than the literally compact space of my car, we were anything but confined. Our adventure existed in the space between where we'd been and where we were headed.

We'd made our travel plans over hot noodles and mind-melding broth. With no job for me get back to, and Lucas having arranged time off from camp, we'd plotted our course and dreamed big.

The mountains of Utah and Colorado big. A longer route back through Kansas, to St. Louis, through Indiana. So many states I'd never visited before, and I got to experience it all with Lucas.

Our trip had been about discovering. New places. Ourselves.

We made our way through the backyard toward the food table, sidestepping children sneak-attacking each other with squirt guns. Lucas scowled. I caught where his gaze landed. Helen, gasping and laughing as another woman spoke while gesturing wildly with her hands.

He shook his head. "Vegas stories. *We* hiked the Rocky Mountains."

I redirected his attention with a gentle touch at his beard. His warm brown eyes settled on mine. "Who cares if Helen thinks our relationship origin story is weird. It's our relationship origin story. I can't imagine anyone else I'd rather have been stuck in a car with after being unfairly hired for a job I had no skills in."

He laughed softly. "The joke's on me. Turns out you're the one with skills. I'm just the handsome face of this partnership." He stroked a hand against his trimmed and expertly groomed facial hair.

"Hey, you two." Jillian approached with her boyfriend Adam attached at the hand. "Did you see Patrick yet? I'm dying to see how he acts around Marcy."

Adam, a lean runner type who owned a home renovation contracting company, kept his gaze on Jillian as he spoke. "How has he been acting?"

Lucas snorted. "Like a fifth grader with a crush."

"Who won't admit he has a crush," Jillian finished.

I scoped the area, but only saw Russos and shrieking children. "I have to admit, it's kind of amusing seeing Patrick get flustered."

Spending time with Lucas the remainder of the summer meant plenty of time spent with his family and friends, all made more convenient while I stayed at Marcy's apartment. Patrick was truly an extension of the Russo family and showed up at all of their family functions. And sometimes at Marcy's doorstep for no apparent reason at all.

Marcy appeared again. "Hey, fam! Jillian, you missed the popsicles. The kids devoured them. But we've got adult beverages and seven kinds of pie coming out in a sec." She took out her phone, muttered a few things as she tapped the keys, then slid it into her back pocket. She scanned the backyard.

I laid a hand at Marcy's arm. "The party is great. Are you able to take a break and enjoy yourself?"

She blinked. "Sure. Enjoy myself. I can do that."

"Marcy!" A woman's voice boomed from beneath the pop-up canopy tent. Three long folding tables were lined up beneath the tent offering seating and trays of food. "ARE MY PIES OUT, MARCY? UNCLE TITO WANTS THE RHUBARB."

Marcy's tight smile surfaced. "Duty calls." She zipped away.

Jillian caught my eye. "She needs us."

I nodded. "Let's go help her."

Lucas stroked my back with a light touch. "Actually, I've got this, if you don't mind. I think I know what's up. Family stuff." He leaned closer to brush his lips across mine. Deep woods mosquito repellent never smelled so desirable.

As Lucas sauntered off, Noah joined our group, a burger in one hand and a wine spritzer in the other. "You two are annoyingly cute," she said to me. She flicked her gaze at Jillian and Adam. "Same for you. Makes a single girl actually want to give the apps another go."

I cringed with sympathy. "The dating apps are rough. Don't you have mutuals back in Chicago who can set you up? Friends of friends to meet up with?"

Noah shrugged. "I'm feeling pretty blah about all of it lately. The job, the city, my existence."

Jillian gasped. "Noah!"

Noah flitted a hand in the air. "I'm *existing*, okay? I'm just blah about it." She gestured to me with the wine spritzer bottle. "Which means I'm down for your experimental adult retreat center. Whenever that opens."

Jillian sucked in air. "When, Hudson? When does it launch? Can I come? Ooh—how about we make it a Mavens event!"

I couldn't help laugh. "You're getting a little ahead of yourself, but yes, the retreat project is for sure happening. Now that the summer season is over, I'll be working with the camp to build a customer base for corporate retreats and restorative yoga weekends. The goal is to bring in groups who pay full price so we can subsidize retreats for local non-profits. Lucas is working with a veteran's group right now as a test case for a hiking and fishing retreat."

Adam nodded, grinning. "Cool idea. I bet my company crew would love to come up there. As a full price retreat, I mean."

Jillian beamed at him.

"Lucas will be thrilled, thank you."

Our time hiking in Colorado had been revelatory for Lucas. He'd loved it. I could sense the energy radiating off of him as we explored small mountain towns and national parks.

Only Lucas couldn't stop talking about camp. About how much potential the camp property had if he took the concepts he'd been excited about doing in Colorado and plugged them in back home.

Back home. He talked about camp like he belonged there. And after mending his friendship with Brycen, the two of them came up with new ideas to grow the camp, while ensuring they kept their own goals front and center.

Which led Lucas to seek out a Michigan-based outdoor adventure company he could work for in short-term stints. Many of the guided trips would take him to the upper peninsula of Michigan, and would last only a week or two at a time. Neither of us wanted to be nailed to one location at the moment, but we also liked a place to call home. Right now, I had several, and that worked for me.

"So are you officially working for the camp?" Jillian asked me.

"I'm part-time, but there's a lot of work on the front end. Branding, marketing, and creating customer packages to hit the markets we're targeting. I've still been staying with Marcy and driving up to camp for a day or two at a time. And then I'm freelancing for a travel blog, and slowly shifting my Beauty Butterfly to more wellness and inspirational content. I didn't want to give up my online identity entirely, but I also don't want to feel obligated to constantly post new content, you know? It just doesn't seem to fit who I am now."

Jillian nodded in agreement. "I spent my twenties in graduate school. I don't know your influencer life, but I definitely know what it's like to be fully consumed by one thing for many years only to have that end. It's weird, but not bad."

She'd found an amazing job in her neuroscience field, which happened to be within a close range of Adam's contracting business he'd built from the ground up.

Change was inevitable. Weird but not bad summed it up. At least, it wasn't bad once embezzlement charges cleared.

Yikes. What a summer.

This moment in time felt transitional, temporary, but in the best way possible. I was spending time with people I cared about, including my parents and siblings. They were incredibly supportive of my move back to Michigan. They didn't quite understand the retreat aspect of the camp just yet, but that's why I planned to invite them to a session. To show them.

Lucas returned to the group. "Everything okay?" I asked him.

He gestured across the yard. "See for yourself."

Marcy and Patrick stood close beneath the large oak shading the backyard, laughing. A snapshot of two long-time friends who clearly trusted each other. Marcy insisted only friendship existed between them. "They'll be arguing within ten seconds, but for now, they're sweet."

"Speaking of sweet." Lucas held out his hand. A slice of pie waited on a clean paper plate. "Peach pie. A Nonna Russo specialty."

"Yum!" I took a forkful and relished the sweet gooey goodness. "Your grandmother is an amazing baker. No wonder Marcy was so geeked to get her hands on her recipes."

Lucas watched me for a beat as I ate. I caught him doing that sometimes, just watching me without commentary. We'd talked about it because he caught me doing the same thing. Sometimes I just looked at Lucas and appreciated who he was and how much I enjoyed being with him.

Now his attention was causing me to blush.

"I promised my nonna I would watch your reaction to her pie," he said finally. "She was very specific that I report back."

I stifled a laugh. "She's right over there. I could just tell her—"

He held up a hand. "She's on one of her, how should I say it…matriarchal streaks. She's been telling my cousins they all need to get married. She's really on Marcy's case about it. It's why I intervened."

More stress for Marcy. I'd heard about Nonna Russo's bossy side. "Does she pressure her brothers or just her?"

"Pretty much all of them." He grunted. "And me."

I froze with my fork midway to my mouth. "She's pressuring you to get married?"

"I gently told her to be patient." His eyes sparkled. "I reminded myself to be patient too."

My heart warmed at his confession. After spending hundreds of hours in a car together (I had no idea the actual number, but it was a lot), we'd covered a lot of ground. Neither of us would be standing here together if we didn't see a future together.

I grinned. "Your nonna likes me, I can tell."

"Probably those skincare samples you gave her."

"Hey, cousin!" Robby, Marcy's youngest brother, clapped a hand on Lucas' back. "Hey, Hudson. Looking *good*."

Lucas' arm immediately hooked around my waist. "Find your own girlfriend."

I snickered. I kind of loved when Lucas got territorial about us—at least with his cousins, where there wasn't any real threat involved.

"I was talking about the pie," Robby claimed. "The pie looks good. You look good too Hudson. I can get my own girls anyway." He wandered off, leaving us laughing.

I set the pie plate on a nearby folding table. "Have I told you lately how much I like you?" I slid my arms up and around Lucas' neck.

He pulled me closer. "Yeah. But I don't mind hearing it again."

He kissed me. A totally appropriate backyard barbecue level kiss, but the sensation of his lips against mine still made my toes curl. My hair probably curled too, which was currently blond with lavender tips.

As dusk settled in, string lights blinked awake hung from the house to posts on the deck. Sparklers emerged, and a fire was lit in a portable fire pit at the far end of the yard.

Our group settled in on camp chairs around the fire. My friends, Lucas and his cousins, and Patrick, all back together again. A fitting to end the summer.

Lucas ran a gentle hand along the back of my neck. I caught his eye and smiled. I felt his affection through that simple look. He was in his element surrounded by the people he cared about most.

And that included me. I loved that it included me.

I didn't want summer to end, but at the same time I couldn't wait for fall. I had my Mavens, my hunky mountain man, and my own quest to make a mark on the world.

In other words, life was anything but settled, but I wouldn't change a thing.

Want to read about Hudson and Lucas' first date on their cross-country road trip? Join my email list for bonus material at stephaniejscott.com

Acknowledgements

When I set about to write a romantic comedy series, I grabbed ideas from everywhere–books I've read and liked, discussions of favorite tropes on Instagram and in discord groups, and movies. The kinds of movies that stick with you, featuring plucky Beverly Hills moms leading their daughter's scout troop, or friends aiming to win a spot on Dance TV. I love the bonkers comedies that center friendship and hope to bring that spirit to this series. I love my love stories, but a good friendship in a book keeps me coming back.

Thank you to early readers Kelly Garcia, Vanessa M. Knight, Robin Skylar, and Rachelle Paige Campbell. I always appreciate the support and brainstorming prowess of Chicago North Romance Writers, and the wonderfully supportive and always interesting Seasonally Booked Up reading group. Thank you to the bookstagram community—you inspire me and fill up my reading list!

Also By Stephanie J. Scott

Lady and the Camp
OMG Christmas Tree
Miss Humbug (coming 2023)
Falling Into Place
Young Adult Books
All Last Summer
Sunset Summer
Big Wild Summer
Free Wheeling Summer
All-Star Love
Alterations
For bonus content, book release news, and discounts, join my
author newsletter at www.stephaniejscott.com

About the Author

Stephanie J. Scott writes light-hearted, quirky romance and young adult. She enjoys dance fitness, everything cats, and has a slight obsession with Instagram. A Midwest girl at heart, she resides outside of Chicago with her tech-of-all-trades husband and fuzzy furbabies.

Photo: Leah Lewis Photography

www.ingramcontent.com/pod-product-compliance
Lightning Source LLC
Chambersburg PA
CBHW051250210726
48287CB00002B/440